Between The Beats

M. E. Cooper

To my family.
For always believing in me.
Especially when I didn't believe in myself.

1

Snap, the rhythmic sound of the drumstick striking the snare. Thump, the resounding of the strings of the bass being plucked. The singer belting a note so long and high, masking the sound of the terrified scream. It was all about the music, the birth of jazz that permeated the air of New Orleans in the 1920s. Nothing else mattered. As long as there was music, everything was right with the world. When the music stopped, that's when bad things would happen.

For as long as Raymond could remember, there was always music playing. The music box his mother would wind up at bedtime, the records she would play throughout the day, or the radio he would listen to while he was working, there was always a soundtrack to his day. Momma had instilled a love of music in him from a young age and when it was silent, the world didn't feel complete.

Raymond always thought of his mother as a strong woman, except when it came to his father. In his mind, she was the picture of beauty, carrying her petite frame proudly, giving her the appearance of height and authority. Her dark hair, pulled back in a twist, showing off her perfectly formed face, and her choice of clothing, flattering to her shape, even though some would think it was simple and plain.

No matter what his father did or where he went away to, she would always take him back when he returned. He would leave them for weeks at a time, only to come home again, with no money, reeking of alcohol, and other women's perfumes. Momma would simply clean up his clothes, run him a hot bath, set out clean towels, and a freshly pressed set of pajamas. Why did that one detail stick in his mind? Freshly pressed pajamas, who ironed the clothes they were going to sleep in any way? But it was one of those things his father demanded, and she supplied.

Raymond learned the hard way to be quiet during these times of reunion. One of his most vivid memories of his father was when he came home after one of these benders, when Raymond was seven years old. Being a curious child, he was asking a lot of questions. Where had daddy been? What was the city like, and the more he inquired, the more agitated his father became, until he reached his breaking point. Without warning, Daddy struck Raymond hard with his fist, sending him tumbling backward, hitting his head on the corner of the table. His mother, hearing the crash, came out and led Raymond to the kitchen, muffling his cries in her apron, all the while trying to soothe not only his bruises, but his damaged pride as well.

She explained that his father just needed time to get settled, that Raymond should do his best to remain as quiet as a mouse, not disturbing daddy until he was ready to acknowledge the family again. Raymond nodded his head, not wanting to make any more noise for fear of upsetting the situation even more. Tiptoeing to his room, he left Momma in the kitchen to finish making supper. Coming out to the dinner table only when called, he found it set with all the foods that his father preferred, and whether Raymond liked it or not, he would do his best to choke down every last bite he was served.

This pattern continued on for the next two years. Daddy would be home for a while, then without notice, he would be gone again. His mother would only say that his father had gone off to work a job in another city for good pay, promising to send money and return as soon as he could, then they would be a family again.

When his father was home during the school year, Raymond found it easy to stay out of daddy's way, keeping busy with school, homework, and other chores. It was during the summer months that proved to be the hardest. Construction was booming throughout the city, but the work to be had was hard labor, made more difficult by the heat and storms that would come rolling through with unpredictable regularity. Why daddy didn't take on some of these jobs was one of many unanswered questions that hung in the air that Raymond knew not to ask. Instead, Raymond would find tasks around the house or at neighbors' homes, just to prove to his father he could indeed be useful, despite daddy telling him otherwise on an almost daily basis.

That fall, when Raymond was eleven, his father announced he was leaving for what he said would be a three-month job. A month and a half later, a letter arrived telling Raymond's mother he was coming home. The job was ending early, and to expect him by the end of the week. The end of the week came and went, and yet there was no sign of him. Halfway into the next week and still no word, Raymond started to give up hope. Not that he held out much to begin with, but he tried to convince his mother he was looking forward to his father's return.

"When do you think Daddy will be home again, Momma?" He inquired one day after school. "I want to show him my drawings."

"I don't know Raymond. I'm guessing work lasted a little longer, and he hasn't had a chance to write and tell us. I'm sure he'll either write or show up soon, though."

Raymond could tell momma was trying to put on a good front for him, but after a couple more weeks, he saw she came to the same realization everyone else had. He wasn't coming back. Over dinner that evening she did her best to explain, but all Raymond only replied with a shrug of his shoulders and a mumble under his breath, "good riddance."

Since he had established a good base of homes in the neighborhood doing odd jobs over the past summers, he could keep earning money into the school year. He continued to learn basic carpentry and painting skills, which allowed him to take on more work, diligently giving his wages to his mother every week, hoping it would help to ease the burden he saw her carrying. He saw she was taking in more laundry and seamstress work, allowing her to be home for him after school. She had told him it was important to her he would have as stable a childhood as possible, knowing what it was like to grow up in the rural South, working too hard at a young age and with not much of an education, and she wanted so much more for him than she ever had.

2

Genevieve Louis met Walter Deacon when she was just fifteen years old. It was love at first sight for her. It was the turn of the century, a new era for everyone. Although slavery had been abolished, she and her family were still living in a sharecropper's cabin, trying to get by on meager wages, and even more meager crops.

Walter was five years older than her, but he swept her off her feet, telling her he would take her to the city, where they could begin a new life together. He was making good money working various jobs, and he knew that with the growth of the city, he would be able to find work and help to support her family too.

A quick marriage and a move into a small house on the edge of New Orleans was more than she could have imagined it would be. But the fairy tale soon came crashing down around her head. The love of music both she and Walter had shared that brought them together in the first place at that seedy juke joint is what would drive them apart.

The first year in the city, when they had a little extra money, Walter would take Genevieve out for a night on the town. They would dress in their best clothes and go out to hear this new music that was taking form. In these moments, they would lose themselves in the rhythm, soaking it all in, feeling it from the tops of their heads to the soles of their feet.

It wasn't until that night when Walter went out by himself and came home later than usual, reeking of alcohol, spewing vile words at her. Trying to figure out what she had done or hadn't done that triggered this outrage, she tried everything she could to appease the monster who stood before her in her husband's skin.

Walter slapped her across the face, a welt quickly rising. She stood and watched in disbelief as he turned and went into the bedroom, locking the door behind him, leaving her to sleep on the old sofa in the living room. Not knowing what else to do, she laid down until morning, getting up early, so when he woke, his favorite breakfast foods were ready on the table. Genevieve sat silently, not saying a word about what had happened the night before.

A month passed before Genevieve and Walter could go out again. The city was growing around them, work was plentiful and Genevieve had tried to put Walter's abuse behind her, hoping it was just a onetime thing. The night they could finally go out, Walter took offense at how some other men were looking at his wife. Instead of interceding in the bar, he dragged Genevieve home, pushing and shoving, blaming her for the leering looks she was getting.

It was then Genevieve realized that when Walter was drinking, he became a different man. This was no longer the man she had met and fallen in love with. But she had no recourse and could see no way out. She tried her best to always appease him, letting him go out more on his own, content to stay home and listen to the music she had there. It wasn't much, but as long as she could play her records, her soul was content.

When she discovered she was pregnant, she was unsure of how Walter would take the news, taking care to keep it hidden as long as she could. Protecting her belly when his fists would fly, until it became obvious, even to him, that she was with child.

Ecstatic at the prospect of becoming a father, Walter promised to clean up his act. He wouldn't go out drinking by himself anymore. He would spend more time at home with her, and he would do his best to find steady work instead of the day jobs he had been picking up.

The abuse abated for the remaining months of her pregnancy and when a son was born, Walter declared he should be named Raymond, after Walter's own father. Raymond would carry on the family name, the family traditions. He would be strong and virile, the first male grandchild born in this new century.

Genevieve watched as Walter held true to his word for the first couple of years of Raymond's childhood. She was convinced that Raymond was the balm to whatever had been troubling Walter and he was once again the man she had fallen in love with.

The summer Raymond turned three, a fire tore through the neighborhood, destroying many of the homes surrounding them. Fortunately, they escaped unharmed, but something in the bleakness of the aftermath of that devastation set Walter off again. He was spending more nights at the bar, stumbling in late, drunk and often smelling of another woman's perfume.

Having learned her lesson, Genevieve simply kept her mouth shut. She took the brunt of whatever punishment Walter would dish out, always protecting Raymond, making sure nothing would happen to him.

That fall, Walter announced he was going to take a job over in Mississippi for two months. He would be gone, but he promised to write and send home money to support his wife and child. For the first two weeks, Genevieve received an envelope containing just enough cash for her and Raymond to survive on. The next six weeks passed, and only one more envelope showed up, with barely enough for her to pay for food. She realized she would have to go back to work again in order to support her son, especially since she didn't know if Walter had any intentions of returning.

Turning to her neighbors, she asked around if anyone knew of any work she could take in at home while continuing to take care of her son. The woman across the street, not much older than Genevieve herself, mentioned she worked for a family in the Garden District and they had some mending that needed tending to. She would bring it by on her way home from work that evening, if Genevieve was willing. She readily accepted, thanking this woman, who she now thought of as her guardian angel.

Thanks to the kindness of neighbors, including Delphine, who soon went from just guardian angel to becoming her friend, she was able to take in enough work to take care of herself and Raymond, and even began to add to her meager music collection again.

Music was the one constant she had in her life that she could not give up. Ever since Raymond was born, she instilled that love into him as well. She would sing to him in the mornings to wake him up, she had a music box that she would play at night when he went to sleep. During the days, she would have records playing. As long as there was a song in the air, all was right in her world.

When Walter returned that winter, he looked haggard and beaten down. Wherever he had been had taken its toll on him, physically and emotionally, and he took it out on both Genevieve and Raymond.

At first the abuse was just verbal, chastising her for overcooking the meat, or yelling at Raymond to be quiet when he went around humming his favorite songs. It then turned physical that spring, when he would slap Genevieve, or whip off his belt and punish Raymond for some minor misbehavior.

Genevieve continued to take in work during this time, in an effort to continue to feed and take care of her family, since Walter didn't seem to have any interest in doing anything. Walter took offense to her working, but didn't seem to mind taking her money and spending it in the bars and gambling rooms.

After having been home for four months, Walter announced he was leaving again. He took all the money that Genevieve had been saving, giving his usual excuses that he would send the money home to take care of them, that her job was to take care of their son, and that he would return when the job was done. Genevieve, having become accustomed to this pattern of behavior now, and just nodded in acquiescence.

3

Genevieve had told Delphine of the many occasions when Walter would beat both her and Raymond, but she hadn't seen with her own eyes just what a monster he could be, until that fateful morning.

Delphine knew Walter hadn't been gone long, maybe just a few days, when she ran into him, returning home, stumbling and reeking of smoke, sweat, and alcohol. He pushed past her, bursting through his front door, yelling incoherent sentences, knocking over anything that got in his way.

Following a few steps behind, she saw him shove Raymond so hard that he fell over backwards, knocking the left side of his head on the corner of the baseboard when he landed. Hearing Genevieve run toward him to make sure he was okay, Delphine hoped that would be the end of it, but before Genevieve could reach him, Walter lashed his fury at her.

A loud crash, followed by the sound of an open hand contacting the delicate skin of a face, shook Delphine out

11

of her stupor. She saw Raymond peering around the corner of the doorway, her eyes then settling on the scene unfolding in the living room. Genevieve was stooped over, picking up the broken pieces of a what used to be a plate or maybe a record, though Delphine couldn't be certain from this vantage point. Walter was just out of his line of sight, but she could still hear him stomping through the house, huffing, and muttering under his breath.

"Damn, woman! How many times do I got to tell you? One more time and you and that no good brat can just go. You hear me?"

"Yes, sir."

"What? What you say? I can't hear you! Speak up dammit!"

"Yes. I hear you. It won't happen again."

"A'right then. Get back in the kitchen an' finish making my breakfast. I need to go soon, and before you go naggin' again, I don't know how long I'll be gone this time. Make sure you pack my good clothes, too. I'm gonna need them where I'm going."

As Genevieve turned her back, Delphine couldn't see the pain in her eyes or the bruise rising on her cheek. What she saw was Genevieve straighten up and return to the kitchen. Sounds of pans being placed on the stove, the smell of bacon and eggs frying, and Walter settling back down at the table were all she could distinguish now. Feeling like an intruder, she crept quietly back onto the steps, as she saw Raymond pass by the window, beginning his morning chores. She was torn whether to return home or stay and make sure things remained quiet.

After a beat, she heard Raymond come back out of his

room and head toward the kitchen, when she heard Walter bark.

"Boy, you need to step it up around here. You hear me? You should've been up an hour ago. What you think this is a vacation home?"

"No, sir. I got my morning chores already done, sir. I'll get to working on the porch just as soon as I finish my meal, sir."

Hearing the sound of the chair being pushed back, Walter grunted and lumbered out of the room.

Deciding that all was calm for the moment, Delphine stepped down to the sidewalk, vowing to return later to make sure her friend and son were okay.

❧

When Raymond heard the slam of the front door, he knew it was finally safe to come out of the kitchen.

Putting on a brave face, he asked, "How long you think he'll be gone this time, Momma?"

"I don't know, dear. He says he's got a job over in Texas. But there's no telling."

He could hear the resignation in her voice, telling him that the conversation was at an end, and no more questions would be answered.

"I cleaned up my breakfast dishes already, and I'll get to work on the painting now, Momma. Why don't you go sit for a minute?"

"Thank you, dear. I think I will." She quietly replied as she continued to stare out the front window.

He paused, wondering if there was something more he should say or do, but decided it was probably just best to let her be and go about doing what needed to be done. After all, what could a ten-year-old boy do? He knew this wasn't how daddies were supposed to treat mommas, but if he dared to speak up, he too suffered found himself on the receiving end of his father's temper and large hand.

He was reminded of this as he set the paint bucket down, his left ear ringing and the latest scars across his back still stinging from the last belting he had taken at daddy's hand.

His father had come home late one night when the following morning Raymond apparently was making too much noise for his father's liking. Having finished his breakfast, he came around the corner, heading back to his room. Entering the doorway, his father grabbed him from behind and whipped him with the ferocity of an overseer lashing a runaway slave. When his daddy slammed his left ear against the wall, his mother stepped in and took the remaining punishment.

Without saying a word, Daddy grabbed Momma by the arm, dragging her into the living room, and throwing her onto the couch. He then picked up and smashed as many records as he could get his hands on, followed by destroying the record player that had just been playing "Darktown Strutters Ball". The force with which he tried to destroy everything his mother loved caused Raymond to run and take cover under the sink for fear of being hit by the flying wax and wood. He heard his mother protest only once, followed by the sound of her body hitting the floor. He peeked out from his hiding spot to see her awkwardly lying on the floor, not moving, but her chest slowly rising and falling, letting him know she was still at least alive.

After destroying what he felt were all the things music

related, Raymond's father took one last look around and stormed back out of the house again. He barely said two words, giving no sign as to why he found it necessary to silence the one thing that brought Raymond and his mother joy and happiness.

Returning to his present chores, he looked around.

"Maybe being dead would be better than living this life," he mused to the bird that had taken a perch on the rafters to watch over his work. The dove, not caring one way or the other, replied with a song before flying off, leaving Raymond alone with his chores and thoughts.

Days soon passed, and Raymond finally stopped asking his mother when she thought his father might return. This time, it felt like things were different. He knew that no money was being sent home as promised, yet there always seemed to be food on the table, though he noticed momma didn't seem to eat as much as she once did. He noted she must have had picked up some extra work too, as there always seemed to be more mending needing to be done.

To the casual observer, life appeared to continue as it always had. Momma was there in the mornings when he woke up, she was there to pick him up after school. What he didn't see were the hours she spent away from the house during the day, cleaning up after someone else's messes, and the hours she spent late into the night, after he had gone to bed, sewing until her fingers bled and she could barely bend her wrists anymore.

This had become their life now. Until that day, she didn't show up to pick him up from school.

4

Ever since that day daddy hit him in the head, Raymond had a hard time hearing on the left side. He tried to hide it from momma as best he could, but it became painfully apparent in school one day, when a little girl hit him with a ball on the left side of his head.

She claimed she had yelled at him to get out of the way, but since he couldn't hear her, he thought she did it on purpose. He retaliated and threw the ball back at her, resulting in them both getting sent to the teacher. It was then his hearing loss became clear to others and he could no longer hide it.

Momma tried to console him at home, making sure when she played music that it was positioned so he could hear it on the right side, even moving his music box to the other side of his room so he could still hear that at night.

It wasn't until a couple of weeks later, when the little girl told some of her friends about his inability to hear, that things took a turn for the worse. He saw a group of them gathering on the other side of the playground, the girl obviously the ringleader of the bunch. She was pointing at him, laughing as she did, then whispering in each child's left ear.

One by one, they came by him, taunting and teasing, always on the left side, knowing he couldn't hear what they were saying. All he could hear was their laughter afterward, resonating across the playground. It wasn't until finally the little girl came by, just as Raymond was about to walk away, when she stuck out her foot and tripped him, then bent over, pretending to offer help, instead announcing loudly that he was just a deaf dummy, who was a momma's boy and would never be anything more.

Despite his telling the teacher what had happened, no one ever received any punishment, and this torment continued until the kids grew bored with him and went to their next target. But Raymond didn't forget. He vowed he would get revenge against Simone, the ringleader of the group. How he would go about it, he had no idea. But somehow, he knew he'd get back at her.

The day his mother disappeared was when the silence began to turn to voices, although at the age of twelve, no one would have guessed then what those dark voices would later lead him to do.

It had been like any other day, he went off to school, and nothing at home was out of the ordinary. When momma wasn't there to pick him up that afternoon, he didn't know what he should do. Sure, there had been days she had missed before, but typically it was because she had been sick in the morning and he knew that before going to school. But this morning, she was fine. There had been no indication she wouldn't pick him up, so he continued to sit on the steps and wait.

Fifteen minutes later, his teacher came out and inquired, "Raymond, why are you still here? Is everything all right?"

Looking up at his teacher, Raymond shrugged. "I think Momma must be running late. I'll wait here a little longer and see if she shows up."

"I'll check back in five minutes. But if you leave before that, please be sure to let someone know."

"Yes ma'am. Thank you."

Sitting and waiting, Raymond looked up and down the street, hoping to see Momma approaching. Not seeing her, he kept himself busy observing the crawling bugs going about their work and listened to a bird singing its song while perched in the cherry tree. Another ten minutes passed when he decided it was time to head on home. As he was leaving, he spotted the janitor picking up rubbish and asked him to please let the teacher know he had left so she wouldn't worry.

Reaching the house, he noticed it was unusually quiet. The front door was closed, he didn't hear any music playing, yet a breeze or some other movement seemed to stir the front room curtains. He sprinted up the steps to the door. Trying the handle, he found it locked. That's not right either. Momma never locks the front door when she's home, and she's always here when I come home from school by myself. His heart pounded faster, a light sweat breaking out across his forehead. 'Where's Momma,' he thought.

Not having a key to the door, he had to find another way in. Stepping over to the front window, he peeked in through a break in the curtain. There must have been an open window somewhere around the back, causing it to rustle. He moved further down the porch, trying to hear or see any signs of his mother, or anyone else, that may have been in the house.

Realizing there was no way of getting in the front, he made his way around the side and to the back. The window above the kitchen sink was wide open, but how was he going to hoist himself up there? Finding a few bricks and a piece of wood, he made a ramp that gave him just enough of a boost to grab hold of the windowsill and pull himself up. Looking in, he saw nothing. The kitchen was clean, no pots on the stove, all the dishes from breakfast had been put away. There was an orange on the counter, but no other food had been left out, something else odd, because Momma always had a snack ready for him when he came home from school.

Dropping back down to the ground, pacing and contemplating how he would get in, he tried the back door, surprised when it opened. Trepidatiously stepping inside, trying to be as quiet as possible, he kept listening for any sounds showing Momma was home, or that someone else was there. The only sound he could hear was the pounding of his heart filling his ears.

Calling out "Momma! Momma, are you home?" Nothing, no response. Again, "Momma! Momma, where are you?" his voice rising, his fear becoming more palpable. He ran from room to room, finding nothing out of place, and still no sign of his mother. He knew something wasn't right, but with no definitive evidence, how could he even begin to know where to look or who to contact? He ran next door to a neighbor's house, but no one had seen his mother since he left for school that morning.

Unsure of what to do next, he returned home and decided to wait. Maybe she was just out running errands and lost track of the time. 'She'll be home soon,' he thought. 'I'll just go ahead and get my chores done. That way, when she does come back, everything will be in its place and she won't have to take care of anything. '

Concentrating on doing his homework and chores, the afternoon turned to evening and still Momma hadn't returned. This was very much out of the ordinary for her. Since it was just the two of them now, she always made sure he knew where she would be, for how long, and when he could expect her to be back. As the evening wore on, his thoughts grew darker along with the night sky. Maybe his father had returned and made good on his one of his many nefarious promises of harming her he so often hurled about when he was home.

5

The morning Raymond went off to school was just like any other day. Genevieve had prepared breakfast and made sure he had all of his school work with him. She knew she had a full day of work outside the house, and a stack of mending that she needed to finish that evening, so she was in a hurry to get her day started.

When Walter came strolling in the front door, just after Raymond had left, she knew her plans for the day were shattered.

"Walter? What are you doing here?" She demanded.

"What do you mean, what am I doing here? This is my house woman. I can come and go whenever I please."

Genevieve stood her ground, glaring at Walter. He hadn't been home for over a year now, and the last thing she expected was for him to return. She had been providing for herself and Raymond that entire time and had come to the decision that if Walter were to ever come back, she would kick him out once and for all. She knew she didn't have the law on her side, being a woman, even in a city like New Orleans, but she was determined to set a better life for her son.

Walter pushed past her, making his way to the kitchen. "Get in here and fix me some breakfast. I'm starving." He shouted as he settled into what had been his chair at the table.

"No. You want something, you fix it yourself. Then you can get your belongings and get out. I'm done with you, Walter. I'm done with your abuse. Thanks to you, our son has lost his hearing in one ear and has had to suffer the consequences ever since."

"That no good boy. Serves him right. You always did coddle him anyway. And in case you forget, my name is still on the deed to this place. So I don't know what you think you are doing ordering me around. If anyone is going to get out, it will be you and that brat of yours." Walter announced as he starting grabbing food from the cupboards, throwing dishes on the table.

Unable to control her temper any longer, Genevieve shrieked. "I am done with you. Get out. Now. Tell me where to send your things and I'll make sure you get what is yours."

Walter stopped, turning toward Genevieve, and picked up the cast-iron skillet that was drying on the counter. "You think you can talk to me that way?" he yelled as he threw the skillet at her. "Woman, you don't know nuthin'."

Without another word, Walter picked up whatever he could lay his hand on, striking out at Genevieve, knocking over the armchair, breaking a glass figurine from the shelf, and finally shoving her into a wall.

Holding her there, he leaned into her face, his breath

reeking, and muttered, "I am taking my things and going back to the boarding house. I have business I need to tend to tonight. But I expect you and Raymond to be gone when I return tomorrow. You are no longer any concern of mine."

Letting her go, Walter stomped off into the bedroom while Genevieve gasped for breath. "You no good, son of a... I'm not going to let you tell me what I can and can't do anymore." A plan was starting to form in her mind, she knew she would have to find someway of keeping him from returning, but how? Maybe Delphine could help? She had offered her help in any way Genevieve had needed. Would she still hold true to that promise? She would have to find out once she got to work that day.

Genevieve arrived at work half an hour late, but at least she was there. She didn't think Walter would leave as easily as he did, but he held true, gathering up a few belongings and departing once again.

She quickly cleaned up the house, knowing that if Raymond came home after school and saw the mess, he would know something was amiss. She didn't want him worrying that his father might be back and what that could mean for them. They had finally settled into a normal life, and even though he had troubles at school with his hearing, he seemed to be finally adapting.

Finding Delphine at lunch, she pulled her friend aside and filled her in on the details of what had happened that morning.

"I have to go to the boarding house and get this taken

care of, but I'm afraid of what he might do when I get there."

"You can't go there alone. Are you sure you can't just drop the stuff off while he's not there?"

"I don't know when he'll be there and when he won't. But I have to take care of this before Raymond gets home from school, too. He can't know that his father is back. Not now."

"Alright, listen. I will cover for you this afternoon. I'm sure Mrs. Batiste won't mind. But you get there and get back home. Don't do anything foolish now. You come find me after I get home from work, too. Then we'll figure out what to do next."

Genevieve hugged her friend, thanking her for understanding, and asked that if anything should happen, that Delphine would keep an eye on Raymond.

6

Raymond knew Delphine's house was just across the street from their house. She lived alone, with no family in the area that she ever spoke of, but she didn't seem to mind. Raymond often heard others whisper behind her back, speculating about why she was still single and what sort of woman must she be. He couldn't understand why people would judge her so. She kept her home neat and tidy and always had a kind word for anyone passing by. More importantly, she was Momma's friend. She had helped them when daddy had attacked momma, and even found her a job, when she realized daddy wasn't coming back.

Jumping down the three stairs from the porch to the sidewalk, he quickly made his way to her house. Approaching the front door, it dawned on him that she was still at work and wouldn't be home. "Right, well, I guess I'll just have to come back later," he told an ant, crossing his path.

Later in the afternoon, when he heard the bustle of

people coming down the road, returning from their jobs, he quickly cleaned up his books and papers and went out onto the front porch to wait. Sitting on the top step, he kept watching for Miss LeClaire. After what felt like the longest ten minutes of his life, he spotted her walking down the street, her distinctive gait giving her away. She was a tall woman who always took long strides when she walked.

Raymond saw she was carrying her usual workbag slung over her shoulder, in addition to what appeared to be grocery bags as well. Not wanting to waste any more time, Raymond ran up to her and offered to carry the bags back to her home. He didn't want to tell her right away the real reason for his chivalrous offer, so he politely answered her questions about school and friends until they had reached the inside of her home and the comfort of the kitchen.

"Miss LeClaire, I?" he started. He wasn't exactly sure how to begin or even explain what he thought might have occurred.

"Yes? Raymond, what is it?" she asked with a note of genuine concern in her voice.

"Ma'am, I'm not sure where momma is," he blurted out. "She hasn't been home since yesterday morning when I left for school. She usually meets me at the end of classes, and we walk home together so I can tell her about my day, and we can run some quick errands on the way. I thought she would be home by suppertime, but then she wasn't, and I waited all evening until I couldn't stay awake any longer. When I woke up this morning, she still wasn't home, so I thought it best to go to school, but when I got home again today, she still wasn't there. Miss LeClaire, I'm scared. I don't know what to do."

He sputtered out his story out so rapidly, it was difficult

at first to understand what he was trying to say. But she pieced it together fairly quickly and told Raymond to sit down at the kitchen table. She poured him a glass of milk and busied herself with preparations to make supper, not wanting to let on her shock at hearing what he had shared.

While chopping vegetables, Delphine told Raymond, "First thing we need to do is get a good meal in you. Then we'll figure out what to do next."

Turning her attention towards him, looking him in the eye and making sure he was hearing her, she continued. "I get why you haven't gone to the police just yet, but you are going to have to let them know soon. Especially considering the disappearance of your father, too. I know he's been gone a while now, but you can't stay on your own for long."

He was about to protest, but before he could say anything, she held up a hand to stop him and added, "But I will go with you to tell them what's going on, and I will offer to take responsibility for you. This way you can stay close to home, continue to go to school, and be here when your mother does return."

Upon hearing her suggest this, relief spread from his face to the rest of his body, feeling as though he could relax for the first time in two days. While she continued to whip up a hearty meal of greens, cornbread, and black-eyed peas, he told her he had kept up with his chores and schoolwork since Momma disappeared. He knew that was what she would have expected him to do, and he didn't want to disappoint her when she returned. Eating ravenously, he gladly accepted seconds when she offered. Her cooking was as good as if not even a little bit better than his mothers, not that he would ever admit that to anyone.

After dinner, Delphine suggested they walk down to the

police station. "Let me explain to the officer what is going on. I will tell them that I will take responsibility for you until either your mother returns or we can find any family who can take you in."

The desk sergeant took her statement and told them, "Son, there isn't much we can do tonight. Most likely your mother will return by morning. If she doesn't, then stop back by the station tomorrow and let someone know."

The sergeant also agreed to Miss LeClaire looking after the boy until his mother returned or other family could be contacted. With a note of finality, he placed the paperwork on top of an already overflowing pile, indicating it was time for them to leave.

On the walk home, Delphine suggested Raymond stop by his house, pick up a few clothes, his schoolwork, and anything else he might need. He should also leave a note for his mother as to his whereabouts, just in case she came home that night and found him gone. "And please, call me Delphine. Miss LeClaire is just too formal, and that's not me."

He took one last look around the house before closing the door behind him. "Come home soon Momma," he said into the emptiness.

Joining Delphine on the sidewalk where she was waiting for him, they didn't speak the rest of the short walk back to her house. Raymond was lost in his thoughts, mostly not good, worrying with each step about what could have befallen his mother.

Since her house was small and there wasn't an extra bedroom, Delphine quietly made up a bed for him in what would have normally been a storage room. It was just big enough for him to keep his things and sleep, as it was only meant to be a temporary solution.

"It's not much, but I hope you'll be comfortable at least," she said as she showed him his bed.

On the verge of tears, he choked out, "I'm sure it will be fine, Miss Le'... er Delphine, sorry. I really appreciate you doing this for me, I honestly don't know what else I would have done."

It was then that the past couple of day's events caught up to him, emotionally, as well as physically. Delphine gave him a hug, a gentle kiss on the head, and left him to have his privacy, allowing him to process what he needed to get through. Later, when Delphine returned to check on him, she found him sound asleep on top of all the blankets. Covering him with one last blanket, she left him alone to sleep through the night.

Raymond awoke the next morning, slightly disoriented, wondering where he was for a moment when it all came rushing back. The smell of breakfast cooking reminded him of the meals his mother would prepare, triggering another round of tears.

He held them back, telling himself, "Be strong, be a man. Everything will work out in the end." Momma will come home, they'll have a good cry, and then eventually in later years, this will become something that they'll laugh over.

He went to the bathroom to wash up and get ready for the day. As it was the weekend, he didn't have to worry about school or questions from his teachers. He would go home, tend to the chores needing to be done, making sure the last of the broccoli, greens, and onions, growing in the fall garden were taken care of, and then walk around seeing if someone, somewhere had seen his momma. He knew

Delphine would be heading to work soon, but he would ask what he could do around her house as well, to at least try to repay some of her generosity.

The weekend passed without a sign of his mother, or even any sign that the police were looking into the case. He managed to contact an aunt and uncle, who had a farm just north of the city, but no one had heard from her, and they had no idea where his father could be either. As far as they were concerned, his father could be dead and they wouldn't care.

"You'll stay with me then. It's not an imposition, it's just a temporary solution," Delphine declared that Sunday evening at dinner. "Besides, I'm still certain your momma will be home soon. And I won't take no for an answer."

"Thank you, ma'am, er, Delphine. I don't know how I'll ever repay you. I hope you're right about Momma. But I don't have a good feeling about this at all."

Delphine shook her head as she placed a plate of food in front of Raymond. She hoped that the positive face she was putting on for him wouldn't betray her sense of unease that was running swift below that facade.

The following Monday afternoon while Raymond was at the house taking care of chores inside when a knock at the door interrupted him. A police officer came bearing news, but not what Raymond was expecting.

When Raymond answered, the officer asked: "Is your mother home, son?"

Shaking his head, hoping the officer wouldn't catch on to his lie, he replied, "No, sir, she's still at work. Can I take a message?" Hoping the officer wouldn't suggest coming back later.

"Yes. Please tell her that according to a new report, your father managed to get into a brawl at a local bar and gambling establishment. It seems he upset the wrong people and wound up on the wrong end of a knife fight. I'm sorry to say, son, he didn't survive. Being next of kin, it's my duty to inform her of his death."

Raymond stood there, unsure of what to say.

The officer continued, "There are a few personal possessions that need collecting. You or your mother can stop by the station to claim them."

Not wanting to let on that his mother was still missing, he simply said, "Thank you, officer. I'll give her the message when she gets home."

Closing the door, Raymond sank down to the floor. Even though he was glad his father had been gone, life had been better without him there, a part of him was still sad that he was now dead. What would this mean for him? Especially since Momma was still missing.

That evening over dinner, he told Delphine the news. Unsure of what could happen next for him, she tried to console Raymond, noticing that he wasn't expressing much emotion when telling her of the news.

"I'm sorry to hear that, Raymond. Your father was, well," she paused, trying to find the right words. Unable to, she continued, "after school tomorrow, you go down to the station and pick up his things. The longer you wait, the more questions it will raise. And you don't need that right now."

Arriving at the police station the next afternoon, Raymond approached the secretary at the main desk. He lied, saying his mother couldn't get off work, and that he was there instead. She called over another officer, who had him sign paperwork, then handed him a brown paper bag. It contained clothes and a set of keys. "Your old man had been staying at a flop house down the street. If you don't want to be charged another night, I suggest you high tail it there and collect the rest of his belongings."

"Yes, sir. I'll take care of that right away. Thank you." Raymond said with a wave, turning to leave before any suspicions could be raised.

He found the boardinghouse just a few blocks from the station. The proprietor led him to the room, explaining even though his father had paid through the month, he hadn't been seen in a few days. Since the police had been by to tell him of the death, he was eager to rent out the room again, so if Raymond would please hurry to clean out the belongings, he'd much appreciate it as he left Raymond alone.

Opening the door and stepping into the room, Raymond found his father had little in the way of belongings. A couple more shirts, another pair of pants, assorted matchbooks with numbers scribbled inside, a half bottle of whiskey and a notebook. Raymond stuffed the whiskey, matchbooks, and notebook into the paper bag and tied up the remaining clothes in one of the shirts. It wasn't much, but maybe something in there would give him an idea of where his father had been and maybe, hoping against hope, that there might be an indication of where his momma might be too.

Returning to Delphine's house, he started going through the pants where he found a pocket watch and wallet that he would hold on to. The matchbooks weren't of much use, most of them were empty, save the numbers written inside. He couldn't figure out what those could have meant. They weren't phone numbers, at least he didn't think they were based on the way they were written. Dollar amounts maybe? A secret code? Something his father used in his gambling habit? Not understanding, he decided he would take them back to his house later and shove them in the bottom drawer where he was keeping other assorted items that weren't of much use.

The notebook, on the other hand, he hoped might hold some clues. Flipping through the pages, he saw a few sketches, one of his mother, another of a mystery woman, and others of what appeared to be buildings. He had no idea that his father had such artistic talent. He tore the picture of his mother out and set it on his nightstand, then continued to look through the rest of the book.

He found stuck in between pages were a couple of unfinished letters his father had written to him and his mother. Raymond read and reread the letters, hoping it would give him more insight into the man, but it was mostly just long-winded blather, not making much sense. Raymond suspected it had written during a drunken stupor, the handwriting was sloppy, and the book reeked of alcohol. Still with no other clues to the whereabouts of Momma, he resolved to keep the journal with him, even though it was only adding it to the ever-growing pile of mysteries and unanswered questions.

As one week passed into the next, Delphine and Raymond found themselves falling into a routine of work, school, and him continuing to pick up odd jobs around the neighborhood. No one seemed to question the living arrangements, most people were unaware or just didn't seem to care.

Fall became winter, which soon turned to spring, and

before long, summer was upon them again. While no one may have noticed his mother being gone during the previous months, her absence would be more noticeable during the summer. Not wanting to raise suspicions, Delphine suggested maybe it was time to get back in touch with his extended family.

Delphine wrote to Raymond's aunt, his father's sister, and fabricated a story that his mother had been called away to take care of a family member up north. Due to an illness in the family, she didn't take Raymond, for fear of him getting sick as well. Yes, it was all rather sudden, and he had been staying with her until school ended, but now with summer upon them, he needed another place to stay, she had explained in the letter.

She didn't go into detail about the police coming to inform them that Raymond's father had been killed or that his mother was actually missing. She was still holding out hope for her return, maybe while Raymond was gone, and didn't feel it was her place to share that news. She also knew from past conversations with Raymond and his mother that if she told the family all there was to know, they would just come and try to take away everything in the house, regardless of whether or not it belonged to them. She hoped to keep some semblance of normalcy for Raymond and his eventual return.

The aunt responded, agreeing to take him in, but just over the summer months. He would be useful working on the farm and could earn his keep that way. They would come for him in a few days.

Raymond didn't want to go, having grown quite fond of Delphine, and he found he was enjoying the life they were living together. It was a tearful goodbye the day he left, but she promised they would see each other again soon, and she would keep an eye on the house. He could return in the fall and would resume school and life as usual.

Although this was his father's sister and her family, to them, he was an imposition, another mouth to feed, body to clothe, taking up precious space that they hardly had to spare. His uncle put him to work in the fields, hard, punishing, laborious work, every day a different job. It wouldn't have been so bad if he had been given one task and could learn to do it well. Instead, it was plowing one day, seeding another, weeding for the next two, and then any other menial task he was ordered to complete. Because he never learned one well enough, he was constantly being yelled at, corrected, and made to do it repeatedly until whoever was in charge was satisfied.

His wages were meager, and paid directly to his uncle, meaning it usually ended up going towards the bottle. The man wasn't a happy drunk either. He would come home from the juke joint down the road, soused, barely able to stand on his own, reeking of the vile abomination they brewed.

If anyone had the misfortune of being awake when he

rolled in, they faced the brunt of his wrath. Raymond tried to stay hidden, feigning sleep in his corner of the room. Most nights, it didn't help. His uncle would often search him out, just to let him know how unwanted he was. The old man was a bully, even worse than Raymond's father had been, and it was commonplace for a few punches to be thrown before he would stumble off to bed.

There were two occasions where with no prompting or logical reasoning when he whipped off the cord that he used for a belt and tried to strangle Raymond. Fortunately for Raymond, his aunt interceded and took the brunt of the consequences until the old drunk collapsed. Raymond often wondered if she only stepped in because she didn't want the hassle of having to explain what happened if her husband had actually killed him. She was a mean woman herself, and he knew that Momma never liked her either. Shoot, Momma didn't like none of Daddy's family, he reminded himself. "But this woman, she doesn't care none for me and I don't care none for her either." He said to a beetle just before smashing it into the floor with the palm of his hand.

This abuse continued throughout the summer, crushing Raymond's body and mental wellbeing, until one afternoon he spotted an opportunity he could use to his advantage to plan his getaway.

The fields were ready for harvest, and extra workers were being brought in on a daily basis. They were towns-people, rounded up in the morning, driven in on a wagon, and taken back in the evening. The overseers that handled these men weren't the most reliable and would try to skip over workers during the headcount at the end of the day. They would attempt to leave some behind, in order to not pay them and pocket the money themselves. It wasn't a fair bargain to begin with, and most days, they would change up their departure times just to confuse the matter even more. These shenanigans resulted in a clamor among the workers when they would realize the wagons were about to leave. It was in this chaos Raymond saw his chance.

One Friday afternoon, after a particularly rough day, the overseers started the process of hitching up the horses. This was the cue for people to stop working and put up their tools. That day, Raymond was working close enough to where the horses were tied up. When he saw the end of day routine starting, he jumped at the chance to blend in with the others. Grabbing the items he had stashed earlier in a corner of the shed, he joined in with the rest of the men.

He didn't care if he got paid or not, though the extra money would have been helpful. On rare occasions, he was able to collect his wages himself and save a little bit instead of handing it over to his uncle. When questioned, he made the excuse that he just didn't get paid that day. He would get beaten for that excuse, but deemed it worthwhile, in order to afford his eventual escape.

Now, amidst the crowd, he squeezed in on the wagon, keeping his head down and only take a quick moment to glance around to make sure someone who might rat him out didn't spot him. It wasn't until the wagon was a good quarter mile down the road he started to breathe normally again, his racing heart settling back down. He didn't want to be too confident that he had actually gotten away. But would they care if he did? He wondered. "It's not like they wanted me here," he muttered to himself. Now he could make his own life on his own terms.

He had no idea what to expect when he got into town

that evening. He just wanted to get as far away as possible from his family and the farm in order to start a new life. Even though he had just turned fourteen, the labor of the months spent in the fields re-shaped his boy's body into that of a young man, no one giving him a second look when he walked off down Main street as everyone else unloaded from the wagon.

He was mildly surprised at how easy it had been to leave the farm. He expected it to be harder, or that he might have been caught anywhere along the way. But here he was, in town, with absolutely no idea where he was going next. He knew he was just over three hours outside of New Orleans, but did he really want to go back there? The house was there, along with the remaining belongings that Delphine had prevented his aunt and uncle from claiming, even though they kept claiming it was rightfully theirs since they were taking him in.

He thought about the life he had lived with Delphine. Had it really only been a few short months ago? She had promised him that the house would be taken care of, and she fully expected him to return that fall. But now he was faced with a decision. If he did decide that's where he would go, how he would get there? It was a three-hour journey, and that was only if he had a reliable form of transportation. Right now, all he could rely on were his own two feet. That would make for a long walk, and in his current state of exhaustion, he'd probably make it a half a mile at best. No, better to find somewhere to stay for the night, he thought, and set off in the morning. By then, the family would realize he was gone. Would anyone come looking for him, just for his uncle to beat him and try to teach him a lesson, or would they just accept the fact that he was no longer a burden to them and move on without a second thought? He hoped for the latter, but only time would tell. In the meantime, he found a cheap room for the night, a hot bath, and the time for him to plan what was next.

He had fallen asleep listening to the music coming from the bar downstairs. If there was one thing he missed more than anything else, it was the music. His aunt didn't believe in anything other than the gospel music they would sing in church on Sundays, and his uncle said singing was a waste of time and energy. If you had time to sing, then you weren't working to the fullest of your ability. The rolling keys of the piano, the beat of the drum, and the horn player who missed more notes than he played comforted Raymond and reminded him of better times.

Waking the next morning, rubbing the sleep from his eyes, he looked around at his surroundings. It took him a minute to remember the events of the day before, when it dawned on him that he had made it through the first night, and there was no one banging down the door, no one shouting to hurry up and get out of bed. Relishing in his newfound freedom, he took his time getting up, languished in the hot bath, and listened to sounds of the house and town coming to life.

Faint strains of music, someone singing downstairs, reached his ears, reminding him of his mother. He wondered if she had returned home, and if she had, why hadn't she come to collect him? Surely, Delphine would have told her where he was. 'Maybe she just couldn't afford to come for me yet, or maybe she was waiting until it was closer to time for school to start,' he thought. He still held out hope, as bleak as it was, that she had come back and that they would be a family again. With that thought, he decided he must head back to New Orleans. If for no other reason than to find out if she was back. If not, maybe he would just pick up a few items and perhaps head out of town to points unknown.

He ambled downstairs to the bar to settle his bill and see what he could find out about getting a ride into the city. The woman behind the bar, noticing how bedraggled he was, took pity and served him a hearty breakfast and a strong cup of coffee at no extra charge. She didn't buy his story that he had gotten separated from his family and was trying to get back, but kept her reservations to herself. She didn't want or need the trouble of getting involved in someone else's business.

When he asked about the best way to get back into New Orleans, she pointed him in the direction of Rudy. He had a wagon that he used to make weekly runs into the city to fetch supplies and was always looking for hands to help load and unload. It would cost Raymond a day's worth of work, but at least he'd get his ride in and that was all he needed. He thanked the woman for her kindness and went to offer his services to Rudy in hopes that they would leave soon. There was no sign yet of anyone looking for him, and the sooner he got out of town, the better off he would feel.

They pulled out just after noon, Rudy, Raymond, and two other men that Rudy regularly hired. No one questioned Raymond about why he was so eager to get into the city where he had come from or anything else about his story. They wouldn't get into the city until late that afternoon, meaning the work would start early the next morning. Rudy told the guys they had a place to bed down for the night and two meals as their payment. The other two didn't care. Based on their conversation during the ride down, they were more interested in the women and booze the city had to offer. This was their way of getting in on someone else's dime, one had explained. Raymond knew he had a place to stay, but he would stick around and fulfill his end of the bargain, if for nothing else than the two meals. He would need his strength for the journey that lay ahead.

The work was hard, but not nearly as exhausting as what he had been subjected to over the summer months. Rudy turned out to be a fair man. He gave the other two the heavy lifting and had Raymond doing what he considered to be the light work. Between the four of them, they finished the load more quickly than expected.

"Looks like we'll make it back to town by sundown this evening, fellas. Let's get goin'. We'll grab grub on the way."

The other two climbed up on the sideboards, but Raymond just stayed where he was standing. "Come on, boy, let's go. Time's a wastin'," Rudy exclaimed as he climbed up on his seat.

"Thank you sir, but no, I'm not goin' back. I have business here I need to tend to. I appreciate you taking me on, but this is where I must say goodbye."

"Your choice, boy. Good luck to ya. Ya gonna need it," was all Rudy said as he urged the horses on with their now empty load.

8

Here he was, back in his city, with all the options it offered, stretched out in front of him. Standing on the street corner, he looked around, dumbfounded at first, then amazed by the fact that two full days had passed, and as far as he could tell, no one had come after him.

Not far from home, he knew he could hop a streetcar, putting him back there in no time. Instead, he chose to walk, giving himself time to take in the smells, sights, and sounds, yes, the glorious sounds. As he walked the streets, a sense of calm came over him for the first time in months. What was it about music that affected him so? Did other people feel this way as well? Although he could only hear it with one ear, he was still taking it all in.

Full of questions and no one around to give him any answers, he arrived home, the sun was hanging low in the sky, casting shadows in all directions. The air was heavy with the late summer humidity, birds circling, looking for places to take shelter for the night. The yard was slightly overgrown, but not so much that it gave the appearance of the house looking abandoned. The paint was peeling on the front rail, just as it had been for months before he left.

"Had I been around this summer, I would have taken care of these chores, keeping it presentable for Momma's return," he muttered. "But I can't worry about that now. Right now, I need to focus on what comes next." Venturing around the back side of the house, he found he could still jimmy the back door open. 'Just another thing on the list of items that needed fixing if I stick around,' he thought.

Assessing his surroundings, he rummaged through the cupboards and was surprised to find a supply of canned food. He thought his family had cleaned it all out as a payment for staying with them. Yet, what he found looked as though it had been recently canned, making him wonder if maybe Momma was finally home and laying in supplies.

As the evening darkness set in, Raymond continued wandering around the small house, not wanting to light any lamps for fear of letting on that he was there. He couldn't say who he was afraid of finding out, he just didn't want to face anyone yet. Wiping a finger across a table, he found a layer of dust on the furniture. He knew if Momma had been here, that would have never met her approval. She would have given the house a good scrubbing from top to bottom before she did anything else.

No, she must not be back yet, but who would leave food in the cupboards if no one is living here? He thought maybe it had been Delphine, but that made little sense to him, either. Why would she leave food here? Wouldn't she expect me to come to her house first when I returned? For now, it would have to remain a mystery. He was happy to have something to eat, one less thing to worry about while he dealt with the most pressing matters at hand.

Walking into Momma's bedroom, he found what remained of her belongings untouched, left exactly as they had been before his life turned upside down. Her bottles were on the nightstand, a nightshirt hanging on the closet doorknob. At least Delphine had kept his aunt and uncle from taking any of her things. After all, she had told them Genevieve was gone just for a while and would return. Crossing over to his room, he found that his clothes, the few items that he had left behind, had been laundered, folded and placed back in his dresser, as though they were awaiting his return.

He stripped out of his dirty work clothes and threw them in a heap in the corner. Right now, all he could think about was sleep. A wave of tired overtaking him, he saw his bed standing there, looking as though it had just been made, inviting him to lie down and succumb to the depths of slumber.

Sleep he did, for, by the time he woke up, it was the middle of the next afternoon. The skies had turned angry overnight, bringing in a storm from the Gulf, lashing its fury on anything that stood in its path. The sound of the back door slamming open and closed, whipped by the wind, roused him out of bed.

Walking across the damp kitchen floor, he latched the backdoor and found a towel to wipe up the water that had blown in. Once satisfied there was no other damage, he turned his attention to his grumbling stomach, silently thanking whoever had left the food.

It didn't take long for him to consume an entire jar of peaches and one of beans. "I'll have to ration the food that's left and maybe lay in a few supplies for the next week. But I expect I'll be gone by the next weekend," he announced to the empty rooms. "There's nothing left for me here now. I don't think Momma's ever coming home."

On his third day back, he ventured out to replenish the dwindling supplies. Trying to avoid being spotted, he kept to the back streets. He still couldn't be sure his aunt and uncle wouldn't come looking for him, and until he made up his mind what he was going to do next, he didn't want to take any chances. Whoever had left the food obviously wasn't returning. Maybe it had been that his aunt didn't grab all of it when they left his home behind. He also needed to pick up some new clothes as well, since a growth spurt that summer caused him to outgrow most of what he had left behind.

During the days, he kept to himself inside, trying to suppress the buildup of uncontrolled emotion and energy. It was unlike anything he had experienced before, as though someone else was living inside his head, whispering dark thoughts, agitating him, telling him he was going to turn out just like his father. Thoughts would turn into panic attacks, and he'd find himself gulping for air, his heart racing. As much as he wanted to listen to the music, in hopes it would calm him down, he couldn't take any chances playing his momma's records just yet. He was sure if anyone heard music coming from the house, it would only attract attention.

At night, nightmares would disturb his sleep, grotesque women laughing at him, bony fingers pointing at him, while their mouths spewed words he could never remember upon waking.

During this time, he had seen Delphine out and about,

but avoided being caught by her eye. The abuse and hard labor he had endured changed him physically, and mentally he was no longer the boy he was when he left.. Now he felt as though he were someone even he himself didn't recognize. Would she still accept him? He wondered. One thing was sure in his mind, he knew he wasn't about to go back to school and the life he lived before.

Unable to contain himself any longer, he knew he had to get out of the house and find somewhere he could hear the music again. Wandering streets of the French Quarter, lingering in the shadows outside the clubs, he stood listening to the music fill the air. The wail of the trumpet, the thump of the bass, the sounds that emanated from the clubs, brought on a sense of calm, easing his jangled nerves, giving him a sense of feeling like himself again, chasing away the darkness, if only for a short time. What was it about the music that affected him this way? Was it the memory of Momma and the songs that she used to play that brought on this calm? He couldn't understand what was happening, what was triggering these dark thoughts and nightmares, and what would be the result if he gave in to their suggestions.

The week he initially planned on staying turned into a month, the month turning into a season, then into a year. He had been careful not to leave anything lying around inside the house that might arouse suspicion should anyone come by and peer in. He was a stickler for detail and made sure that everything was always put away in the exact place it belonged. He also left the outside mostly unattended as well, giving the house an un-lived in look.

There were a couple other times when he almost ran into Delphine. She had been true to her word and the promise she made when he left, to come by the house every few weeks to check in, making sure everything was still as it should be.

Having watched her come and go, he wondered if she noticed anything and what she must have thought about the food being gone. He speculated maybe she thought that maybe his aunt came back by again and took it as continued payment for taking him in. But even that thought brought no consolation, he just couldn't be sure.

The closest he came to being discovered was one day, while he was in the kitchen, he heard footsteps on the front porch. He ducked out the back door just as Delphine came in the front. Upon his return, he found there was a fresh supply of canned food again, answering that one question that lingered.

"Surely she must think something amiss, since what she left last time was gone," he said to an empty chair. Getting no response, he continued, "I suppose I ought to go thank her at some point, though. Try to explain why I haven't come by. She deserves at least that much."

When another month had passed, he found a box on the front porch, this time filled with canned vegetables and fruits, and a note that read: "For whatever reason, you don't want me knowing you are here, and I'll respect your wishes. Please take care of yourself. Delphine."

He sat down on the porch next to the box and began to weep. So she knew all this time. "How long has she known?" he whispered through his tears. "Does she know it's me, or does she think it's Momma?" For just a moment, he considered going and thanking her for the generosity, but even after all this time, he still wasn't ready. For whatever reason, he didn't want her to see him this emotional or have to explain why he hadn't come to her when he returned. He knew he didn't have a suitable answer.

Instead, he continued to spend his time picking up odd jobs here and there, earning enough to pay for his food and to put a little away for when he was ready to leave. Not returning to school, having finished eighth grade before he had left that summer, made him decide that was enough book learning, instead he was now preferred to learn his lessons on the streets.

After more than a year of this clandestine living, he decided it was time to move on. Counting up his savings, he found he had enough for a train ticket that would get him to Galveston and work could be found there. It wouldn't be easy, he'd have to lie about his age if asked since he was still a couple of months short of his sixteenth birthday, but at least he would be able to survive, support himself, and start a new life.

His last day in New Orleans he spent covering up the furniture, making sure everything was put away in its place, and packing what belongings he would need in a beat up suitcase he picked up for this journey. Maybe one day, some time in the future, he might return. Yet, he didn't hold out any hope as he walked out, took one last look across the street, and set off for the station.

9

Life is full of moments and the memories of those moments are stored in the lyrics of the songs. Some killers took physical trophies from their victims, such as a lock of hair or piece of jewelry. He, on the other hand, took their songs. What was playing when they met, when they danced, or the last song she heard before the last glimmer of life left her eyes. And when he wanted to remember her, all he had to do was play that one song.

Arriving in Galveston, Raymond found it easier than expected to find work. Showing up on the docks one morning, a foreman asked why he was there. "I'm looking to work, sir." He replied. The foreman, pointing to a ship that had just come in, told him, "go help unload that one. See me at the end of the day and you'll get paid then. Show up again tomorrow, same deal."

No questions asked, Raymond obliged and worked

alongside the others, day in and day out. It was arduous, exhausting work, but the other dockworkers didn't ask questions, and he found he could live life on his own terms.

The opportunities to hear good music weren't as plentiful as they had been in New Orleans, but eventually he found a spot he could go and get his fill.

The first night he happened upon the place was shortly after he had arrived. Standing on the sidewalk, just outside the front door, he was listening to the band that was playing inside. He wasn't bothering anyone coming or going, but the guy working the door didn't like him being there, "music was for paying customers only," he declared, forcefully showing Raymond the way back down the street. Physically bruised and his ego battered, Raymond vowed to get back at him, somehow, some way, but the doorman just laughed and shoved him further down the block.

The deep need to hear the groove of the bass, the wail of the horns, the snap and beat of the drums, the rolling of the keys on the piano, the music he had grown up listening to, was ever present in his mind. "That's what music is supposed to sound like," he said to no one that night as he rubbed at the bruises forming on his arms.

Wandering down the alley that ran behind the bar where he had just been, he found an old crate he could use as a seat, allowing him to hide in the shadows, letting the music drown out everything else, washing away all the problems of the day. This became his routine: work, home, dinner, alley, night after night, month after month, year after year for the next three and a half years. The bands would come and go, the patrons would change, but the music always remained. This was his solace in an otherwise mundane life.

One night, while hiding in his darkened corner, he heard the band play something that sounded like a riff on "The Memphis Blues," which brought back the memory of his first night there, being taunted and beaten by the doorman. That memory turned into another of the pain of the abuse at the hands of his uncle and his father. It was then the voices he thought he had left behind in New Orleans returned. Those dark thoughts taunting him again.

Was this the same song Momma had been listening to, recalling the first experiencing of abuse he suffered at his father's hands? But why did his mind now associate it with these other men, too?

Continuing down this train of thought, he found himself falling further and further into darker places in his mind. The voices that used to taunt him in his sleep were now present in his waking mind, telling him that women were weak, despite what he once thought about Momma and Delphine. That men were to be strong and should show their strength through whatever means was necessary.

These were the same feelings he had experienced before when he had first returned to New Orleans. The sinister voice had woken him from his sleep one night, whispering in his ear, filling his thoughts with vile schemes, that encouraged the idea of revenge against his daddy and even whoever may have been responsible for Momma's disappearance.

Now the voice was back, plaguing him again.

"Look for an opportunity to hurt the brute. Find the one he cares about and do to her what your daddy did to your momma. All women are weak, and at their core, so are the men that love them." He heard the voice screech.

Suddenly scared by what he was feeling and the suggestions of what the voice was telling him to do, he ran off, trying to shut out the noise. Running home to the room he kept, he still heard the voice deriding him, "you're just a weak, scared little boy. When are you going to grow up and prove that you're a man?" It wasn't until early the next morning when he finally fell into a fitful sleep that a sense of quiet returned.

Now Raymond had grown into a man, found his own style, and carried himself in a way that radiated confidence and charm. As he strode into the bar for the first time, right past the doorman who had chased him off all those years ago, he turned the heads of the ladies, those with and without dates, but he didn't seem to notice or care.

He didn't say much to anyone, limiting himself to just one drink that night, preferring to find a spot in the corner and spend the evening watching, listening, taking it all in, as though he were a man living his last days. This became his routine for the next two weeks.

What went unnoticed by the other patrons was the careful attention he paid to a certain waitress, the girlfriend of the brute, working the door. Even though time had passed since that night when the doorman threw Raymond down the street, he hadn't forgotten the pain and humiliation he had experienced. Raymond knew she would be instrumental to his revenge for the wrong done to him and it made crafting this newly hatched idea, all the more satisfying, as he thought it through.

That fateful night, all the pieces fell into place, as though some higher power had ordained it. The band began playing La Pas La Ma as he saw her walking toward the restrooms. Knowing there was a door at the end of the hallway that led to the back alley where he had spent so much time, he was trying to figure out how to get her outside without being spotted. Seeing everyone else focused on the band or their own business, he made his way down the hall, stopping just short of the outer door.

Seeing her exiting the restroom, he called to her, "excuse me. I seem to have dropped my wallet outside, just behind a crate that I can't move and I can't fit my hand back there to reach it. I need someone with a more delicate touch. Do you mind helping me?"

Laughing at his calamity, she replied, "Of course."

"Thank you so much. It's just right over here," pointing at the darkest spot in the alley.

Once he had her outside, and away from the now closed door, it took little for him to overpower her. Finding his hands around her throat, he continued choking the breath out of what he thought to be her worthless body, while listening to the music fill his ears.

It was then Raymond felt a sense of euphoria, as though an enormous weight had been lifted from his chest, a burden that had been making it difficult to breathe all those years. He could hear every note, the beauty and the sadness, the emotion contained in each and every fragment of that song. It was as though through her death, she had given him a new life, a new appreciation for music, and much-needed soul sustenance.

In that fraction of a moment between the beats, when she gasped for her last breath, he took what felt like his first, and he knew his life would never be the same again. Later, he would find that he could relive this feeling, again and again, whenever he heard that song being played. Time would pass and while the memory of her would live on in other people's hearts and minds, for him the memory of what he had done, what he had found out about himself, would live on in the music.

Even though it was dark in the alley, he thought it best to drag over a few empty crates to hide her body. Once finished, he leaned up against the wall and continued to listen as the band played on, savoring every last note. When they finished, he knew his best course of action was not to go back inside. Instead, he wanted to continue enjoying this feeling, hearing the music clearly again, for as long as he could. Walking home, he hummed the tune over and over again.

Returning later that week, Raymond found the mood still somber and her death still the talk around the bar. Taking a seat at the bar, he overheard the bartender telling another patron the details of how she had been found.

"The band had just finished their set and was taking a break when one of the guys, the sax player I think it was, went out back for some air. He sat down on a crate, and when he leaned back against the wall, he saw her there. Scared the poor guy half to death himself. Could barely understand what he was tryin' to tell us, 'til he finally just dragged Joe over there out to see for himself."

"She was such a lovely person," commented the patron, while others were nodding in agreement.

"She was just so sweet," said a waitress, crying inconsolably. "Why would anyone do this to her?"

"If I ever find the guy, I'll kill the son of a bitch myself," the doorman fumed.

The barman continued to explain they were questioned

by the police, but no one had a clue as to who would have done something like this. How could they have not noticed or heard anything, either, was the question that weighing heavily on everyone's mind.

Satisfied he was in the clear, Raymond tossed back his drink and turned his attention back to the band. A smile crossing his face as he heard the band play the first notes of "The Memphis Blues". Taking this as a sign, he made the decision then, it was time to return home.

10

Nothing changes, everything stays the same. Everything changes, nothing stays the same.

Back in New Orleans for the first time in almost four years, Raymond stood in front of the house noticing that not much had changed since he had left, yet somehow everything had changed. The man standing here was no longer the little boy that had grown up in this house, who tried valiantly to protect his mother, who survived his father's torment and abuse. Now in his early twenties, he was living life on his terms, discovering who he was and wanted to be. He no longer defined himself by the words and opinions of others, what they said or thought of him didn't matter anymore.

What did matter was the music. As long as he could hear the music, everything was right in his world.

Approaching the door, he hesitated. The nerves of facing

the unknown churning in stomach, his heart racing, and for a moment he found he was holding his breath. 'Had Momma returned? What would he find inside?' Questions he knew could only be answered by opening the door were racing through his mind.

As far as he could tell, his family had never come looking for him and probably assumed he was dead in a ditch somewhere. The only person he was worrying about running into now was Delphine. Despite having been gone for as long as he had been, she was still the one he was afraid of disappointing. In retrospect, it had only been a relatively short time since they had lived together, yet she had been kinder to him than anyone else, and he didn't know how she would react to the man that he'd become.

"Later, I'll try and find out if she is still in the neighborhood. Perhaps she's still working at that same house in the Garden District. Or maybe she had finally met someone and moved on," he said to the spider who had taken up residence in the doorframe. "But first I need to tend to the house, both inside and out."

Pushing open the front door, a layer of dust, cobwebs, and a musty odor greeted him. It was obvious no one had been in since the last time he set foot in here, everything was still exactly where he had stored it when he left. His ever mercurial attention to detail would have caused him to notice if even a record was out of place.

The last shred of hope that he had been holding onto all these years, that Momma might have returned, now died as well. Faced with no idea what happened to her, other than she never came home that day, he could only speculate, and that still would not get him any closer to finding the truth.

The only thing this train of thought would do was continue to water the seed of disappointment regarding his view of women and just how weak they were, giving substance to what the voices in his head had been telling him all along.

Not wasting any time, he walked back to his old bedroom, throwing his bag on the bed, digging around in the dresser drawers until he found a couple of old t-shirts, many sizes too small now, tearing them into rags. These, along with the old red napkins, would do to clean up the decay that the years had inflicted upon the house. For the next three days, he cleaned, repaired, and repainted, until finally, instead of an empty shell, it began to feel like home again.

He worked to clear a patch in the backyard where he would put in a garden, just as his momma had done all those years before. He weeded the front yard and planted a few new gardenia bushes, too. It was always a favorite scent of his, evoking sweet memories of what he tried to remember as an innocent childhood that seemed like a lifetime ago.

One evening, while working along the side of the house, he saw Delphine walking by. She looked as though she hadn't aged a day, wearing that same maid's uniform, her hair pulled back from her face, carrying that old tote of hers, and humming a tune he sometimes heard in his dreams. Had she noticed the changes around the house, he wondered?

Keeping out of sight, he saw her glancing at the yard, the look on her face showing she had questions. He was wondering what she might be thinking. Was she was trying to figure out if maybe Raymond had returned, or maybe it was it another family member who had decided to take over the property after all these years?

He knew it wasn't her style to be nosy, so he wasn't surprised when she didn't approach the front steps. He watched as she smiled and took in a deep breath of the sweet fragrance coming from the fresh blooms.

For a moment he considered whether he should come around the corner when he overheard her say in a voice just loud enough for him to hear, "I do hope whoever is there is enjoying the house and that it serves as a welcome home to them for many years to come."

Deciding it best to remain hidden in the shadows a little while longer, Raymond smiled and watched as she continued across the street to her house.

11

Spotting the blonde in the corner, the deep emerald green dress she was wearing catching Raymond's eye, he found himself reminiscent of one his mother wore so many years ago.

He watched her looking around, following the movement of her eyes as she searched the crowd in the packed club. Was that a look of disappointment crossing her face? He wondered. Had she been stood up? Taking this as a sign, he turned to the bartender, ordered a shot of whiskey and inquired about the mystery woman. The bartender shrugged as if to say she was just another customer, no one of any importance.

Glancing in the mirror behind the bar, he straightened his navy blue tie and matching pocket square and buttoned the grey silk jacket. He took pride in his appearance, something he noted many of the other men there didn't seem to do.

Striding up to the table, his confidence high, he took the

mystery woman's hand. "Good evening, Dove. Waiting on someone?"

"I was waiting for someone, but it would seem that I've been stood up. Again. I guess the tables presented a more seductive offer than I do this evening." She answered sharply.

Reaching for the back of the chair across from her in an unasked question, he replied, "Well, then he is a fool. I, for one, find you much more attractive than any game ever could be. Allow me to buy you a drink, at least, and perhaps one dance before the night is over?" The charm in his voice never wavering.

Without missing a beat, she agreed. "Gin Rickey, if you please. And my name is-"

Interrupting her with a wave of his hand, "For now, I shall call you Dove, because you must be a divine angel, and to know your name would ruin the mood of the evening. A Gin Rickey for the lady please, and a martini for me," he said, turning toward the passing waitress.

"Will you at least tell me your name so I can properly thank you?" Dove inquired.

"Just call me Raymond. And there is no need to thank me, I simply cannot abide by seeing a beautiful woman sitting alone with sadness creeping into her eyes, especially on such an evening as this."

"You are too kind then, Raymond, but I'm afraid I don't understand what makes this evening any more special than any other night of the week. It's just another Thursday, not a holiday or special event I am aware of."

Reaching over and taking her hand gently in his, he leaned in closer so only she could hear him. "It is special because it is the first time I have met someone as enthralling as you, Dove. And it will be a night that I will remember and cherish for many years to come." His voice was rhapsodic and charming, as though he were caressing each syllable.

Settling back into his chair, he watched as she lifted the drink to her blush pink lips. He noted a pause before she drank and raised his glass in return. The band had returned to the stage and the tempo of the music had picked up, encouraging the patrons to fill the dance floor. As she finished her drink, he asked if she would like another or would she prefer to take him up on a dance.

He was hoping for something slower, a foxtrot maybe, if the partner was willing. That would allow for more physical contact, and the opportunity for him to take in the sights and smells of his companion for the evening. But sensing her apprehension when they first met, he decided perhaps a quicker paced dance such as the Charleston to start off with would set her at ease before moving on to something more intimate.

She giggled, "I warn you now, I have two left feet and very little sense of rhythm, but I'll give it a try if you don't mind me embarrassing you out there."

"Nothing you could do would embarrass me, Dove. Allow me," he said, standing and offering her his hand.

He led her to the dance floor confidently, with a style and grace, a perfect gentleman and dance partner.

As the evening wore on, Raymond kept hoping the music he was hearing internally wouldn't end. It was keeping the voices at bay, and he wanted so much to just enjoy the evening. He knew this Dove wasn't "the one", but she was pleasant enough company. He didn't want to consider what could happen next. Knowing if the music stopped, this dove here wouldn't be around for too much longer. And that was a shame, she seemed to be a sweet young thing, with a bright future ahead of her.

After another dance, Dove excused herself to the powder room, allowing Raymond the time to reflect on the events of the evening so far. He noted after her initial hesitation, which most women had when approached by a stranger, she became more comfortable in his presence, letting little bits of information about her life slip out in between dances. She had consumed two more Gin Rickey's, and as far as he could tell, she had not noticed that he had stopped drinking after his first martini. He knew he would need to have a clear head for what was to come later.

When she returned from the powder room, he suggested, "perhaps one more drink before the evening ends?"

"I suppose one more couldn't hurt, but I really must stop after that. I have to be in to open the store on time tomorrow morning, or there's no telling what my boss will do."

Instead of waiting for the waitress, he excused himself from the table, insisting he get the drinks. Striding confidently up to the bar, ordered her Gin Rickey and a glass of water for himself. Staying out of her line of sight, he reached into his coat pocket and retrieved a small vial. Hiding it in the palm of his hand, he slipped a few drops of bromide into her drink, swirling it gently to mix it in as he returned to the table.

Finishing their drinks, he asked, "May I see you home safely, or at least allow me to escort you to the streetcar? I wouldn't want anything to happen to you, even if home is just a short distance away."

He watched as she pondered his suggestion for a minute after a beat, acquiescing and allowing him to retrieve her wrap from the coat check as they made their way out of the club. "I don't live that far from here, really. We could just walk if that would be okay with you," she slurred. "I think the fresh air may do me some good, too. I'm suddenly feeling so much more tired than I was just a little while ago."

"Of course, Dove, if that would make you feel better, by all means, let's walk."

Strolling down the sidewalk, Raymond watched as the Bromide took full effect. Dove was now stumbling and becoming more unsteady on her feet. "I don't know what's wrong with me. Usually Gin Rickey's don't affect me this way. I am terribly sorry, but I think I need to stop for a minute."

Seeing the opportunity presenting itself, he steered her down a walkway leading back to a courtyard for the surrounding apartments, finding a little bench where they could sit down. Dove was trying to speak, but all that came out was a series of mumbled syllables, nothing that was making any sense.

"There, there, Dove, just relax. Everything is going to be just fine." It was then she could see in his eyes that every-thing wasn't going to be just fine.

12

The Gibson was a club just on the edge of the Back
O' Town, set away from the raucous crowds and
illicit gambling houses that permeated the rest of
the neighborhood. Located on a corner, it had windows that
opened on both sides, filling the night air with its songs.
The sign, weathered and faded, added to its unassuming
appearance. This place was a true hidden gem, where you
could find some of the best musicians the city had to offer.
There was no pretense allowed when you were here, egos
were checked at the door. Skin color was no barrier, wealth
and stature didn't account for anything, either. The love of
the music, plain and simple, is what brought the kindred
souls together.

When the group of friends arrived that evening, they
found the place already hopping. The band was in full
swing, evoking the mood of a tempest. The music befitting
the night was steamy and sultry, a storm churning off in the
distance in the Gulf.

Delphine could feel the music through her entire body,

from the follicles of her hair, down to the soles on her calloused feet. A bead of sweat trickled down the small of her back, reminiscent of a soft rain running down a drainpipe. She watched the piano player as his fingers caressed the keys, the trombone player slid in low and slow, and the drummer set the tempo. As a drug addict needs his next fix from his dealer, the audience is held captive by the musicians, first given just a little taste to get them hooked, then reeling them in for the final score. It was times like this when she forgot everything and everyone else and just allowed the sounds to permeate every inch of her being.

Walking to the last empty table, Delphine looked around, noticing a man standing alone at the end of the bar, a feeling of déjà vu coming over her. It wasn't until they were sitting down when she turned to Evelyn and asked, "Over in the corner of the bar, do you recognize that guy over there? It feels like there's something familiar about him."

Glancing over her shoulder, Evelyn shrugged. "I don't know him. But then again, I'm not here as often as the rest of you. Do you think he is cause for concern?"

"No. It's just me being foolish. I just can't place the face, but I feel like I should know him from somewhere."

"Well, he is a handsome fellow, I'll give you that. Maybe you should go introduce yourself." Evelyn teased.

Giving her friend a look as if to say, 'I'd rather die,' Delphine turned her attention back to her friends and the band.

When the band started their next song, the group was on their feet and moving toward the dance floor. Evelyn was enjoying a much needed night out with her husband David, while Delphine, who didn't normally dance much, also joined in the festivities, taking turns dancing with David and a couple of other fellows from work who had joined them, when she found herself face to face with the stranger who had previously been in the corner.

No words were exchanged between them, and after a few quick turns, he moved on to the next partner. Leaving her to wonder just who this stranger was and why he seemed so familiar.

When the band took a break, the group made their way back to the table to catch their breath and refresh their drinks. Shifting her chair to gain a better vantage point, Delphine glanced around the room in an attempt to find the mystery man again. She couldn't shake the feeling she first had when she saw him and was now convinced that she must know him, but from where?

Thinking she saw him in the hall by the restrooms, she started to get up when Evelyn stopped her.

"I know that look, Delphine. What are you up to?"

"Nothing. I just..." Delphine trailed off.

"That look says more than nothing. You need to sit back down and think about whatever it is you're about to do."

Delphine looked at her friend and the rest of the group at the table. Knowing Evelyn was right, she took one last look down the hall, seeing nothing, nodded and took her seat again.

When the band returned and the rest of the friends got up to dance, Delphine and Evelyn stayed behind at the table, Delphine feigning fatigue, Evelyn saying she'd stay to keep her company. Once David and the others were out of earshot, she turned and moved closer to Delphine in order to be heard over the music.

"Okay. You haven't been yourself all evening. What has gotten into you?"

"I don't know. When we came in I spotted that guy at the bar, and well, just something about him set my hair on end. Then we came face to face on the dance floor, well face to side of face, he wouldn't actually look at me. Which was odd. And well, I haven't said anything before this, because I wasn't certain, and I'm still not, but Evelyn, I think Raymond may be back in town."

Taking a beat to consider what she just heard, Evelyn declared, "Well, that's good news, right? If he's back, then you don't need to keep taking care of the house like you've been and now you can focus on you. But what's got you so disturbed by that?"

Looking at her friend as though she had lost her mind, she asked, "Do you not remember, all those years ago..."

Met with a blank stare, Delphine continued.

"Ever since Genevieve disappeared, life has not been the same for Raymond. First, she doesn't come home, then his daddy winds up dead just after that. I know Raymond came back for a little while after the summer I sent him away. And Evelyn, I still feel bad about that. Looking back, I shouldn't have done that. But after that last episode at school, when he beat up that girl, I didn't think I could handle him. Especially knowing what a monster his father had been. I was afraid he was going to turn into him."

Interrupting, Evelyn held up a hand. "But I don't understand, what does this have to do with the mystery man?"

"I'm getting to that. Like I said, I think he's back in town again. I've seen some movement at the house, and it appears someone has a garden growing in the back again, too. At first, I thought maybe Genevieve came home. But if she had, why wouldn't she come tell any of us? My next thought was maybe other family had decided to come take over the place. But surely I would have seen people coming and going if that were true. So, that only leads me to believe that Raymond must be back, but doesn't want anyone, at least me anyway, knowing. Which begs the question, why? What is he hiding? Which brings me back to the mystery man. I think it could have been him. I mean, it's been years since I've seen him, and I didn't get a good look at his eyes, but the more I think about it, the more is seems like it could be."

"Okay, so say Raymond is back. So what? Delphine, you did all you could those years ago. What more can you do now?"

"I don't know. I just feel like all those years ago Genevieve was trying to tell me something that last day before she disappeared. It's like she knew she wasn't going to be able to take care of him anymore. All these years, I've been left wondering if she had something to do with Walter's death. Or maybe he killed her first? I don't know. But there is something wrong, and I mean to get to the bottom of it."

Before she could say anymore, in that brief moment between the beats of the song, she thought she heard a scream off in the distance. Looking around, she tried to pinpoint where it was coming from, but the band was playing on and she decided she must be hearing things that weren't there. Turning back to Evelyn and the band, she said, "Maybe I'm just tired. I think it's time for me to go home and just leave this night behind me. Maybe things will look clearer tomorrow."

13

Laying in bed, Delphine spent the night tossing and turning, haunted by the memories of events from years gone by.

One in particular was the day Raymond was sent home from school for beating up one of his classmates. He claimed she had been the one to start it, always trying to talk into his bad ear, knowing full well he couldn't hear. Usually it would wind up with the teacher telling them both to be quiet, but on this day, having had enough, he turned around and punched her, knocking her out of her seat and onto the floor. Once down, he continued kicking her in the stomach and calling her names until the teacher could pull him off. He was immediately sent to the principal's office, who called the house where Genevieve was supposed to be working.

Delphine intercepted the call and said she would make sure someone came to pick Raymond up right away. Upon retrieving him, she could see a darkness in him that had not shown itself before. His eyes were blazing, his fists balled up, and he stomped his way back to his makeshift room when they returned home. She tried to talk to him, in an attempt to find out what had happened, but all he would say was, "she had it coming." Words that she had heard uttered by Genevieve when she spoke of the abuse that she had suffered at Walter's hand.

Knowing that she wouldn't be able to control Raymond if his behavior like this continued, she decided then that when summer came, he would have to go live with other family. She would make some excuse to them why, to not raise too many questions. She convinced herself it was what would be best for him and perhaps by then Genevieve would have returned and the point would then be moot.

Her thoughts turned to Genevieve, and speculation about what had happened to her. Delphine had found out shortly after Walter's death that a woman had been at the bar when Walter was killed. Based on the description the bartender had shared with her, she guessed it had to have been Genevieve. But if she was still alive after Walter's death, why had she not returned home? Did she have something to do with it? Would anyone have blamed her? He was a vile man, and the world, especially Raymond and Genevieve's would have been better without him around.

Then there was the letter she had received a year after she had sent Raymond away. There was no return address, no sign it was even mailed. Just an envelope in her mailbox with her name printed on the front. The handwriting was hard to read, some words smudged, perhaps even tear stained, and the content rambled on. The writer was trying to apologize without saying exactly what they had done or needed forgiveness for. Delphine thought it was from Genevieve, but she couldn't fathom why her friend just didn't come home. Why would she stay away from her son and her home for so long?

Unable to glean much information from the letter, Delphine tucked it away in a drawer, thinking maybe someday she would find the answers. Otherwise, out of sight would be out of mind for her.

Rolling over, Delphine tried to go back to sleep, knowing sooner, rather than later, she would have to come face to face with her questions, and quite possibly, Raymond too.

14

Lost in his train of thought, Raymond wasn't paying attention to anyone else on the street. Had he been, he would have seen Delphine approaching from a block away, and noticed the look of determination on her face, as though she were a woman on a mission.

"Hello." She said, stopping him in his tracks.

"I, um, excuse me." He stammered, not fully aware of who he had just bumped into.

"Raymond, is that really you? After all these years?"

Raymond paused, first taking notice of a look of questioning, then disbelief, then impatience crossing Delphine's face.

"Yes. Hello, Delphine. It's n-nice to see you again," he stammered. "H-how have you been?"

He was finding it difficult, trying to maintain his composure with the stampede of thoughts and emotions that he was experiencing, leaving him confused and disoriented.

Delphine appeared taken aback by his brief response, as

though she had been expecting something more, recognition, remorse, heartfelt, she wasn't sure.

"How have I been? That's all you have to say for yourself, Raymond? How have I been? I don't even know where to begin. I..." Smiling, she took another step, arms open and ready to embrace him.

Before she could hug him, Raymond gathered his wits and interrupted, "I'm sorry. I guess I should have stopped by when I got back into town and let you know I was back. That was my mistake. I do owe you more of an explanation, but I'm in a bit of a hurry right now. I don't mean to be rude, but can we meet later? Perhaps coffee or dinner, and then I can explain."

Trying to extricate himself from the situation as quickly as possible, not wanting to accidentally blurt out more than he should, he knew he needed to have his story straight in his mind before he could face the well-meaning inquisition that was sure to come.

Delphine raised her eyebrows in question, but instead suggested, "Sure. Why don't you stop by the house later then and you can fill me in on what's been going on in your life? We certainly have a lot of life to catch up on."

"Coffee it is then," he agreed, resuming his walk down the street, continuing on past his house to make it appear as though he were on his way to somewhere else, hoping this would appease her for his erratic behavior this time.

'What is it about her that is so unsettling to me? She's never done me any harm, but yet it feels as though she sees right through me or that she knows something more than she's saying, but what could it be?' He pondered as he continued to wander around the neighborhood. 'Does she know something about Momma's disappearance? Did she recognize me that night at the Gibson? Could she have seen what I did?'

Too many questions flying around his mind were causing his heart to race and a cold sweat to break out across his brow.

'I have to get home and figure out how I'm going to handle this. I can't go in blind, but I can't do anything to raise any suspicions either.'

Returning to her home, Delphine began preparing for Raymond's visit. Crying and overcome with emotion, she was unsure if they were tears of happiness or sorrow. Thinking back to his childhood brought about another pang of guilt, should she have done more for him all those years ago?

Reaching for the coffee cups, it was then she realized it had been him she saw at the Gibson. Her feelings of guilt were now being replaced by even more questions. Why would he never have said anything? What did he want to hide from me? Surely I've never given him cause to doubt that my home was a safe place and that I would always be here for him, even after sending him away. Where has he been all these years?

Thinking back to just a few nights before, she knew there had been something unsettling about him when she had seen him in the club, but she couldn't put her finger on what exactly it was. Was it just the note of familiarity, a remembrance of who he had been as a child, but that she didn't recognize him as an adult? What had happened in his life during the time he had been gone? Who had he become? Had he found out about the secret she had been keeping all this time?

Continuing with her preparations, she wondered if she should call Evelyn and David to come over, too. No, best not, she decided. Having someone else here might not make him feel comfortable enough to give her the answers she needed to the questions that she knew she had to ask. Besides, what reason would she have to not feel safe with him around? It would just be the two of them, having a cup of coffee, catching up on the years that had elapsed between them.

Raymond walked around the block twice more before finally approaching Delphine's door. No matter what he told himself, he still felt like a disappointment to her after all these years, and he didn't want to find out what her reaction would be if she knew what he had been up to.

Pushing aside the nagging thoughts of inadequacy, he knocked on the screen door. Delphine was quick to answer. He saw her wiping her hands on her apron as she approached and invited him in. As he entered, he looked around the room and noticed not much had changed over the years. It was as though he stepped right back into his childhood once again, and he found himself overcome by questions and the emotions of where his mother might be and why she never returned.

"Raymond, please, come in and have a seat. It's so good to see you after all these years." He heard Delphine saying, bringing him back to the present moment.

"Yes, I... well..." Raymond was trying his best to find the right words to explain what had taken place all those years.

"Please, let me get the coffee and I've got some cake, too.

It's not much. But we can at least enjoy a little something while sit and talk. There's no need to rush, unless, of course, you have somewhere you need to be later?"

"No, no. I'm sorry. It's just been so long since I was last here and suddenly the memories of Momma, the music that she used to always have playing, her disappearance and, well... everything. It's just a little overwhelming. I'm fine. Please, let me help you with that," he offered, as she came back out with a tray.

Settling down in the living room, Delphine started. "I have so many questions, Raymond. Where do I begin?"

Raymond interrupted, hoping to control the conversation and what information he would share, "Let me see if I can fill in some of the blanks for you first."

He told her of his time on the family farm, but not of the abuse he endured there, accepting Delphine's apology for not checking in on him and reassuring her it wasn't her fault or her responsibility to have taken care of him. She, after all, had her own life. It wasn't as though he was related to her, she shouldn't feel any guilt for not knowing.

"But when you came back to the house, why didn't you let me know you were here? I could have helped out."

"You did help out, though. You left food for me, which I cannot thank you enough for. You also, for whatever reason, chose not to come asking questions. I know I should have come to you sooner and told you I was back. But I kept holding out hope that Momma was going to return any day. After a while, I just came to the conclusion that she was never coming back."

Pausing, he thought back on the young boy that left, wondering how much different life would have been had he sought out Delphine's help instead of trying to live on his own.

He looked at Delphine as she sat, considering all that he had just told her. What could she be thinking? Was she questioning her decision now, to leave a young boy like that to his own devices? He could see something was weighing heavily on her mind.

"Delphine, is there something bothering you? You look as though you've seen a ghost."

"No, I'm sorry. I was just taking in all that you've told me. Wondering if I should have stepped in sooner. Or not sent you away in the first place. Would life have turned out differently for you? But it seems that you've made it okay. But I do have to ask, that was you at the Gibson. Why didn't you say anything?"

"I don't know. I don't have a good answer for that. I suppose I didn't want to intrude on your life. I was just there to hear the music." It was a weak excuse, and he knew it.

"Well, it wouldn't have been an intrusion at all. I was there with my friends and coworkers, and I'm sure they would love to meet you too. Next time you're there and you see us, please, do come over and join us, at least for a drink."

Considering the implications of this proposition, he just said, "Yes, of course, the next time I see you there, I will try to stop by."

Continuing to talk over the next hour, Delphine shared she had continued to monitor the house while he had been gone, looking for his mother's return or that of any other family. But no one ever came by. She asked if he had ever found out anything more regarding his father's death.

"No, I took a chance and stopped by the boarding house. The old man that runs the place remembered him, but what little information he offered was of no help."

"I see. And from what you've told me, no word on your momma either. Raymond, I am so sorry. I wish there was something more I could do or say to set your mind at ease," Delphine sighed.

Pausing for a moment to mull over what he thought he heard, he replied tersely, "Yes, I've come to accept the fact that she's just gone and that it will always be an unanswered question in my life."

Looking at Delphine, he wondered if there was something more she wasn't saying. Did she know something about his mother? Had Momma come back during the years he was away? If so, why didn't she stay? Once again, he found himself with even more questions than he first arrived with.

Abruptly getting to his feet, he declared, "Thank you for a lovely visit. I apologize again for not coming by sooner. I honestly have no good reason why I didn't. You have always been so kind to me, Delphine, I don't know if I could ever repay you. But now I won't keep you any longer."

Taken aback at the suddenness, Delphine rose as well. "Don't be such a stranger anymore. Please. I'm here if you need anything. And remember, the next time you are at the Gibson, I expect you to come say hello. I know everyone would love to meet you."

Walking to the door, Raymond took one last look around. "Yes, well, good night then," he said as he let the screen door slam behind him.

15

It wasn't until the following Thursday afternoon on her way home from work that she saw signs of life at Raymond's house again. The windows were open, a ladder was leaning against the front porch, and a paint can perched precariously on a step. Seeing this as an opportunity to approach the house without raising suspicion, she walked up to the steps and bent down to push the can back against the handrail. As she stood, she found herself face to face with Raymond, brush in one hand, and a glass of lemonade in the other.

"Well, Delphine, we meet again." Raymond spat.

"Raymond, I'm sorry. I didn't mean to disturb you. I just noticed the can looked as though it was about to fall off the step. I didn't think you'd want the mess of paint running all over the place," she tried to explain.

"Oh, yes, well thank you for that," his tone softening. "I had just gone in the house for a drink. Guess I wasn't paying attention to where I set it down."

"So, how have you been since our last visit? Looks like

you are sprucing the place up. Does this mean you are planning on staying?" Delphine said, trying to be as cordial as she could without coming across as though she was digging for information.

Glancing over her shoulder as though there were something on the street that held more interest, he said, "Well, as I mentioned during our visit, I'm back for a while. I don't really know how long exactly. I guess until the wind blows and the music changes."

His mention of music caused the hairs on the back of her neck to stand up. For a second time this week, someone referring to music caused her to experience a twinge of disquiet. Trying to not let it show on her face, she smiled.

"I see, well I should let you get back to your chores. But you really must come over some evening for supper, it will give us a chance to catch up some more."

"Of course. Thank you. Maybe one day next week we can do that," he offered, his tone not quite genuine.

"Yes, that would be lovely. You just let me know what day works best for you, and I'll fix your favorites. You are still partial to catfish and greens?"

Taken aback at her mention of his childhood favorites, he finally looked her in the eye. "Even after all these years, you still remember that? Yes, ma'am, still one of my favorites. And I still haven't found anyone else who makes it quite the way you do."

Blushing, Delphine offered a smile as she picked up her bag. "Then next week it is. In the meantime, if there's anything else you need, you don't hesitate to come by, understand?"

Attempting to hide his confusion as thoughts began

bubbling in his head, he replied, "Yes, ma'am. Thank you again."

Crossing the street to her home, she quickly closed the front door and collapsed into a chair. Even that brief encounter with him had set her on edge. She now knew in her gut there was something off about him, but she still couldn't identify what bothered her so. Had the short time away with his extended family affected him that much? Or had something else happened during those years away to change the sweet young boy into this man she hardly recognized anymore?

As he stood there, watching Delphine return to her home, Raymond could feel his anxiety building. He knew he would have to go over sometime soon for dinner, or she'd keep coming around until he finally acquiesced. Setting the glass of lemonade down on the rail, he was reminded of the happy time he spent at her house as a young boy. How different life had been back then. Even with the turmoil of his momma missing, life had been mostly good, the music still sounded pure, his future ahead of him unblemished.

He shook his head, trying to push the memories and the voices back down, reminding himself to focus on the here and now. From inside, he heard the radio announcer interrupting the steady stream of music with what he figured could only be bad news.

"Police issue a statement regarding the latest body found. No new leads, or suspects, this one just adding to the rising number of young women found dead outside of various clubs. The police urge caution and ask anyone with information to please come forward."

Reflecting for a moment on what he knew he had done, a slight smile crossed Raymond's face as he recalled some songs he had collected so far, "Farewell Blues," "Deed I Do," and his favorite, "Squeeze Me."

Looking back across the street at Delphine's house, his smile turning down, he whispered, "I'm not proud of what I've done, I know it's wrong. But soon it will stop. Simone will pay for what she did. The voices will finally shut up, and the music will play the way it should once again."

16

That night at the Gibson was the second time Raymond thought he had seen her. A grown-up version of the girl from his childhood, Simone, the one that taunted him and always got him in trouble. But he still couldn't be sure. It had been so long ago. Yet after all these years, he found it was her voice that he heard screaming the dark thoughts in his sleep and her face, twisted and grotesque, that haunted his dreams.

Why her though? She had only been in his life for a short time. He had suffered more abuse at the hands of his father and uncle. What was it about her that brought out this darkness in him?

After the night at the Gibson, he decided to pay a visit to the house in the Garden District. He knew Delphine had worked there as a child, and perhaps she was still working there. He didn't want to come face to face with there, but he had too many questions and knew he needed to find answers. He was taking a chance being so close, sure he was going to spotted. Creeping up the side porch, he was considering taking a step inside, just for a quick peek, when he heard someone approaching. In his haste to leave, he dropped a red napkin that he had been clutching in his hand.

It was then he saw Simone for the first time. She walked into the room he had just stepped out of and watched as she picked up the napkin from the floor. He could hear her questioning someone else about it, but couldn't decipher who it was that answered her. Hearing her voice, suddenly all the previous years were erased, and he was back in the schoolyard once again. With his head spinning, he found his vision turning cloudy, as though the humidity and heaviness in the air of the impending storm was casting a veil over the city as well as what was directly in front of him.

The taunting voices telling him indeed, she was the same person from the playground, then perhaps punishing her for what she did all those years ago would bring him some peace. Maybe if he could do to her what she did to him, then he could hear the music for what it was and he wouldn't have to satiate this inner darkness any longer.

Stepping back off the porch, Raymond tried to push these thoughts from his mind. But the harder he tried, the louder they became. Just as he was leaving, he heard her laugh above the other night sounds and knew exactly who she was and what he needed to do.

17

Over a week had passed after his run in with Delphine and during that time he thought it best if he not set foot back in the Gibson. He knew he still would have to go over for dinner and didn't want to give her any other chances to confront him and raise more questions before he was ready. When he knew he couldn't put her off any longer, he made sure to be outside one afternoon when she was coming home from work. This would be the evening when he would control the narrative and finally face her and his past.

Going to greet her as she made her way down from the streetcar stop, he put on a show of offering to help with her bags, acting as though nothing had ever changed between the two of them. Raising the idea that this evening would be good for him to accept her invitation to dinner, she agreed this would be a fine time for them to share a meal.

"Give me an hour to get things prepped, then you come on over." She told him when as they approached her door.

An hour later, on the dot, he trepidatiously approached

the door and knocked. Delphine promptly answered and as she opened the door Raymond could smell the greens simmering and the catfish frying, smells immediately transporting him back to childhood.

Ushering him in, she said, "Raymond, I'm so glad we can finally share a meal. Please, make yourself comfortable. I need to tend to the fish before they burn. Can I offer you tea or lemonade to drink?"

Taken aback by the genuineness of her demeanor, he stuttered, "Um, tea is fine, thank you."

"Wonderful. Have a seat, supper will be ready shortly. You remember where everything is, I'm sure."

As Delphine returned to the kitchen, Raymond took a moment to look around, observing that not much had changed over the years. The house still looked and smelled the same as when he was a boy, everything neatly in its place. He noted a few areas of disrepair, but that was expected of a single woman living on her own. Perhaps if he offered to take care of those chores for her, it would give him the opportunity to probe for more information regarding Simone without it seeming too awkward.

"I'm sorry it's taken me a while to take you up on the offer. I know I said I would be over last week, but time just got away from me." He called to her in the kitchen.

"Of course, I understand how that is. You must be busy with work and all."

"Yes, well. That's been sporadic, but chores around the house have kept me occupied too. I see there are a few things around here that look as though they could stand to be fixed. I could help you out with that if you like. You know, to repay you for all your kindness over the years. I feel I at least owe you that."

Poking his head around the corner, he saw her wiping her hands on her apron. "That's kind of you, Raymond, really. You don't owe me anything, but the help would be appreciated. I've been so overwhelmed at work lately, I just haven't had the energy to take care of anything once I'm home. But let's save that conversation for later. Right now, dinner is ready, please," she said with a wave at the table, already set.

The greens were cooked and seasoned to perfection, the catfish flaky and tender, with just the right amount of heat in the crust. He had forgotten how much he missed her and his momma's cooking all these years. The meal was complete with cornbread and a side of black-eyed peas. For dessert, he spotted a peach cobbler sitting on the kitchen counter. It was as though she knew he would be here this evening.

"Delphine, you have outdone yourself. Surely you didn't just happen to make all this food—even the cobbler—in just an hour's time?"

"No, I just - well, call it intuition if you will. Somehow, I just knew that you'd be over tonight. But enough about my food, please, let's sit somewhere more comfortable while we enjoy our dessert. There's so much to catch up on."

Raymond wanted to run. He wanted to leave now before the evening took a turn, he could feel the darkness stirring. But before he could make any excuses about it being time for him to leave, Delphine handed him a plate of cobbler and pushed him in the direction of the living room. Knowing she wouldn't have it any other way, he replied, "Yes, ma'am."

Raymond sat rigid in the straight-back chair in hopes of it helping to contain what he was feeling inside. He waited as Delphine took her time to settle on the couch across from him. He was watching her as she was looking back at him.

"Now, before we go about getting caught up, I have to apologize to you, Raymond. I had no idea what your family was like when I sent you off that summer and had I known, I would have kept you here with me. For that, I am truly sorry."

Sitting still for what felt like an eternity, Raymond took in what she said, trying to appear more interested in his cobbler, that had so far remained untouched. Hoping that his face wouldn't give away the confusion clouding his mind, he was trying to figure out how could she have known what he suffered through that summer? He had told of his time on the farm, but not about the abuse he suffered at the hands of his aunt and uncle. Who could have told her about that? And more importantly, what else did she know about his past?

"I don't understand Delphine. What do you have to apologize for? You thought you were doing what was best for me, sending me to be with family. While they weren't ideal replacements for my parents, they treated me fairly enough," he said, trying his best to not let on what a lie he was trying to pass off.

"Oh, well, I'm glad to hear that. I just thought, well, I thought you had come back home after that summer, but since you didn't come by here to let me know, I thought maybe you were mad at me for sending you away and that maybe something terrible had happened. They seemed nice enough when they picked you up, but I also had a sense that perhaps that had been just for my benefit. I'm glad to hear that things went okay for you that summer," Delphine said, trying to backpedal her words, realizing that he knew she wouldn't have had any first-hand knowledge of what she had alluded to.

"Yes, it was fine. And yes, as you know, I did come back for a time. Again, I can't thank you enough for the food you left. It definitely helped me through those lean days. I had every intention of coming over and letting you know I was back. I even thought about going back to finish my last couple of years of school. But then time just seemed to get away from me, and I thought it best to leave town. It was apparent to me that Momma wasn't coming back and Daddy was dead, so there wasn't any reason for me to stay."

"But," Delphine interrupted.

"No. Really, it's fine. I wound up in Galveston for a few years. I found work there pretty easily, and it gave me the chance to grow up a bit too. There were too many memories around town here, a fresh start was what I needed. While it was rough at first, but eventually, I found my way. I grew up, learned the ropes of the construction trade, and then, when it was time, I decided I was ready to come back home." Raymond was trying his best to control the conversation, not letting too much information slip, but giving her just enough that he hoped it would pacify her inquisition before it had a chance to get to out of hand.

"Well, that's not something such a young boy should have to go through. I do wish you would have let me help out more. But I'm glad to see you back now. Not too much worse for the wear I can see. You seem to have done fine for yourself."

"Yes, ma'am. I have. My only wish still is to know what could have happened to Momma all those years ago. Do you know if they ever found anything more?"

Delphine paused, taking a sip of her tea, as he noticed her hand shaking. "No, I'm sorry dear. I periodically stopped back by the precinct, but as you know, the police around here don't place a high priority on the disappearance of any woman. Even now, with all those young girls they've been finding around town, they don't seem to be doing a lot to solve those either."

Raymond was taken aback by her matter-of-factness at how she was speaking about his killings. Again, it felt to him as though she knew something, but he couldn't quite figure out what or how to ask. Shifting slightly in his chair, he raised his hands to adjust his tie, hoping to camouflage anything that might betray what he was thinking.

"I figured as much. I guess I'll just have to accept the fact that I'll never know what happened to her or who could have killed Daddy."

"Raymond, I wish I could speak words that would take away your pain. All I can tell you is that I believe your momma is living a better life now. Not that it makes it any easier, but hopefully it will bring you a little solace." Delphine softly replied.

There was something about Delphine's inflection when she said Momma was living a better life, it felt as though she were talking about her still in the present tense. Fidgeting in his seat, unable to sit still any longer, he was finding himself with more questions and still no answers, the noise that he had managed to keep quiet all evening, starting to swell. He shook his head in an attempt to quiet it, but it didn't seem to help.

Rising abruptly, he thanked Delphine. "It was a wonderful meal and delightful company. Thank you again for the invitation, but I really must be going now. I've taken up too much of your time already."

Taken aback at his sudden change, Delphine rose and offered, "Any time, Raymond. You are always welcome here, you should know that."

"Yes, well, good night then," Raymond said, striding to the door and out into the cool night.

The breeze felt soothing against his hot face, but he knew it wouldn't be enough to pacify the storm that was now raging within. He attempted to walk as casually as he could back to his house, knowing that Delphine was probably watching. Her words had been casual enough, yet he could feel there was an underlying current of information that she wasn't going to share, at least not readily. Faced with more questions, he walked into his house, closed the door, and drew the curtains, before heading into the kitchen and retrieving the hidden bottle from the top shelf in the cabinet.

Sinking to the floor with bottle in hand, he was wishing the strong drink would help quiet the clamor and give him a chance to process all that he had learned that evening. Was it possible that Momma was still alive after all these years? What difference would that make in his life now, though? And more importantly, how did Simone fit into this picture? He still knew nothing more about her. What was it about her that made him think she had what it took to quiet his mind and soul?

18

The only thing the whiskey accomplished that night was knocking Raymond out. His nightmares, even more vivid than before, the faces of the girls he had killed so far, intermingled with those of Delphine, Momma and Simone.

Waking the next morning, Raymond returned to the courtyard, reliving the events that had taken place there, hoping that maybe he would find solace and possibly some answers. The physicality of what he had done there repulsed him. He had taken three lives now. Each time choking the life from their bodies, then collecting their last songs. Yet it was in these brief moments he found a respite, a sense of calm and that all was right with the world. He could hear the music the world had to offer, and that at least made him feel happy once again. But in the background, the demons were still tormenting him, raising their voices in quiet moments, reminding him all was not quiet in his world.

Watching the fountain spill over its sides, he continued

pondering. 'Perhaps if I got answers regarding Momma's disappearance, then maybe life could return to normal. Maybe then the voices would stop. I could sleep through the night without the horrible dreams and then I could truly hear the music once again.'

Deciding that he had to face facts once and for all, he left behind the fountain and all the thoughts he had there, and made his way to the same police station he first visited as a child. He found himself wishfully thinking that maybe someone had come forward with new information or perhaps the case had been solved, but no one ever told him. Either way, he knew he had to find out, so he could put this awful worry behind him.

Much to his dismay, the desk sergeant on duty wasn't much help. He dug out a file, what appeared to be no more than two pieces of paper. "Based on the family history that I see here, I'd guess your daddy came back and took care of her once and for all. I also see he's met his demise as well. Pretty open and shut to me," he said with a grunt as he returned the paperwork to a pile standing ready to topple off the corner of his desk.

It was obvious to Raymond that they had put no effort into the investigation, which came as no surprise to him, either. After all, it was just another poor colored woman who went missing, not a high priority case as far as they were concerned.

"I see. Well, thank you, sir, for your help in the matter," Raymond replied icily. "I won't take any more of your time then."

Leaving the station, he wondered if his victims would wind up in that same pile. Nameless faces, forgotten by everyone else, except for those who were closest to them.

He found this thought unsettling somehow. They deserved more respect than that. Feeling the chaos rising, he knew it wouldn't be long now before he'd have to hear the music again.

⚜

Having found no success when he asked the police for help in finding his mother, Raymond decided it was time to try a different tactic to find out what happened to her. Maybe Daddy's journal will give me a clue, he thought. Digging through what remained of his father's belongings, he found the tattered book, right where he left all those years ago.

Walking back out to the living room, he settled down in the old, straight-backed chair his father used to occupy when he had been home. Reading through the scrawled entries as best he could was an uncomfortable experience. Some entries were difficult to decipher because of his father's handwriting, others partly due to stains on the page that Raymond could only assume resulted from spilled alcohol, and some entries were just downright vulgar.

Many of these accounts were boasts or laments about his winnings and losings at the gambling tables and the conquests of unwitting women. Yet in between there were sporadic writings that gave Raymond insight into the man who his mother had first fallen in love with.

Raymond teared up when he read the written missives on how his father missed his mother's beautiful face, how he longed to taste again the meals that she so lovingly prepared. He read an entry where daddy reminisced about a time when he and momma must have been dating and they went on a picnic one summer afternoon. Just the two of them, sharing a lunch that she had prepared, as they spread out on a quilt within a stone's throw of a pond where the ducks swam lazily in circles, oblivious to the two lovers on the banks. He described with flourish what she had been wearing that day, how she smiled when he tried to coax a duck over to eat a piece of bread and instead got bitten, and how he knew then that he wanted to spend the rest of his life with her.

There was an extensively detailed entry devoted entirely to the songs that they had danced to during their courtship and the first years of their marriage. Raymond was seeing a side of his parents that he never knew existed. A couple that would go out, dance until their feet couldn't take any more, and shared a love of music, a love which had been instilled in him as well.

He thought to himself, 'maybe this was why momma always had music playing when daddy wasn't around. Maybe it reminded her of the better days, happier times before life took the turn it had. Was this also why his father tried to destroy anything musically related when he smashed all her records that day all those years ago?'

Because he had been so young at the time, he didn't have any clear memories of what went on outside of his little worldview. What could have happened then to cause this downward spiral? What must have snapped in the man to treat his wife and son the way he did? Was this a trait that passed on from father to son? Was it in his blood, too? Or was it something learned?

Pausing for a moment, he reflected on the Doves he had met and killed. 'Maybe it is hereditary. Why else would I feel the need to do what it is that I do?'

Picking the journal up again, he came to the last entry. The penmanship he found it was unlike any of the other pages. This page was devoid of any stains or smudges, printed in very straight letters, as though someone else had written the words that were now floating in front of his eyes. He read, "It's too quiet these days. I can't hear anything anymore." No other explanation, no date showing when it was written, no more insight into why, when, or who penned this last declaration.

Now faced with even more questions than when he began, he recalled the letters his father had started, but never sent. The dates showed they hadn't been written long before his death, and the return address was that of the boarding house where he last stayed. Had he actually gone off to wherever he said he was going, or had he been in New Orleans that entire time? Would anyone still be there at the boardinghouse who would remember the man after all these years?

Perhaps this place would hold the answers. Maybe the proprietor was still around and could shed some light on how long his father had been living there and what he had been doing during that time.

19

Raymond stood outside the old house, suddenly unsure whether he should abandon this mission. He was feeling like the child who went there all those years ago to collect his daddy's belongings, scared and alone. Deciding it was probably a fool's errand, he started to turn to walk away, when a grizzled old man came out and yelled at him. "What business you got here, son?"

"Sorry sir, I was just trying to find out some information about a resident who would have been living here some years ago. I don't mean to trouble you any," Raymond replied politely.

"Who you looking for, boy?"

"My Father, sir. It's been some years now. He was killed in a bar fight when I was just a young boy. I came to collect his belongings back then, but I doubt you'd remember that, though."

"How could I forget that damn drunk? He caused more trouble than he was worth. Didn't surprise me none when he wound up dead. Just surprised it took as long as it did."

"I'm sorry, sir. But can you tell me how long he was here before he died?"

"Let's see," he paused, spitting something from his teeth, "I think he got here in October. Hung around a couple of months. Left for a while, then came back again in the spring, March or April maybe? Was killed just before that next Christmas I believe." Narrowing his eyes and looking Raymond up and down, "Yeah, I remember you now. Came by to pick up his stuff. Scrawny little thing you were. Tryin' to be a big man, weren't ya, son? Sorry for your loss, I guess. But he was a son of a bitch. He was."

Raymond shook his head, trying to wrap his mind around the details the man offered. This new information was only adding to the questions, not giving him the answers he so desperately hoped he'd find.

"Thank you, sir. You've been a great help."

"If you don't mind my sayin', boy, you's probably better off without that man in your life. If he was any sort of father, he wouldn't a been here, and he sure as hell wouldn't have gone gettin' his self kilt in a bar fight."

With a tip of his hat in acknowledgement, he agreed. "Yes, sir. You're probably right. Thank you for your time. A good day to you."

Walking home, he was trying to fit the new pieces of information into place. He now knew his father had been around long before and at the time Momma disappeared. While he didn't have conclusive proof that his daddy might have been responsible for that, it gave him something else to consider.

This next part he knew was going to prove to be more difficult. Tracking down the guy that killed his father, or even the bar where it happened. He had the information that he gleaned from the police report, and that would be where he would start.

⚜

Arriving home, Raymond continued his erratic pacing, unable to find any comfort from being in a more familiar environment. Inside he could feel the remaining bits of any control he had shattering, spiraling out of control. He kept seeing Simone laughing when she mocked him on the playground, only to have that interrupted by the memory of the noise of albums breaking when his father tried so hard to silence the music. Try as he might, he couldn't stay focused on any one person or memory for more than a few seconds.

Despite the abuse and humiliation he suffered at the hands of men throughout his life, his daddy's beatings, the time spent on his uncle's farm, and that brute that chased him off back in Galveston, he found himself identifying with them and their strength. He aspired to be strong like them, never to be bullied again. Women, who he had once thought to be strong, now had become weak in his mind, and should be shown their place. Now they were simply a means to an end. Until he could determine if Simone was the same person as that little girl and what revenge he would seek, he knew he would continue to kill others for their songs and the moments of peace that they brought him.

Walking to the coffee table, he picked up his father's journal and turned to the last page, rereading the last sentence over and over again. "It's too quiet these days. I can't hear anything anymore."

'Who wrote this?' he wondered. 'Why is the penmanship

101

so different from everything else written in this book?' He couldn't imagine that his father would try to disguise his handwriting, what point would that serve? But who else would have known about this journal, and why would they find it necessary to write something so cryptic?

Unless... stopping his train of thought, thinking what he was about to propose was impossible, could it be his mother's handwriting? The letters were too straight and perfect, not the loopy open handwriting that he remembered hers looking like.

Tearing the house apart, he went looking for anything that would have a sample of her writing. An old envelope that held a letter that never got sent before she disappeared, or old school work of his that she would have signed, maybe. Rummaging through the desk, it was then he came across a list of songs written out, stuck to one of her old letters.

Looking at it, he saw the writing on this list was very straight and deliberate, just like on the last page of the journal. But where had this come from, and why hadn't he ever seen it before? He thought he had organized all of her old papers, only keeping important documents or sentimental keepsakes, and threw away most everything else. Yet this list, he knew he had never seen it before. Was this proof that it was her handwriting in the journal? But why would she try to disguise it? What reason would she have to write something like that? In Daddy's journal?

Dropping to the couch, staring at the paper, turning it over and over in his hands, nothing was making sense. He told himself, "I have to go at this more logically if I'm going to find any answers."

Standing back up, he took one step at a time, crossing

the room. With each step, he thought back on each event that had taken place. Step - 'Momma disappeared shortly before Daddy died.' Step. 'Could it be that she was responsible for his death?' Step. 'No, that wasn't possible. The police report stated he was killed in a bar fight.' Turn and step. 'There's no way she could overpower him, even if she had a knife. Had she hired someone?'

Continuing to find a way to put the pieces together in a way that made sense, he now knew his father had left them, but hadn't left the city. Instead, he had holed up in that boarding house, drinking, gambling, womanizing the entire time. But how would Momma have known? What happened that pushed her over the edge? To possibly do something like this? More importantly, why would she care if it she knew it had been going on for years?

Unable to stand any longer, Raymond laid down on the couch, turning his head to look at the cabinet standing in the corner of the room. It reminded him of yet another day, shortly before her disappearance, when she hadn't been there to meet him after school. He had come home to find her at the house, disheveled in her appearance. He asked why she hadn't been at the school to pick him up. She meekly replied she had been caught up in chores around the house and had lost track of time. She continued on, saying that she had been up on the step-stool trying to clean the top of the cabinet and lost her balance, briefly knocking herself out in the fall. She knew he would make his way home and everything was fine now, so he shouldn't worry about it at all.

As he replayed the scene and her words repeatedly, he recalled noticing a broken lamp in the trash, was that what she knocked over when she fell? But there was something else, too. What was it? Her words and behavior somehow didn't fit with what she was telling him. She wouldn't make eye contact with him, she kept wrapping a dishrag around her hands, tying them together, then loosening it again. He had spotted something in the corner, too. Blood? Glass? It struck him as out of place when he recounted the story she had told him. If she had been doing chores and cleaning, why wouldn't she have cleaned that up too?

Standing up again, he started walking around the room, trying to reenact what she had described as taking place. If she had been trying to clean the top of the cabinet, as she said she was, she would have struck the coffee table. The end table with the lamp was at the other end of the couch, too far from where she said she fell. But this still didn't explain the reason for broken glass and what looked like blood in the corner, either. Suddenly, none of what she said happened could have possibly been true.

What was beginning to make sense now was the thought that maybe his father had come back? His father would have known that he was at school, so he could come in and take what he wanted without any interference from Raymond. His mother had never fought back, she knew she didn't stand a chance against the brute of a man that he was when he was angry. But did she fight back this time? Had she cracked him over the skull with the lamp? Whose blood was that then?

Still, none of this explained the odd journal entry. She would have had to find daddy at the boarding house, locate the journal and pen the entry. How would she have figured out where he was staying? Why would she bother to track him down like that? Weren't they better off with him gone? Had he threatened her? Had he threatened Raymond?

What could have happened that made her search him out? And if she wrote that, the biggest question remaining was why?

Reluctantly, he found himself concluding that maybe Momma did have something to do with his father's death, and now he was going to have to pay yet another visit to the boarding house. He couldn't be sure the proprietor would have any more answers than what he had been given before, but he had to ask the questions. Had she been there? And if so, was it before or after his father was killed?

Now he found himself questioning everything else, every other choice that he had made over the past years since she disappeared. Had he not been sent to the farm and suffered the beatings there, had he not run away, had he not spent time in Galveston, had he not committed his first kill, and all the others that followed, would any of this have happened if Momma had just come home?

20

Delphine was on edge ever since her meeting with Raymond, and it was showing on her face and in her demeanor at work. Frowning at simple tasks, snapping when people would ask her a question, even when Simone questioned if something was wrong, all she could muster was a grunt and a firm shake of her head. She knew she couldn't bear to burden her friend with the knowledge of this long-held secret that was eating away at her.

Delphine had been keeping this information to herself for so long, and now, with Raymond's return, she wasn't sure how much longer she could hold out. It had been easy when he was gone, there was no one left in the city that the keeping of this information affected. But now that he was back and living at the house again with no sign that he'd be leaving anytime soon, well, that changed everything.

She knew she would have to get in touch with Genevieve. But how? To the best of her knowledge, Genevieve was no longer in New Orleans. Maybe Evelyn would know, since she seemed to keep up with everyone better than Delphine ever had.

Evelyn had been the rock through it all.. Had it not been for her wisdom and guidance, Delphine didn't think she would have had the strength to cope with that awful situation all those years ago. But here they were now, years past that awful man's death, and the memories that used to haunt her nights returned as well.

Resolving to speak to Evelyn as soon as she could find a moment, she knew Evelyn would know what to do once Delphine shared the information and questions that she now possessed.

The following morning, Delphine found Evelyn in the kitchen, helping Cook with the day's meal preparations. Glancing around to make sure no one else was in earshot, she spoke in a low, tense voice. "Oh good, you're both here. We need to talk."

"What's going on Delphine? You look absolutely awful," Evelyn responded.

The apprehension in her voice even caused Cook to turn as Delphine explained, "Ladies, I have to tell you, Raymond is back and I think he's starting to ask questions regarding his father again."

Telling them about her running into him on the sidewalk, meeting later for coffee and then finally the dinner at her house, "I thought I had seen him around, but wasn't sure if it was him or not. He's even shown up at the Gibson a few times, though I didn't realize at the time it was him. And well, something is just not quite right about that boy. I can't say for certain, but I think he's got more of his daddy in him than we know."

"But what makes you think he's looking into his daddy's death? Wouldn't he concern himself more with his momma's disappearance?" Cook inquired.

"I rode past that old boarding house a couple of days ago. I saw Raymond talking to the old man that runs the place. Of course I couldn't hear anything, being on the streetcar. But it was clear that something was going on. When Raymond and I had dinner, he asked a couple of questions about his Momma, but seemed, I don't know, resigned to the fact that she was gone and never coming back. As if he didn't have much interest in finding out anything more about her disappearance. He didn't say anything to me about his daddy, of course, I thought he had resolved that long ago before he had left town the first time. But now, well, there's just something not right. Evelyn, I know you've been in touch with her, is it time for Genevieve to come back?"

At the mention of that name, Cook dropped her knife and Evelyn stopped mixing the dough she was kneading, and looked directly at Delphine. "Why would you suggest such a thing? If you think he's as dangerous as his daddy was, do you really think now is the time for her to be coming back around?"

"I don't know. Maybe you're right. But I think she needs to know her son is back in town. What if she were to come back and find him at the house? What do you think would happen then? If he is as short-tempered as that old bastard was, well, there's no telling..." she trailed off.

Cook, ever the voice of reason, chimed in, "I don't know Evelyn, I think Delphine might be right this time.

Genevieve should know her son is back. Maybe it's time for her to come back too? She can talk to him, explain why things went the way they did. Isn't he at least owed that much? From what we know of his past, and what little more we know now, the boy has been through enough in his lifetime already. And it's certainly not Delphine's place to tell him, either."

Before Evelyn could answer, Simone strolled into the kitchen, smiling ear to ear. Noting the tension in the room, her smile quickly faded, only to be replaced with a look of question and concern.

"What's going on, ladies? Everything okay?" Simone inquired.

"Oh, no dear, everything is fine," Evelyn chirped a little too cheerfully. "Cook dropped her knife, and we thought she had cut herself at first. Turns out it was just tomato juice on her fingers."

Simone looked pointedly at Delphine and asked, "Are you sure that's all?"

"Yes, dear. Really. Everything is fine. Now, what are you so smiley about just now?"

Simone explained, "Nothing in particular. It's just a good day. The children are being cooperative, the sun is shining. I just have a good feeling about today."

Evelyn effused, "Well, that's wonderful, dear, but I think the children are waiting for their rides, are they not?"

Looking at the three ladies, sensing something was wrong, but not getting any other answers, Simone replied. "Yes ma'am," as she left to go find the children.

Once Simone was gone, Delphine turned back to Cook and Evelyn and asked in a low voice, "Okay, now that she's gone, what are we going to do about Raymond and

Genevieve? My good face is starting to crack and Simone keeps asking if something is wrong. Ladies, I've seen the way Raymond was looking at her at the club too and somehow I don't think it would be good for her to know, well, any of this."

Evelyn, contemplating it all, asked, "Has he made mention of her at all?"

"No. Nothing when we talked. But there's just something about him and his hanging around the Gibson that makes me feel uncomfortable. And I'm not saying he has anything to do with this, I'm sure it's just a coincidence, but those girls they've been finding, well, that just gives me another reason to be concerned."

"I agree. David and I have been wondering about how safe it's been lately. It seems the police don't seem to care much about these cases, either."

"But what does any of this have to do with Simone? There's no connection between them, is there?" Cook asked, looking back and forth between the other two.

Pausing, Delphine took a deep breath, knowing this piece of information would be news to her friends. "Well... actually, there is. Though I don't know that he's recognized her. But Simone is the one who got him into so much trouble in school. You know, he lost some of his hearing in one ear, one of the times Walter beat both Genevieve and him so badly. Anyway, it seems that Simone would mercilessly tease him on the playground, always trying to talk in his bad ear and then tattling when he would react. Usually he just said mean things to her, but one day, he snapped and started hitting her. It was hard enough to give her a bloody nose, and it took two teachers to pull him off of her. It was shortly before I sent him away to live with that awful family. But surely, after all these years, he doesn't know that's her."

Leaning back against the counter, Evelyn eyed Delphine. "Why didn't you ever tell me this? Is that why you got Simone the job here?"

Shaking her head, Delphine said, "No. It really was just a coincidence that she came by and applied. I didn't even put it together at first either. But one day when we were talking, she told me about where she went to school as a child. I just put two and two together. I've never even asked her about it. I figured it was just better off left in the past. But now it seems the past is coming back to haunt us all."

Shifting her weight from one foot to the other, Evelyn hung her head.

"Oh Delphine. I guess we all have our secrets that are coming to light. I promised her I wouldn't say anything, but it seems now you need to know. Genevieve is back in New Orleans. And before you say anything, it wasn't my place to tell either of you. She's been trying to start a new life. These past years haven't been easy on her either. But, based on what you've told me, she needs to face the past. I'll stop by this afternoon and see if she's around. But Delphine, you're going to have to be the one to tell her what's been going on and justify your concerns about her son."

Glaring at Evelyn, Delphine shot her a look as if to say, 'I don't want to do that.' But instead agreed, "I know. See if she can come and meet me at my house on Saturday. Since the Batistes will be gone this weekend, I plan to stay home and tend to my long-neglected chores. I realize her coming there is taking a chance that Raymond will spot her, but I can't spare the time away from home either. Anywhere else I fear would be too public of a place."

"I'll have her there Saturday if I have to drive her there myself," Evelyn said, standing at attention, prompting a hearty laugh from Cook and Delphine for the first time that morning.

"Oh dear, based on the last time you drove, I don't think David will allow that," Cook chortled, reaching for the next tomato to slice.

21

Unable to sit still any longer, Raymond left the house and began walking. All the puzzle pieces were floating in front of him, but he didn't have the complete picture to figure out how they fit together. He was certain that Delphine knew more than she was telling, but what was her role in all of this? Did she know all these years what happened to Momma? Why wouldn't she have just told him?

Having not paid attention to where he was going, Raymond looked around and found himself in the Garden District. He wasn't far from the house where Delphine and Simone both worked. Should he go there and confront Delphine? Should he say something to Simone? What could he possibly say? The last time he was there observing, he had almost been caught. Surely it wouldn't be as simple as just walking up to the door and asking her point blank what either of them knew.

Walking down the opposite side of the street, he stopped one house short and looked over at the old, grand home. He had a recollection of a visit there when he was a child. The backdoor leading directly into the kitchen, where he had sat and ate an afternoon snack while Delphine finished her work for the day. There had been others there, the cook, and another lady who he remembered seeing at the Gibson too. They were all so nice to him, stopping to check on him, to make sure he was taken care of. When he saw the other woman walking down the sidewalk across the street, he knew he was in the right place. But who else would he find there? The voices telling him maybe this wasn't such a good idea after all.

Gathering up his nerve and pushing past his uncertainty, he crossed the street and started to make his way down the side of the house. Passing by an open window on his right, he heard laughter and voices coming from inside. He immediately recognized one of them belonging to Delphine, but it was when he heard the other voice that one of the puzzle pieces fell into place. While the voice had changed slightly over the years, he now knew with certainty it was the voice of that girl from his childhood, the one that still haunted his nightmares. But why was she here, too? What connection did she have with Delphine?

Peering in the window, he saw Delphine and Simone standing across the room. He recognized her as the same person he had seen that night at the Gibson. After all these years, the face of his childhood tormenter was right there in front of him again. Feeling the darkness swelling, a deafening roar began to consume him. What started out as him being able to hear all that was going on around him now made him feel as though he was underwater, unable to hear anything at all.

Unable to contain the rage he felt burning, he ran off,

not stopping until he arrived home. Drenched in sweat, heart pounding, he closed the door behind him.

Once inside, Raymond continued his erratic pacing, unable to find any comfort in being in a more familiar environment. Inside, he felt shattered, as though he was spiraling out of control. He kept seeing Simone laughing, only to have that interrupted by the memory of the noise of albums breaking when his father tried so hard to silence the music, then remembering the day Momma disappeared. Try as he might, he couldn't stay focused on any one person for more than a few seconds.

He didn't want to believe that Delphine knew more than she was letting on, or that she had befriended Simone after what she had done to him. He could feel the bile rising from his stomach, leaving a bitter taste in his mouth.

Maybe the only way to quiet these voices once and for all was to confront Simone. Call her out for her behavior all those years ago. If he could just do that, maybe then he would find peace, stop the nightmares, and be able to enjoy the music again.

But before he could confront her, perhaps it was time for a little payback. Something to set her on edge, disrupt her bucolic life a bit. While he knew little about her or her life these days, aside from the fact that she worked at the house in the Garden District and seemed to enjoy going to the Gibson, he had an idea of what he could do to begin.

22

True to her word, Evelyn got in touch with Genevieve and set up a meeting with her and Delphine for Saturday morning.

Anxious about Genevieve's arrival, Delphine alternated between waiting by the door and peering out the front curtains. She hoped nothing would stop Genevieve from coming, but at the same time, she wished she wouldn't. When Delphine heard the knock on her door announcing Genevieve's arrival, it assuaged some, but not all of her doubts. Quickly urging her inside, she didn't want to leave anything to chance today.

Leading her to the kitchen, they sat down at the table, far enough away from the front windows to avoid any inquiring eyes. Delphine had partially drawn the curtains, but wondered if it was enough. She knew it was necessary to leave them open, not only for the daylight to come in, but to keep the nosy neighbors away. Had they been completely drawn, they would come by to make sure everything was okay. It was one of those advantages and disadvantages of living in the close community that she did. Everyone knew everyone else's comings and goings, regardless of whether or not you wanted them to.

Once they were seated, the tea and cake served, Delphine shifted in her seat, obvious in her discomfort and full of questions. "Genevieve, I don't know where to start. I mean, how long have you been back? Why didn't you come by and tell me? I mean, thank you for coming here today. I know this must not be easy for you. But then again, it's not easy for any of us these days."

"Delphine. I, I well, I'm sorry. I should have come sooner. Evelyn even told me as much. You had every right to know that I was back. And yet, today I almost didn't come. You have no idea how many times I changed my mind between home and here. And then when I got off the streetcar and saw Raymond outside the house... Well, I almost turned tail and ran then, too. But here I am."

Agitated, Delphine leapt from her chair. "Wait, you saw Raymond? Did he see you? Did he see you coming here?"

"I don't think so. I stayed to this side of the street and, from what I could tell, his back was to me the entire time. I tried not to stare at him. But Delphine, my god, he's no longer a little boy. He's a full grown man over there."

Delphine stood, considering for a long minute the woman who was sitting in front of her. The details of the secret they shared, scrambling about in her mind. She had thought she had buried it far enough away that it would never have to be revisited again. She had made peace with her role. But now here was Genevieve, back in the city, back in the neighborhood and Raymond just across the street too, that peace was no longer assured.

"Okay. Well, let's hope he didn't see you. Or things could

go downhill quickly." Sitting back down in her seat, Delphine took a sip of her tea.

"Delphine, I owe you an explanation. And well, an apology too. I -"

Delphine held up a hand, stopping Genevieve's ramblings.

"Before we dig up long held secrets and you tell me anything about, well, anything, I need you to hear this first. I don't know how much or what Evelyn has told you, so please, hear me out and, for god's sake, try not to overreact. As you now know, Raymond is back. He's been back for some time now. And for whatever reason, he was trying to keep himself hidden from me. It was only by chance that we ran into each other when we did. He did come over for dinner once and he was courteous enough during our visit, but Genevieve, there's something off about him. He's not the same person he was all those years ago. He wouldn't give me much in the way of any details of his life since you disappeared. I had expected that he would have come back here after that summer to return to school and home. Of course, I had expected you to be back by then as well."

Genevieve interrupted, "I know. I was trying to come back. But I got so sick at the end of that summer that by the time I was well, it was almost Christmas again. I realize I should have come back then, too. But I don't understand what you mean about Raymond."

"Maybe you know, maybe you don't. I know you've been in touch with Evelyn all these years, so I'm guessing you have some idea of what took place. When Raymond did come back, I did what I could to help him without sticking my nose in too far. Maybe I should have been more proactive and taken him back in, but I didn't and I have always felt bad about that decision. Then, one day, he was just gone again. I kept looking for him to return. Determined that when he came back, I would make sure to not make the same mistake and try to give him a stable home or whatever it was that he needed. But this time, that departure turned into years of him being gone. After a while I just went on with my life, expecting that to be the end of it all, trying to put it all behind me."

Taking a deep breath, knowing what she would say next would open many old wounds and memories, Delphine watched as Genevieve toyed with her food. Trying to read her expression, Delphine found Genevieve sitting there, stoic and unmoved by her story.

"But here we are now, these years later, and old unanswered questions are being raised again. I'm hearing that Raymond is asking questions at the boarding house and the police station. I've also seen him hanging around the Gibson, always watching the crowd as though he's looking for someone in particular, yet always keeping to himself. I don't know how else to explain, other than to say it's all a bit unsettling."

Genevieve straightened up in her chair, staring at Delphine, while her hands were playing with a loose button on her sweater, betraying her composure. Delphine knew what Genevieve's husband had been capable of, she had seen the bruises and the scars. She also knew the mental wounds of that ran deep as well. But what would have kept her away from her son for all those years? What could she possibly be thinking that staying away was the best solution? Did she think she was protecting him?

When Delphine realized Genevieve would not offer any information, she leaned forward, her voice taking on a more demanding tone. "Something is not adding up here, and I don't have all the details like you and Evelyn. But what little I do know and what else I have pieced together is starting to give me pause. It's also affecting me in ways I don't like." Taking a deep breath, she asked, "Which brings me to the hardest question of all... Did you do what I think you did?"

Dropping her hands into her lap, Genevieve smoothed out her skirt and said, "No, well, sort of, not directly... But I suppose I should go back to the beginning and explain."

23

Genevieve stood up and stretched, thinking the chair was about as comfortable as the events that she was about to explain. Pacing around the small kitchen, she stopped to wash her hands in the sink, then turned her attention towards the back door, looking out at the garden. Trying to gather her thoughts before launching into her story, she now found herself unable to look directly at Delphine, instead, keeping her back turned as she began.

"That day I disappeared, I had every intention of coming back home. I was only going to go to the boarding house, find that no good excuse of a man, and try to talk to him. Tell him it was over, that he should never come back home, and to forget that he even had a wife or son. I was through with his abuse and I wasn't about to let his behavior turn Raymond into a monster, either.

"I left work after I had talked to you and got there just before noon. Marching up to his room, only to find he wasn't there, I thought maybe, just maybe, he was working for a change. Right? Who am I kidding? When I went back downstairs, the man running the place said he was probably just at the bar around the corner. From what he knew of his comings and goings, Walter had been spending most of his time there and at the racetrack. Of course, this came as no surprise to me that those were the two places he would have been.

"He always did have a strong love for the bottle and the ponies. I debated whether to go and confront him. I didn't know what state he'd be in, or who else would be there. It was only the middle of the day, after all. Thinking back now, I guess whatever money he did send home never came from an actual job, either."

Stopping to catch her breath, she turned to face Delphine and was met with an inscrutable look. She couldn't tell if Delphine was upset, sympathetic, or didn't believe a word of what she was saying. Determined to finish her story now, she returned to the table and sat down. Her posture softened a bit, but her voice still contained a tone of apprehension.

"I gathered my wits about me, straightened my hat, and marched down to the bar. I knew if I didn't confront him then and there, he'd just be back again and the abuse would continue until he killed me or Raymond, or both of us. I walked in to find it was only him and two other guys sitting at the opposite end of the bar. I guess the bartender could tell by the look on my face that I was there to drag him out, so he simply stepped back and let events unfold. It was obvious he didn't want to get involved. Walter, ever the bastard, looked up, saw me, and spat. Nice greeting, huh?" A stilted laugh punctuating her last sentence.

Delphine nodded, not saying anything more as she sat, waiting for Genevieve to continue.

Picking up and putting down her glass, Genevieve's voice took on a new strength Delphine had not heard before. "I don't know where this new found determination came from, but I didn't give him a chance to say anything. I lit into him, telling him in no uncertain terms that he was to stay away from the house and me and Raymond. He had left home for the last time. I would have what little remained of his belongings sent to the boarding house, but he was not to set foot back on the property. Oh, he tried to protest, saying it was his house, but I was having none of it. Then he changed his tone and tried sweet-talking me, but this time I stood my ground."

Unable to sit still, squirming as if the chair were shocking her, Genevieve stood and began pacing again.

"He started cussing up a storm, telling me I was a no-good wife and mother, using words I won't repeat here. During his tirade, he had gotten up off the barstool and took an unsteady step towards me. It was then the other two guys got up. They could see it was about to take a turn, and for whatever reason, they weren't going to stand for it. They started to come towards Walter as I took a step back. Mind you, I didn't know these two guys from any other Joe on the street, but had it not been for them, well, I probably wouldn't be here now."

She stopped pacing, and was standing behind the chair she had first occupied, gripping the back so tight, that Delphine was afraid that if it was any harder, she would break the chair in two.

"The younger of the two men walked over to me and asked if everything was okay. Walter told him to mind his own business and get lost. The older man had stopped off to the side, just watching, biding his time, it seemed. The younger man that had been keeping Walter's attention turned back towards me and asked if I was in need of any assistance. I told him I was fine, I was just about to be on my way. He offered to see me home, or at least to the streetcar stop, if I preferred. By now, his friend had taken a step closer to Walter, which made me feel uneasy."

Shaking her head at the memory, Genevieve continued. "I don't know why, but I agreed to let the younger man walk me to the streetcar stop. I had said my piece and didn't see any need to stay any longer. The rest was going to be up to Walter now. I could see he was furious, about to boil over, and if I said anything more, I'm sure it would come to blows there, regardless of who was around.

"As I was walking out the door, I heard the older man approach Walter and say a few words. He spoke so low that I couldn't make out what exactly he said. But when I looked back based on the look I saw on Walter's face, well, let's just say, it seemed to put him in his place.

"As we walked to the streetcar stop, Samuel introduced himself to me. As the trolley approached, I thanked him for his kindness. Still, I was unable to hide the anger and hatred I was feeling. As I said, I hoped that was the last I would see of that no good excuse of a man."

Delphine finally finding her voice, interrupted and asked, "So he was still alive when you left then? But I thought..."

Genevieve, either not hearing the question or just choosing to ignore it, continued. "As I found a seat, I watched Samuel walk back into the bar. There was something about the look on his face that gave me chills. What was it about those two and their interest in Walter? I wondered. It seemed odd that whatever the older one had said shut him down, fast. Did they know each other? All the thoughts that started swirling through my head at that point were just too much for me to process. I tried to focus on just getting home and back to Raymond, but I couldn't shake the feeling that something was suddenly, terribly wrong."

Dropping back into her seat, she looked at Delphine, waiting for her to ask the next obvious question. When none came, Genevieve just shrugged her shoulders.

"I don't know why or what came over me, but I got off at the next stop. All I could think was I didn't want to see any harm come to Walter, I just wanted him out of our lives. I crossed the tracks and waited for the next car to arrive, and went straight back to the bar. I had no idea what I was going to do, why I was even doing it, or what I expected to find. I just knew I had to do something.

"When I finally got there, he was gone. The bartender told me he had left with Samuel and the other man, who he identified as Lawrence, but that he didn't know where they went.

"It didn't take long for me to find Walter. I went around the corner and down the alley, and there he was. A bloody mess, almost unrecognizable. I stood there just looking at him, unsure of what to do next. I couldn't find my voice to scream, my hands were trembling. I bent down to see if maybe he was still breathing, but it came as no surprise that he wasn't. I thought about going back to the bar again, but what good would that do? I wasn't sure what I was supposed to feel at the moment. All I could think of was Raymond. Then, as if my feet knew where to go next, I hurried back to the boarding house. That's when I ran into them again."

Delphine shifted to the edge of her chair and reached across the table to take Genevieve's hand. It was the first comforting gesture she had offered since her arrival, and it had an overwhelming effect. Tears welled in Genevieve's eyes as she struggled to continue.

"It seems that he owed a lot of money to Lawrence, shocker, I know. And when they saw how he was treating me, well, that was the final straw for them. Once Samuel had made sure I was on the streetcar, they took Walter out of the bar and back to the alley. They took what little money he had on him and then preceded to beat the daylights out of him, leaving him for dead or close to it, they thought. Lawrence apologized for any trouble that it may cause me, but he would not stand to see a woman treated the way I was being at that moment. He had seen his mother beaten to death and immediately recognized what Walter was going to do next. He didn't care anymore about the debt, as far as he was concerned, we were square. He only asked that I not go telling the police anything."

"But Genevieve, all these years, why did you let everyone think you were gone, and that you were responsible for Walter's death?"

"I don't know. I guess I thought I was protecting Raymond that way. I didn't have any trouble not telling the police. After all, it wasn't like they were going to do anything about it. They never did anything all the times when he beat me either.

"Looking back, I should have come straight home. I don't know why I went back to the boarding house instead. I guess I thought if I went there, I could take what money I could find, that maybe it would help support Raymond and me for at least a little while. Had I not gone there, I would have never encountered those two again. It was then that Lawrence and Samuel had suggested that I not come home, but that I hide out for a few days until things settled down. I figured what money I had found would help cover the cost. They didn't think the police would come ask me questions since he was just another dead drunk. Neither Lawrence nor Samuel made mention or indicated that they had any idea about Raymond, and I sure wasn't about to tell them about him. I had to protect my son. I only expected to stay gone for a few days at most. But then that's when things went from bad to worse."

24

Genevieve was tired, but knowing that Delphine had to hear the entire story, she mustered her strength and picked up where she left off.

"I had every intention of coming home after a couple of days of lying low. I even came back through the neighborhood one afternoon, saw that Raymond was with you and that he was safe. As far as I could tell, Lawrence and Samuel didn't know about him and I meant to keep it that way." Pausing, she took a sip of her tea.

"Three days later, I had finally decided it was time to come back home. As I was getting ready to leave, there was a knock at the door of my room. I had found a cheap place to stay at old Mabel's house, just a few blocks from here. I didn't think anyone knew where I was, and of course, I wasn't expecting anyone. When I opened the door to it more than surprised me to find Lawrence and Samuel standing there. I thought we were square, at least that's what they had told me anyway, so when they showed back up, I got scared all over again. Turns out, I was right to be."

Noting that her hands were shaking almost uncontrollably now, Delphine reached back across the table and took both of Genevieve's hands in hers.

"It's okay dear. Just stop a minute and catch your breath. Before you go any further, just know that they never came around here. Raymond was safe all those years. Well, as far as I know. I kept him with me until the school year was up and then contacted Walter's family to come and take him to the farm. After his troubles at school, I didn't think it was right for me to try and keep him any longer. He needed to be with kin. He came back for a short while after that summer, but I was so busy with work and all that I neglected to keep up after him. I left food on the porch a couple of times, figuring maybe he would come by after that. But he never did. Then one day he was gone again."

Genevieve looked aghast at Delphine. "Oh, my poor boy. How could you let them take him?"

"They're family. I thought..." Delphine trailed off.

"That family is awful. They are just as bad as Walter was, maybe even worse. At least when Walter wasn't drinking he wasn't mean, but his brother, that man is pure evil all the time."

"I'm sorry, Genevieve, I had no idea. I mean, you hadn't come back, I didn't know what else I was supposed to do. But you have to understand, I couldn't keep him with me any longer. He was getting into trouble at school, and I knew the summer months were going to be busy at the Batiste house. I was already working extra hours, having to take him there with me at times. Also, neighbors would have started asking questions, and how was I to explain you being gone? I did what I could. So now, finish, and tell me, what exactly kept you away?"

"Alright. I'm sorry. I shouldn't blame you. You did what you could for him and I do appreciate that. I just had hoped that Raymond had been protected from that evil and hate that runs through Walter's family. I tried so hard to protect him and keep him from turning into another one of them. Of course, had any of my family been around, then this would all have been completely different."

Rising from her seat, Genevieve resumed pacing, taking measured steps, punctuating her story.

"Lawrence told me they needed my help, just for a few days he said. And since they had taken care of Walter, it was only fair for me to repay the favor. He told me it wouldn't be long that I'd have to be away, then I could return to my life here, or start a new one, somewhere else, where no one would know me. What he neglected to tell me was that we'd be leaving not only New Orleans, but the state of Louisiana as well, and getting back would be no easy task."

"It turned out that Samuel and Lawrence worked for a lady in Kansas who had a whorehouse and gambling establishment. Every few weeks, they were sent to New Orleans, Baton Rouge, and Jackson to find new girls. Enticing those they found with the ideas of quick money and a better life. It didn't take much to convince those young, naive girls. I thought if I just did what I was told, I would repay my debt quickly and could return home.

"I started out serving drinks to the men, mostly where the gaming took place. Surely I told myself this was all I had to do and they wouldn't keep me long. I also didn't think that they would make me to do anything I didn't want to do. Then a month turned into two, and I was not given a choice in what I was told to do next.

"Before long, six months had gone by, my spirit and will had been completely crushed and any thoughts of returning home were long gone. I cried myself to sleep every night until I had no more tears left to cry. The only way I could survive was to become a shell of who I used to be. How could I even think of coming back to my son and our home now? Would he even recognize me?

"It wasn't until I was back here, accompanying Lawrence on a trip, that I ran into Evelyn. I hadn't seen her since that day she was here at your house, after one of Walter's more awful beatings. If you remember, she wasn't at work that day and well... It was just one of those situations where she saw the awful state that I was in, I had lost weight, and according to her, my eyes were dead. She slipped a piece of paper into my pocket with her address and told me to write her when I could, to let her know where I was and who I was with.

"It was months of clandestine letter writing, often times weeks went by in between letters. I was never sure if the letters I was sending were being intercepted or if they actually reached her until I would get a reply from Evelyn. Eventually Samuel, Lawrence, some of the other girls, and I returned once again to New Orleans. But there was no way for me to get another letter to Evelyn to let her know of this change. I suppose it was fate intervening that I ran into her again. We were still here in New Orleans when a few weeks went by. Then one day without warning, I was freed. Of course, despite being let go, there was still the nagging thought that I was going to come around a corner and there would be Lawrence or Samuel or one of the others and they would drag me back to that life or just kill me."

Shocked at hearing the sordid details, Delphine also

found herself saddened. Not just for Genevieve, but for Raymond as well. All the years he had lost, not knowing that his mother was still alive, still left Delphine with questions.

"So you are who Evelyn and Cook have been protecting all this time? She never told me exactly who you were, she just enlisted my help from time to time gathering clothing or extra food. All she would tell me was that she was helping someone who needed it, and that was all I needed to know."

"Yes, they've both been so kind to me. After a month of rest and Cook's amazing food, I was able to move out and get a room of my own. They had found me a job with a family across town. No one knew me over there, or my history, so I could start over again. I still kept looking for Lawrence and Samuel, but over time, I finally began to relax, realizing that maybe I was finally free of it all. I so wanted to come back and find Raymond again, but I just couldn't bring myself to face him and what I'd done. I'm ashamed of it all." Genevieve slumped down into her chair, head hanging low, her shame filling the space in between the two women.

"Genevieve, I have no words to express how sorry I feel for you and all that you have been through. No one should have to live a life like that, much less twice, as you have. I've told you what little I know of what happened with Raymond after you left. But you have to listen to me now. What I'm going to say is not going to be easy for you to hear. I'm concerned about him now. He's back, and he's grown, but there's something off about him too. I fear he's got more of Walter in him than either of us would like to think. I know it's not my place to interfere, but I do think it's time you came back home. The boy still needs his momma."

Genevieve whipped her head up, looking at Delphine defiantly. "What do you mean 'off'? What has he done? What have you seen?"

"It's nothing I can put my finger on. It's just a feeling I get when he's around. I don't know, maybe I'm just on edge with all those girls that have been killed lately, but he's not the same person I knew all those years ago. Something in his demeanor..." she stopped as she saw the tears welling up in Genevieve's eyes.

"Delphine, no. I can't believe that Raymond would be responsible for any of that. Sure, he spent time with that miserable family and he yeah, he has his daddy's blood in him too. But this is my son you're talking about here. The sweet boy who wouldn't hurt a fly."

Considering her next words, Delphine looked at Genevieve. She wanted to believe that she was wrong, but she still felt in her gut, something wasn't right. She knew she had to tell Genevieve about his troubles at school.

"Genevieve, I'm sorry. But there is something else you need to know."

"After you left, Raymond was staying with me, and we settled into a routine of him going to school while I was at work, then coming back to your home in the afternoon. He was good about taking care of the house, and I certainly wasn't about to let him fall behind in his studies, either. We both believed you'd be back soon enough, or at least that some answers regarding your disappearance would come to light. The police came by one afternoon and told Raymond about his daddy's death. He didn't seem to have much reaction to that, but that didn't surprise me either.

What did surprise me was what started happening at school shortly after that. At first it was just little things he was getting in trouble for. Apparently, there were some kids who would pick on him because he couldn't hear out of his left ear. He would retaliate, calling them names, but nothing more.

"It wasn't until one day when I got a message at work, he had, well, he had punched one of girls in the nose. I came to find out that she was the one who had instigated the teasing. Despite my having talked to him about it, trying to tell him to just ignore them, I guess he couldn't hold back any longer. When I asked him about it that night, there was something in his eyes, something I had seen in Walter's eyes too. At that moment, I knew I couldn't take care of him much longer. He needed more than I could give. That's when I reached out to the family. I did not know they were such miserable people. I mean, sure, when they came to pick him up, they tried to take a lot of what was left behind in the house as 'payment', they said. It was mostly foodstuff and a few of Walter's things. I convinced them you were eventually coming back and that haughty woman left your things alone.

"After he left, I went back to my normal routine. I kept watch over your house. I kept expecting you to show up and at the end of the summer, I expected Raymond would return as well. And he did, though he didn't let me know. After he disappeared again, and it was apparent you weren't returning, I tried to put it all behind me. I didn't have any answers to the questions that remained, and I tried to tell myself it wasn't my place, anyway.

"It wasn't until less than a year ago, when a young girl came to work at the Batiste house, when old secrets started resurfacing. A few months into her being there, I was finding out things that I hadn't known before. It turns out that she, Simone, is her name, she is the same girl who was behind the teasing that Raymond had suffered at school. She doesn't know that I know this. In fact, she has no idea of the connection I have to him, or you, or anything. Then a few weeks ago, when we were out at for a night at the Gibson, I saw Raymond again. I also saw him looking at Simone, and it was then that all these dark memories started taking their toll on me. I had to go to Evelyn and tell her of my concerns. That's when she filled me in on what she knew of you being back and, well, here we are now."

Genevieve, furious now at what Delphine was implying, trying not to shout, growled at Delphine. "But that doesn't explain why you think he's turned into his father? You have no proof of anything other than he's back. Maybe he did recognize Simone. So what? Has he done anything to hurt her?"

"Well no. But you have to understand, we're all just a little on edge around here. Girls have been showing up dead in that courtyard not far from the Gibson, and as usual, the cops don't care. And I'm concerned about Simone. You weren't there and didn't see the way he was looking at her. Well, it just ain't right."

Genevieve yanked her hands away from Delphine's, stood up, straightening her dress and smoothing out her hair. Wiping her face, she turned to Delphine and declared, "I will not sit here and listen to you speak that way about my son. I may not have been around to raise him these last years, but I know my boy. He's a good boy, despite it all. He is not his father." Gathering up her coat and purse, she started toward the front door.

Pausing, her stance softening slightly, she added, "Please do not say anything to him about my visit. I promise I will come back around to him in my own time. But it has to be on my terms, and when I'm ready."

Delphine, noting this sudden change in Genevieve's tone and attitude, nodded and watched as Genevieve strode out the door. Delphine continued sitting a few minutes longer, contemplating what her next move should be. She knew she would have to talk with Evelyn and Cook, but also wondered also if it was time to pay another visit to Raymond too.

25

Returning to this neighborhood stirred up many emotions for Genevieve. The minute she stepped off the streetcar, a flood of memories overcame her. From the first day she and her new husband set foot in the house, to the day her son was born. His first steps, the tumble he took down the front stairs, her garden in the backyard. She could see them all as clear as if it were happening right in front of her all over again.

Despite the fact that the city was booming and new construction was taking place everywhere else, here the houses and yards still looked the same. Maintained well enough at a first glance, but looking more closely you could see the peeling paint, rotting wood, and other repairs often left neglected.

She, on the other hand, was definitely a different person now, both in her physical appearance and mental state. She patted her newly cut hair, the long locks that she had worked so hard to maintain all those years now in a trash bin. The curves she once was proud to display also had disappeared. Now she was rail-thin, more angular someone had said, her cheekbones the most pronounced feature on her face. Gone was the naïve young woman who spent all her time trying to please her husband, make the best home for her family, and raise her son the best way she knew. Now a strong, determined woman stood in her place, one who wasn't about to allow the emotion of the past to cloud her judgment in the present. She knew in her heart the decision she made all those years before was what was best for both her and Raymond, no matter how much it had hurt them both.

She considered turning around and taking the next streetcar home, backing out on her meeting with Delphine. Later, she would explain to Evelyn that she thought it best to not be involved at all. She would suggest that they all just forget that she ever came into their lives and act as though she had died all those years ago. Raymond didn't know any better and wouldn't need to know any different, either. It was then she saw him come around the side of the house and her resolve melted.

The little boy she once knew had now grown into a man. She saw a flicker of her young son in his eyes, but the body had changed over the years. Noting he had the build of his father, her thoughts filled with the hope that he still possessed her compassion and love of music. Those were the two most important things she tried to instill in him, and she hoped he hadn't forgotten those, at least.

When she saw him look in her direction, she turned away as fast as she could. Genevieve couldn't take the chance that he might recognize her after all these years. Despite her newfound determination, she wasn't ready to explain to him all the whys. Why she left him, where she's been all these years, why she never came back.

Hurrying down the street, staying on the opposite side to keep what should be enough distance between them, she made her way to Delphine's. Knocking on the door, she was greeted and ushered into the house. She dared not look back, for the fear if she did, he might try to approach her and she could only imagine where that would go.

After having been away from New Orleans for more than three years, Lawrence and Samuel brought her and some of the other girls back to the city for what they were told would be an extended stay. Most days they were kept inside the house, only being let out to run errands if they were accompanied by one of the men. Yet, for whatever reason, this trip and, more importantly, this day, was turning out to be different all the way around.

That afternoon, Lawrence told her she would be allowed an evening out by herself. "You have a curfew of midnight, Cinderella," he joked. "I'm trusting you'll be back by then and not make me come looking for you." She recognized the look on his face as one similar to what she had seen when he took care of Walter and just nodded her head in agreement.

Feeling as though this might be her starting chance to get back to her normal life, she made her way into the French Quarter. Like a moth attracted to lamplight, when she heard music playing, she entered the first place she came upon, giddy with excitement. Oh, how she had missed this. The crowd of bodies jammed together on the makeshift dance floor, the smell of tobacco and alcohol hanging heavy in the air, and the feel of the music washing over her as she stood taking it all in. Yes, the music is what she missed most of all.

Music had been her salvation all those years ago, her one escape from the abuse, and here she was, able finally to have the chance to experience it once again. She longed to stay there all night, but knew her time was limited.

Across the room, she spotted a woman who she recognized as the one that had reached out to her the last time she had been in the city. Though she never came face to face with her again on that trip, they had communicated through a few letters. The hope that she had felt when she first met this woman had been fleeting. But now here she was, in the same place as Genevieve. Could it be fate was working in her favor?

She approached, gently tapping the woman on the shoulder. "Excuse me? I don't know if you remember me," she began when the woman turned around.

"Of course, Genevieve. My goodness, I'm surprised to see you here."

Recognition flooded her brain as she burst with excitement. "Evelyn! Yes, I've been back a few months now, but haven't been allowed out until now. I had wanted to get a letter to you to let you know what happened, but there was just no way. I don't know what I've done, but I guess I've gained enough trust that they felt they could let me out for the evening. Though I do have a curfew." Pausing, she looked around, as though she expected it all to be a dream. "But oh, it feels so good to be out amongst people and hearing music once again."

Recovering from the surprise, Evelyn apologized. "I'm

sorry, I'm being terribly rude. Please let me introduce my husband, David. David, this is Genevieve. You remember me telling you about her?"

"Of course. It's a pleasure to meet you," David declared, as he gently shook her hand. "Allow me to get you ladies drinks, while you two get caught up."

"Thank you. I really shouldn't. I just wanted to say hello." Genevieve tried to reply as he strode off toward the bar.

Not willing to take no for an answer, Evelyn led Genevieve towards a table. "Well, at least come sit with us and enjoy the band as long as you can. And don't worry about getting back in time. David will drive and make sure you are back by your curfew."

"I can't impose like that," Genevieve protested.

"It's not an imposition at all. It's the least we can do. Besides, this will give us a chance to talk and see what we can do to get you out of that situation sooner rather than later."

As David returned to the table with drinks for all three of them, Genevieve was sharing what had transpired over the past months and years.

"We'd been in Kansas going on two years when suddenly we were told that we were going to move. I was surprised, to say the least, when I found out we were coming back to Louisiana. We spent almost a year up in Baton Rouge before coming to New Orleans. Apparently, Lawrence got into some trouble with another fellow who had connections to the local police. Since he wasn't from around there, well, let's just say, it wasn't going to go well for him."

"That explains why the letters stopped coming then. I

had written to you a couple more times but never received any response. I tried not to think the worst, but of course..."

"I know. I should have written when it all happened. But they kept me under lock and key for most of the time. By the time we got here, it was always a couple of the other girls that were sent out to do the shopping. They weren't from around here, so I guess they figured they couldn't be recognized. Even Samuel and Lawrence didn't go out for the first month we were back. And there was no way I could risk trying to get a letter out. After a while, it seemed that whatever was causing them such distress diminished, and they started letting us out within a couple of blocks of the house. Being that I was the oldest of the bunch, I was usually assigned the role of chaperone to the rest of the girls."

Taking a sip of her drink, Genevieve noticed that David and Evelyn looking at her with only compassion and not an ounce of judgment on their faces.

"I guess I've proven myself trustworthy now, that even since we're back here, I haven't run off. So maybe they are letting me have a little more freedom. I don't know how long it will last. Or how much longer I'll last. I'm just so tired. And it breaks my heart every day knowing that I'm back here and can't even attempt to find my son, or return to my home."

Reaching over and taking her hand, Evelyn looked Genevieve in the eye. "Oh Genevieve, dear. Please know that we will do whatever we can to help you," she declared. "But enough about all that for now. You came out to enjoy the music, and that is precisely what you will do."

⚜

Had it not been for that fateful night, and David and Evelyn's generosity and persistence, Genevieve probably still would have found herself indentured to those two men and the woman they worked for.

Over the next months, Evelyn somehow found ways of getting messages of encouragement to her, telling her they were working on a way to get her out of there and back home, where she belonged.

One afternoon, coming back from her errands, Samuel met her on the front porch. At his feet she found her bag packed, and in his hand a piece of paper with an address.

"Go here. Don't come back. Don't ever speak of this. You got it?" He demanded.

Unsure of exactly what was happening, she nodded while reaching down and taking her bag in one hand and the paper in the other. She knew not to ask questions. Questions only brought about pain. Turning around, she hurried back to the streetcar stop from which she had just come. It wasn't until she reached the corner that she took the time to look at the address on the paper and saw that it was somewhere in the Garden District. What it was, or who would be waiting there for her, she had no idea. For a brief moment, she considered going back to her home, but unsure of what or who she would find there, she opted to do as she was told. She had to be sure that she wasn't being sent to yet another nightmare, another gambling and whorehouse, where if she didn't show up, they would only come looking for her again.

As she arrived at the grand home, she was instantly overwhelmed by a flood of thoughts as to what awaited her there. Walking around the side of the house to the back entrance, she timidly knocked on the door. Cook immediately answered, took one look at who was standing before her, and bellowed for Evelyn.

Ushering Genevieve inside, Cook took her bag, setting it under the table, and placed a plate of food in front of her. Evelyn came running into the kitchen in a huff, asking, "What on earth are you hollering for?"

When she saw Genevieve sitting at the table, looking around in awe at the commotion that suddenly filled the room, she rushed over.

"Genevieve! You're here! Oh, wait until David hears the news," Evelyn said excitedly as she ran around the room. To the casual observer, it would have appeared as though she was at a loss for what to do next, yet somehow Genevieve was comforted by this erratic behavior as Evelyn went on saying, "Plans have been put into motion now."

"Evelyn, I don't understand. What plans? Why am I here? How is this even possible?" Genevieve had so many questions, she didn't know where to begin.

Cook encouraged her to continue eating as Evelyn came and sat down at the table with her. Taking one of Genevieve's hands in her own, she settled down, saying, "All that matters right now is that you are safe and free. You don't have to return to that house or those people ever again. We'll take care of you, put some meat on those bones again, and get you settled back into a normal life here. But, you can't go home. No, not yet."

Genevieve protested, but Evelyn continued on. "No, I'm sorry, but that is how it has to be. You will come and stay with David and me for a while. I can't say anymore, it's for your own good. Understand?"

"No, not really, but who am I to disagree at this point? I'm so tired, I feel like I could sleep for a week."

Genevieve still couldn't believe the kindness shown to her by Evelyn, David, and Cook during her time of recovery and restoration. Here she was now, almost a year later, on her own and remaking her life again. She still had not returned home on the strict orders of Evelyn and Cook. Even if she had been told she could, she just couldn't find it in herself to muster up the nerve to return and come face to face with Raymond. But at least now she was finally feeling more secure in the fact that she didn't have to look over her shoulder every time she went somewhere.

Even after all this time, she couldn't get a straight answer from Evelyn or Cook when she asked about how she suddenly got her freedom. What had they done? Why wouldn't they tell her? She hoped one day to repay them. But how? She had no idea.

On more than one occasion, Evelyn had invited her to join them for a night out, telling her about all the bands that performed there, the fun they always had. Instead, she always made some excuse why she couldn't go, knowing full well that it was never a good explanation, but Evelyn didn't press the matter either, and for that, Genevieve was thankful.

Tonight, though, that would change. She was going to go out and hear live music again, and that was truly going to be the highlight of the evening for her. Listening to live music again, she knew her body and soul would be filled and nourished by the sounds of instruments and the players that coaxed them into doing their bidding. Music had always been her escape, and tonight she hoped she could regain that feeling once again.

26

That evening, as the staff at the Batiste house was sitting down to dinner, there was a knock at the backdoor.

Going to answer it, Delphine found a box sitting on the step addressed to Simone.

"Simone, were you expecting a package, dear?"

"No. Not that I'm aware of. Who does it say it's from?"

"There's no sign. It just has your name on it."

Rising from the table, Simone went to the counter and untied the string. Opening the box revealed a children's book.

"Well, that certainly is odd. Why would someone send me this? I haven't seen it since grade school."

Delphine came over and looked over her shoulder. "Strange. Is there any sort of note or anything?"

Opening the front cover, Simone noticed an inscription. "I hope this brings back the same memories for you as it does for me." She read out loud to the group. "Well, that isn't helpful at all. Are you sure this isn't just a joke one of you is playing?"

Looking around at all the staff, she was met with blank stares and shaking heads.

"No, honey. None of us," Cook replied.

"Well, I guess we just have a mystery on our hands then. Perhaps a note will follow and it will be solved. After dinner I'll just put this in my mending basket. Maybe one of the children will enjoy it."

After dinner, Delphine followed Simone to her room, when she spotted a red piece of fabric in Simone's mending basket.

"Simone, dear, where did that red fabric come from?"

"Oh, that. It's actually a napkin I found it in the parlor one night, just before that big storm blew through. I guess the wind must have carried it in. I asked around, but no one seems to know who it belongs to. Why?"

Trying to hide her discomfort, Delphine replied, "oh, it's nothing. I've just been looking for a piece of red fabric to mend a skirt. But I don't think that would do. No, not at all."

"Are you sure? You're welcome to take it and see if it's a match. Like I said, no one else seems to have any use for it. It's just been sitting there for a few weeks now."

Picking it up, Delphine handled it gently, turning it over as she considered her suspicions. Maybe it was just her memory playing tricks on her, but she was sure she had seen one just like it many years ago.

There was an evening when she and Raymond had been

back at his house, getting some of his clothes and other necessities when she found him in the kitchen. He was holding what appeared to be a red napkin to his face, wiping away tears she was sure he hadn't wanted her to see. Not wanting to disturb him, she tiptoed back to the living room and waited until he finished.

"Thank you. Maybe I will take this home and see if it's a match. You know how hard it is to find just the right shade of red," Delphine laughed, trying to change the subject.

"Are you sure you're okay, Delphine?" Simone asked. "You don't look so well."

"No dear, I'm fine. It's just been a long day and I guess I'm more tired than I realized. A hot bath and a good night's sleep I'm sure will take care of what ails me. Thank you again for the fabric. I'll let you know how it works out."

Stepping out of the room, she made her way back down to the kitchen. She considered telling Evelyn of her concerns, but decided instead it was best just to go home. Making her way out the back door into the night air, Delphine wondered, was it possible that Raymond was stalking her? Or was he there for Simone? What would he have been doing there in the first place? None of this was making any sense, and the knot in her stomach only tightened more as she made her way home.

While on the streetcar, she decided her first stop needed to be at Genevieve's before returning home. She wasn't sure Genevieve would want to see her after their last visit, but she hoped she would at least be able to tell her if the napkin was hers or not. Maybe then it would give her some answers.

Arriving at the boardinghouse, she found no one was around. It was still early in the evening, so she wasn't too surprised and concluded that Genevieve must still be at work, or maybe running errands on the way home. Choosing not to wait, she scrawled a quick note and slipped it under Genevieve's door, asking her to please get in touch with her as soon as she could. She was vague as to the reason, not wanting to raise any alarms, especially since their last meeting had ended on such an acrimonious note. Delphine knew she had to make peace with Genevieve if they were all going to move forward in their lives. Continuing to carry around this bitterness wasn't doing anyone any good.

Approaching her own home, she noted the front door of Raymond's house was open and loud music was emanating from inside. 'How out of character for him, as he normally keeps the volume low, and the door closed,' she thought, the hairs on the back of Delphine's neck responding to her heightened sense of apprehension, she made her way across the street.

Calling out to Raymond as she approached, not wanting to startle him as she came through the door, she received no response. Stepping inside the front door, she was shocked to find Genevieve sitting on the couch, her back to the door, and a half empty bottle of whiskey on the table in front of her.

"Genevieve, what are you doing here?" Delphine exclaimed, looking around the room for any signs of Raymond or anything else out of place.

"Delphine! I didn't hear you come in," Genevieve drunkenly replied.

"Of course you didn't. You have the music up so loud, I imagine you can't hear anything," Delphine shouted, in an attempt to be heard over the music.

Genevieve, trying to stand, fell back down onto her seat, regained her composure, and got up again. She stumbled over to the phonograph, tripping as she walked, and clumsily lifted the needle off the record. "Better?" She asked, tottering back to her seat.

Delphine made her way across the room to the chair next to the couch and sat down. "Are you alright? What on earth is going on? Where is Raymond?"

"I don't know. I came here looking for him, hoping that I could get some answers, as well as maybe his forgiveness. He wasn't here, so I let myself in. I started looking through things. I found a few of my old things still in the dresser, the records that Walter didn't destroy were still stored on the shelf, and then I found this bottle, hidden away on the top shelf of a kitchen cabinet. I put on one of the records and sat down to listen. One minute I was deep into the music, the next I found myself pouring a drink. Delphine, honest, I don't drink like this. I don't know what's come over me. Something about being back in this house and the ghosts that still haunt this place." Genevieve said, her head dropping to her chest, tears rolling down her cheeks.

Delphine sat, staring at her in disbelief. She only had ever seen Genevieve have one drink when they went out, and that had been years ago. Her being drunk now was something new and seemed definitely out of character for her. Knowing that they couldn't stay there, especially if Raymond came home and found his mother in this state,

Delphine started to clean up the mess that Genevieve had made. While putting away the records, closing drawers, and tidying the kitchen, she instructed Genevieve to gather her belongings. "Don't think about taking anything else other than what you brought in with you. No need putting ideas in Raymond's head that someone's been here. I'm taking you back to my house. We'll get a hot meal in you and then you need to lie down and sleep this off. You're not going to like how you feel later, but believe me when I tell you, this is for the best right now."

Genevieve looked at Delphine as a small child would look at their mother when they've been scolded. "I didn't mean any harm."

"I know you didn't, but if Raymond comes home and finds you here like this, what do you think he'd do?"

"I don't know. I just feel so bad. I just want him to understand what happened all those years ago. His daddy was a mean, mean man."

"Come on, let's go. We can discuss this more over dinner." Delphine said, helping Genevieve out the door.

Not long after they had returned to her house, as Delphine was preparing dinner, she saw Raymond return home. Hoping he wouldn't find anything amiss, she reassured herself she had done her best to return everything to its proper place. She saw a light turn on in the living room, and his shadow pass by the windows. Aside from what appeared to be his normal movements, she couldn't see any sign that he noticed anything out of the ordinary. Breathing a sigh of relief, she went back to finishing the meal preparations.

Over dinner, Delphine did her best to sober up Genevieve. Knowing they still had to have a tough conversation, Genevieve's drunken state didn't give Delphine much confidence that anything said would be remembered the next day.

Genevieve spent most of the time lamenting her leaving all those years ago, wringing her hands in guilt over abandoning her baby boy. She alluded to a couple of episodes when the abuse at the hands of her husband had been especially bad. But she insisted she hadn't wanted him dead, just out of their lives. The guilt of her involvement with that deed still hung heavy over her every day, even though years had passed and most people had long forgotten him.

After dinner, while sitting in the living room, Delphine decided it was time to have the dreaded conversation.

"Genevieve, we really need to talk. I have some serious concerns about Raymond and his behavior. I know you aren't going to want to hear what I have to say, but it's about time you do."

Genevieve, looking up at her with the look of someone still feeling the effects of too much alcohol and the tiredness of a hard, lived life, slowly nodded her head as if to show she understood. But before Delphine could continue, Genevieve slid down further in her seat and succumbed to the unconsciousness that was overtaking her.

'Well, that didn't go as planned,' thought Delphine as she helped Genevieve up from the chair and over to the couch, covering her with a blanket.

Adjusting the pillow beneath the sleeping Genevieve's head, Delphine quietly said, "I suppose tomorrow will be soon enough for us to have this conversation. Maybe then clearer heads will prevail and you'll be able to see your son for the man he's become, not who you want him to be."

"Make it stop. Make it stop." Genevieve called from the living room.

Entering the room, Delphine found her friend, slumped over, head in hands, and trembling uncontrollably.

"Oh, you're awake, I see. Guess you're not feeling too well after your bit of drinking yesterday?"

"Oh god, Delphine. What have I done? I barely remember anything. Just one minute I was at the house, the next I'm waking up here. What's going on?"

"First off, breakfast. Let's get some food in your stomach and see if that helps. Then we can talk." Delphine said, as she led her back to the kitchen.

Once they finished their meal, and feeling like she actually had Genevieve's attention, Delphine cleared her throat. "This is not going to be easy, but you need to hear this."

"I don't -"

"No, you are going to listen and hear me out." Delphine interrupted before Genevieve could protest any further. "First off, what were you thinking going over there like that? No. Never mind, that's not what's important right now. What we need to do is get you home without being noticed by Raymond. I've already seen him up and working outside this morning. As long as he is out there, there's no good way to get you to the streetcar."

"Delphine, listen to me. I know you have your doubts about Raymond. You've made that clear already. But you have no proof. And sooner or later, he's going to find out that I'm back. I either need to go over there and tell him myself, or, well, I don't know. I guess that really is the only way. I can't expect you or anyone else to shoulder that responsibility any longer."

"Genevieve, stop. You have to hear this. Since our last conversation, I've discovered something else. It seems that Simone found this napkin in the parlor of the Batiste house a few weeks ago, and well, it looks awfully familiar to me. I'm pretty sure you'll recognize it as well."

Handing over the fabric to Genevieve, Delphine watched to see if there was any sign of recognition.

"I suppose that could be one of mine. I mean, it looks enough like the ones we used to have. But surely there are plenty of people who had those. What is so significant about it? Or even about Simone finding it?"

Exasperated, Delphine shook her head. "Because it was in the Batiste house. Weren't you listening to me? It wasn't as though it was just on the porch, it was inside the parlor. And there is no way the wind just blew it in there. Some-one, and I think that someone was Raymond, was in the room. What would he be doing there Genevieve? Surely you can see my concern now?"

"Honestly, Delphine, I think you are just trying to make things up now. Even you can't come up with a good reason he would be there. Maybe someone else had it with them when they were there visiting the family, and just dropped it without realizing. Why are you so determined to turn Raymond into his father?" Genevieve shouted. "I'm done listening to this. Nothing you have said to me substantiates any of your claims. My poor boy has been through enough. It's time for me to go home, get cleaned up, and then come back here and face my past. Thank you for taking care of me last night. In that regard, you are right. It would not have been good for Raymond to find me like that. But this matter is no longer any of your concern. Any guilt or whatever you may be feeling is forgiven. None of it is your fault. You did what you could for him. But now, now it's time for you to mind your own business. I will be on my way, and should we cross paths again, well, just stay to your side of the street."

Before Delphine could respond, Genevieve was on her feet, putting on her coat and covering her head with her scarf. Grabbing the door handle, she looked around, turning back to Delphine as if to say something more, before turning and storming out the door.

27

Trying to clear his mind, Raymond put the New Orleans Rhythm Kings on the turntable, hoping that hearing the music would calm the cacophony he was currently experiencing. Setting the needle down, he heard the opening refrain of "She's Crying For Me" as the darkness continued to grow, the demons taking control.

Dressing quickly, Raymond headed out for the evening. Perhaps live music and being around others would be the balm he so desperately needed.

Arriving at the club, he walked straight up to the bar and ordered a double shot. The bartender gave him an inquiring look, set down a glass and poured. Raymond slammed it back and ordered another.

"That's a bit unusual for you. I'd take it easy if I were you, pal," he offered.

"Mind your own business," Raymond growled.

Shrugging, the bartender poured again, then turned his attention to the next customer, leaving Raymond with his drink and dark thoughts. Looking around, he was unsure of what or who he was looking for. Maybe he'd see Simone, and this would be his chance to settle his score with her.

"Why her?" he muttered under his breath, turning back to the bar to demonstrate his desire for another drink. The bartender delivered, this time with no additional commentary. Raymond toyed with it as he returned his attention to the room.

Spotting a leggy brunette dancing alone with a drink tipping back and forth in her hand, he could tell based on her spasmodic movements she had started her drinking earlier than everyone else. Keeping an eye on her for the remainder of the set, he noted she appeared to be there alone. Perhaps she was what he needed to clear his head. Getting the attention of a waitress, he sent a drink over to test the waters. Upon the brunette receiving it and being shown the identity of the sender, she looked his way and responded with a smile.

Taking this as a good sign, Raymond made his way towards her. 'Take it slow,' he reminded himself.

"Thank you for the drink," she slurred as he approached. "I was feeling a bit parched there."

"Good evening, Dove. I'm glad I could oblige."

"Oh please, call me," she started. But Raymond gently put a finger to her lips before she could tell him her name.

"No, please, I prefer to call you Dove. You are as beautiful and graceful as a bird in flight. I couldn't take my eyes off of you as you were dancing. I was just surprised to see you all by your lonesome out there."

Shrugging and laughing at his gesture, she replied, "I was supposed to meet up with friends, but they all bailed on me at the last minute. So I decided to go ahead with the party by myself. No sense in letting a perfectly good evening go to waste, now is there?" Her inhibitions relaxed by the drinks, she continued her muddled babbling until the band returned for the next set.

Taking this opportunity, Raymond suggested a dance. She teetered a bit as they made their way to the floor, the effects of the alcohol becoming more apparent with each step. Helping to steady her, he held her hand as they joined the other dancers on the floor. Giggling, she let go and launched into her own version of a dance, leaving Raymond to look about, assessing his best path to getting her out the door without too much notice.

Because of her exuberance, it concerned him she would draw too much attention to the two of them, so he took a couple of steps back and allowed her the freedom to continue her gyrations. As the songs became more sultry and hypnotic, the dancers began pairing off, their attention and focus now on one another, not those around them. Raymond took this moment to take her in his arms, steering her towards the side of the stage and towards the door that was at the end of the little hall.

Whispering in her ear as they moved, though she couldn't make out what exactly he was saying, he could see in her eyes that she suddenly felt as though she had made a mistake.

Waking the next morning, Raymond looked out to see grey skies and ominous looking clouds building in the distance. As he lay in bed a moment longer, replaying the scene and song from the night before, he found his heartbeat steady, the dark voices silent. Deciding he would tackle the outside projects on the house that he had been neglecting, he got up and walked out to the kitchen. Rummaging around, he threw together a quick breakfast and decided he would try to get done with what he could before the weather set in.

Outside, as he was leaning a ladder alongside the porch, he noticed a woman hurrying down the opposite side of the street, away from Delphine's house. 'Odd,' he thought, 'how can she see where she's going with that scarf around her head and face like that?' Yet there was something familiar about her gait, an energy in her step he found mildly disconcerting. He couldn't recall seeing someone like her around the neighborhood before. And that was one thing he did, his meticulous attention to details allowed him to stay informed on who was still living here and who had left since he had moved back. He had been careful to maintain a low profile and didn't want some nosy neighbor speculating on his comings and goings or what he might be up to.

He continued watching until the approaching streetcar blocked her from his view. When the trolley pulled away, he no longer saw her, assuming that she must have boarded when it stopped. Try as he might, he couldn't shake the opposing feelings of uncertainty and recognition. Something about her was familiar, yet at the same time foreign.

This was an altogether unique feeling than he had ever experienced before, something new, not like when the music would turn from song to cacophony. When that happened, it was akin to the panic, cold sweats, and the terror that he felt as a child when his father beat him and took away his hearing.

Finding himself overwhelmed by the emotional response that had surfaced upon seeing the stranger leaving Delphine's home, Raymond sat down on the front porch, afraid he would otherwise succumb to the dizziness, sweating, and the feeling of his knees about to give way under him. The noise in his head was like nothing he had ever experienced before. As though someone was standing next to him shooting a gun, rapid fire, punctuated by an occasional cannon blast.

Who was this stranger that had been visiting Delphine? There was something familiar about her walk though, and for a moment, he thought it could be Momma. But surely, if it had been her, after all these years, wouldn't she come to their house first? Did she not see him outside? Wouldn't she want to know if that was him, all grown up now?

Finding his strength, he dragged himself inside, locking the door, closing all the curtains, and allowing the darkness to envelop him and his spiraling thoughts. Shuffling towards the kitchen, he reached for a bottle of whiskey that he kept high in the cabinet. Noticing how low the level was, he scratched his chin. He knew there had been more in there the last time he placed it back on the shelf. But how did it get this low? He hadn't drunk that much.

It was then he walked back out to the living room, when he noticed one record sticking out a fraction from the others on the shelf where they were stored. 'That's odd. I don't remember that being like that when I left the house yesterday,' he thought. He was always a stickler for details, especially when it came to his music and storing his collections properly.

His suspicions were now high. He knew someone had been in the house. But who? And why did they drink his booze? Aside from a record out of place and the half empty whiskey bottle, he didn't see anything else out of order. As he felt his anxiety level rising again, the peace he had felt the night before now leaving his head began to spin, the questions mounting. 'Who would have done this? Had Momma been here? And if it was her, then what was she doing and why wasn't she here now?'

Sitting down abruptly on the chair before he lost his balance, he tried to catch his breath. What had started as a quiet morning was rapidly escalating into a cacophony of overwhelming emotions and noise.

Memories of his childhood intermingled with snippets of the songs he collected from his Doves. Visions of their faces overlapped with images of his life at school and home all those years ago. Shaking his head, as if to clear his mind, he was attempting to focus on just one thought at a time. But the more he tried, the more riotous it became. A thousand reminders of all that he had experienced, places he lived, lives he had taken, and the songs he collected and treasured. One song after another ran together, the notes clashing, creating a discord that he couldn't stop hearing.

All the faces started melting into one another, creating a grotesque image in his mind's eye. That image eventually gave way to that one face that had haunted him day and night all those years, that of his tormentor. He tried to change his focus and think of his latest kill as an attempt to calm himself down. Taking a few deep breaths, he found he could quiet the visual and auditory noise down enough that now the only two remaining images were that of his mother and the last time he saw Simone.

Rubbing his hands over his face, as to clear the pictures from his mind, Raymond tried to return to the present. "Could the mystery woman I just saw be Momma? Was she here last night while I was gone? Why wouldn't she stay? Why wouldn't she tell me she was home?"

Looking at the whisky bottle in his hands, he took a large gulp, hoping that would be enough to settle his nerves. The liquor burned its way down his throat, hitting his stomach with a fire that felt as though it would burn through to his shirt. A few more slugs and the numbness he was so desperately searching for finally overtook him. Moving from the chair to the couch, he slid down and set about trying to figure out what he would do next.

It was time to send another package. But what could he send this time? He knew he needed to include a note as well. But it had to be worded just so.

28

Knowing it was a chance she had to take, Genevieve decided a night out at the Gibson was in order. Figuring she had burnt her bridges with Delphine, she hoped she could at least salvage her friendship with Evelyn, and maybe even see Raymond there. Perhaps if they were to meet on neutral territory, he would at least give her the chance to talk to him, to try and explain.

Walking in the front door of the Gibson, Genevieve saw the band and patrons already in full party mode. The dance floor was packed with bodies, swaying, grinding, allowing the rhythm to syncopate their movements. The wail of the saxophone startled her, bringing her attention back to the faces in the room.

Scanning the crowd, she caught David's eye when she saw him walking towards her. Taking her hand, he lead her back to the table where the group of friends had just sat down, taking a break and catching their breath.

Clearing his throat to get their attention, he began.

"Please, everyone. For those who don't already know her, I'd like you to meet someone."

As he pulled out a chair for her to sit, he gestured, "this is Simone, and Frederick. Of course, you already know my lovely wife, Evelyn, and Delphine."

Simone and Frederick both offer welcoming hands and smiles while Delphine acknowledged her with a flat, "Nice to see you again."

Looking directly at Delphine, Genevieve replied, "Thank you all for letting me join your party. I don't mean to intrude."

"Not at all. We're always happy to have new friends join us. And you picked a great night too. These guys are some of the best the city has to offer." Simone replied, oblivious to the rising tension.

The waitress stopping by the table to take orders, provided a much needed break, giving everyone else a chance to regroup and Genevieve to take in all that she was experiencing.

"Delphine, you're being awfully quiet this evening. Is everything alright?" asked Simone.

"Yes, I..." she started to say, stopping mid-sentence, her attention captured by something across the room. "I'm sorry. I need to excuse myself for a moment."

Simone shrugged, unsure what to make of Delphine's behavior. Turning towards Genevieve, she said, "I love your dress. I actually had my eye on something just like it a while back. Wherever did you find it?"

"Thank you. I found it in a little shop in the Garden District some time ago. I had no idea why I was buying it at the time, I certainly didn't have anywhere to wear it until now, that is."

"Oh, my! It must be the same dress then if it's the same shop I'm thinking of. They have such wonderful creations there, like nothing I've seen anywhere else. I'm so glad you found it. It looks absolutely stunning on you."

"Thank you. You are too kind. I feel a little silly all dressed up like this. I guess it's just been so long since I've been out for a night on the town. I forgot what it was like and what fun it could be."

"Well, I think all the women look exceptionally stunning this evening," said Frederick. "And it would be my pleasure to accompany each and every one of you to the dance floor."

"Always the charmer, aren't you, Frederick," says Evelyn, while elbowing David in the ribs.

The band had regrouped and was starting their next set, prompting Frederick to extend his hand to Genevieve. "Please, allow me to share this first dance with you." Genevieve nodding her approval as they headed towards the dance floor. David and Evelyn soon followed, leaving Simone alone at the table.

Scanning the room, in an effort to locate Delphine, she instead locked eyes with a gentleman by the bar who she thought appeared to be watching her. The look on his face sent a shiver down her spine, making her more than uncomfortable. Trying her best not to be obvious, she turned back around toward the band, to see if maybe it was someone else that he was looking at instead. Finding no one else that would have been in his line of sight, she turned her focus back to the dance floor, looking for Frederick and her friends, instead finding Delphine returning, visibly distraught.

"Delphine, what on earth is wrong? You look as though you've seen a ghost."

"Simone, I need to tell you something. But here is not the place for it. Where are the others?"

"On the dance floor. Frederick took Genevieve to dance, then David and Evelyn followed. But that's not what's important right now. Your tone and your face, you're scaring me. I can't say I've ever seen you like this before."

Moving her seat closer to Simone, Delphine began, "Alright. Don't turn around, just listen carefully. There is a guy at the bar. No, don't turn," Delphine reprimanded. "I know you'll know who I'm talking about in a minute. Sharp dresser, a step above the other guys, but not flamboyant. Not one of the 'regulars' we always see here, but he's been here before. Small scar on the side of his face that you'd remember. Usually alone, as far as I can tell. Though I guess I can say I've seen him with a few women, but never the same one twice. Typically, he doesn't dance, but I think you may have danced with him once."

"Okay, now this is getting creepy. Who is this guy and why do you know so much about him? And what concern is it of mine?"

Steeling herself, Delphine leaned in and lowered her voice, not wanting to be overheard. "Remember me telling you some time back about the young boy that stayed with me for some months? His momma went missing, and his father, well, he never showed back up either. Well, that's him at the bar. His name is Raymond, and after being gone for so many years, well, now he's back."

"I'm still confused. What does that have to do with anything?"

"Ugh, I didn't want to discuss this here. Well, I didn't

want to discuss this at all. It's not my place, but I guess you'll eventually find out, anyway." She paused, taking a sip of her now watered down drink, trying to find the courage to continue. "Genevieve is his mother. As I said before, she's been missing for years and now suddenly, she's back, too. And I think you may have known him too, years ago. Before you go asking questions, there are too many details to go into now. But I can say I don't think he knows she's alive. And of course, now she's here. And he's here. And this could get quite awkward in a hurry if they are to come face to face."

"Wow, I... I don't know or remember. I certainly don't recognize him, but how..." Simone whipped her head around, first towards the bar, then back to the dancers and the band.

As though the band sensed a change in the air, the tempo of the music dropped, the music took on a more somber timbre. Frederick and Genevieve returned to the table, noting the look of consternation on the faces of those sitting there.

"Everything all right?" Genevieve asked.

"No, not at all," Delphine replied.

Genevieve quickly picking up on the concern in her voice, sat down next to her and said, "Raymond?"

"Yes. Here. At the bar. From what I can see, his back is turned to us at the moment, but I wouldn't count on it staying that way for long."

Frederick interrupted, "Can someone tell me what's going on here?"

Simone leaned over and, in a hushed voice, quickly caught him up on the details he had missed.

Looking pointedly at Delphine, Frederick asked. "Okay,

so what exactly does he have to do with us? Aside from Genevieve here."

"Recently, I've had a couple of conversations with him. Even had dinner with him a few weeks back. I told him I had seen him here and asked why he never stopped by to say hello. He couldn't give me a suitable answer, and as a result, I told him that next time he was here, he should at least come over and introduce himself. It also left me with an unsettled feeling. Like there was something else. But that was before I knew that both he and Genevieve would be here at the same time and..." she trailed off.

Genevieve started gathering her belongings. "I have to go over to him. I can't involve you all in my business any more than I have. I admit I've put this off for too long. If there's to be any fallout, I don't want any of you getting caught up in it."

"Genevieve, wait! Are you sure that's such a good idea?" Evelyn asked, reaching an arm up to stop her.

Shuddering at the touch of her hand, she pushed it away and looked at her. "Good idea or not, I have to face the music sometime. Might as well be now."

"You can't possibly think going over there alone is a good idea. At least let one of us go with you," David implored.

"No. I'm putting my foot down for once. I realize this is something I should have done long ago, and if I had perhaps a lot of things that happened to me, to him, to all of you, wouldn't have." Tossing back the last of her drink, she turned, ready to head towards the bar and whatever fate may await her. Looking to where Raymond had been standing, she now found an empty space, the bartender wiping off the counter where his drink had been.

29

"That can't be...?" Raymond was thinking to himself. He had seen this woman come in, but hadn't given her another thought until he spotted her sitting at the table with Delphine and the others. "Momma?" He questioned. "But, after all these years? And at the Gibson? What exactly was going on here?" All these questions were making his head spin and his hands shake as he set his glass down on the bar.

Turning his back to the group, hoping he wouldn't be recognized, he saw Delphine get up and head toward the back hall. 'Did she know something, or was she maybe just headed to the restroom? Was she on to him?' The longer he stood there, the more his anxiety increased. He had to get out before anyone could approach him or cause a scene.

Pushing his way through the crowd, he made his way to the front door and lunging out, gasping at the air. He was pacing up and down the block, keeping just enough distance away from the club where he could still see anyone coming out the door. The night air was doing nothing to quiet the brewing internal storm. He knew he couldn't take a chance that one of them might come out and run directly into him.

If indeed that was Momma, there were a lot of questions that needed answering. Surely, after all these years, if she was really in the city, she would have come home right away. So what was she doing at a nightclub, in that dress, with those people? Did she know Simone? What did connection did she have to her?

Clutching his head, trying to avoid the overwhelming feelings, Raymond leaned against the wall. In that split second, his attention diverted away from the door, he didn't see Genevieve exiting the club and approaching him.

Noting that his back was turned, Genevieve breathed a thankful sigh of relief that he hadn't yet seen her. She didn't want to shock him any more than necessary, knowing that this was going to be a staggering surprise to begin with. She was experiencing a tidal wave of emotion, comprising guilt, shame, loss, and love all at once. She had no idea what she was going to say, and certainly no idea how Raymond was going to react, either. But now she was committed to the reunion that was about to take place.

As she walked, the sound of her heels striking the sidewalk gave her away, prompting Raymond to turn around. Here she was, face to face with her son for the first time in years. Words failing her, all she could do was weep at the sight of him, taking a long moment to stare into his eyes. She raised her arms, as if to hug him, then dropped them again to her side, unsure what the right move was.

She saw the eyes staring back at her, looking as though they belonged to someone else. Eyes that used to be tender and filled with love were now filled with a sight she recognized all too well. A despair, longing, sadness and it frightened her. Standing before her was no longer the little boy she had left behind. Now there was a man. A man she no longer knew, didn't know if he wanted to know her.

Regaining her composure, she straightened her back and said, "Hello, son."

Looking bewildered and unsure of the woman standing before him, he replied, "Momma? Is that you?"

Taking a step closer, Genevieve said, "Yes, Raymond, it's me."

Gaping at the woman standing before him, sweat beading on his forehead, hands clenching and unclenching, Raymond growled. "But what are you doing here? I thought you were dead? Where have you been? Why didn't you come home?" The questions tumbling out of his mouth in rapid succession as though they were trying to choke him and stop him from breathing.

"I know you have a lot of questions, and you deserve answers. But here, this sidewalk, is not the place to have this conversation. Please, let me take you home. I promise to not leave until you have all the answers you need."

"I don't know. I mean, I suppose so. I guess it's still your home. But..." his head shaking back and forth. He could feel the noise in his head had intensified to a cacophony of clashing cymbals and screeching horns, making it difficult to form even a complete thought or sentence.

Gently taking his arm, Genevieve steered him toward the streetcar that would return them to the home where it all began. "It will be okay, Raymond. Momma's here now and I'm not going anywhere."

Raymond was quiet the entire ride back, too quiet, Genevieve thought. She watched his eyes darting back and forth, first to her, then out the window, then back at her again. Hearing him mutter a few words under his breath as they got off the streetcar, it was nothing she could understand. He was walking as if in a drunken stupor, and she instinctively held out her hand to catch him should he fall, as if he were still a little boy.

Arriving at the house, Genevieve was taken aback. Nothing had changed since she had left, yet there was still something unsettling about being back again. The long ago memories of time spent living there, the abuse, the music, and even the laughter, it all came back to her the instant she took the first step inside. She could see he had changed nothing and had kept the house in order, offering her a sliver of hope that her Raymond, the one she carried in her memory, was still in there, somewhere.

She watched as Raymond made a beeline to the kitchen, rummaging around for what she didn't know, knocking over anything that happened to be in his way. After a minute of this, she surmised he found what he had been looking for when she heard the clink of bottle hitting glass. Walking into the kitchen, she found him pouring a drink and gulping it down. Seeing him drinking like this set her back a step. Had he grown into his father, after all?

"How long have you been back here?" He shouted. "Why now? All these years, I thought you were dead. Why didn't you just stay that way?" His eyes boring into her, a coldness filling the space between them.

Startled by his shouting, she dropped her handbag and took another step back, her response rushing out in a torrent.

"I don't expect you to understand, Raymond. I had no intention of being gone as long as I was. The day I disappeared, I had gone looking for your father. Only when I found him things didn't turn out so well. I fell in with the wrong people, got mixed up in some things I shouldn't have, and when it was all said and done... I thought you'd be better off without me around. Believe me, son, it was the hardest decision I've ever had to make. It broke my heart every day thinking about you. But I had seen you with Delphine and knew she was taking good care of you. It wasn't until after I got back that I found out about you staying with your aunt and uncle and for that, I am so sorry. I know they were worse than your daddy and had I known that was going to happen, I would have found a way to come back sooner. But son, I'm back now. I want you to know I never stopped loving you. I never stopped thinking about you."

Walking towards her, he looked at her and spat out the words she didn't want to hear. "I don't want you here. Get out."

"But Raymond, please, let me explain."

"No, I don't want your excuses. You left once before. It should be easy for you to do again."

Genevieve, recognizing the look in Raymond's eyes as one she had seen before in her husband, knew better than to argue any further. She picked up her handbag from where it had fallen on the floor and took one last look around. Turning back to Raymond, she pleaded, "I won't beg. But I'm in town for good now. I do hope you'll find it in your heart someday to talk to me. I love you, son. I always will."

She was met with only a glare that sent a chill down her spine. Knowing that there was nothing else to say, she kept her eyes on him, hoping to see the boy she once knew still in him somewhere, as she moved towards the door, not wanting to turn her back until the very last second. Stepping out onto the porch, she gently closed the door behind her.

⚜

Raymond picked up the glass he had left on the table and drank down what remained. The whiskey burning its way down, delivering a punch to his stomach. He was hoping it would be enough to get his wits back and give him the courage to face the truth of his mother's return.

Instead, he could feel the rage continuing to build. While there was a conflicting emotion simmering underneath, trying to push past the anger and fear he was feeling. Shaking his head, he tried clearing the confusion, but it didn't help. Grabbing the glass, he threw it against the wall. The crash making a satisfying sound but did little else to ease what was boiling inside of him.

He tried screaming, wishing the sound of his own voice would drown out the noise. Most of the words were indecipherable, but shouts of "stop the noise," "she will be mine," and a long wailing "no" broke through the air that hung heavily in the room.

Exhausted, Raymond sunk to the floor, feebly pounding

the hardwood with his fists, scraping his hands until the skin was raw and exposed. Why had his mother returned now? Where had she been all those years? She did little to answer any of these questions during the short time she was there. Maybe he should have let her stay and share her story. But would he have actually believed her?

He was so close to making his move, to getting his revenge against Simone. Knowing that once he dealt with her, it would calm the cacophony in his mind. He wouldn't have to keep on killing to find his peace anymore. He would be able to hear the music as the world had always intended.

Pausing on the front porch, Genevieve was wondering what to do next. Seeing lights on at Delphine's house, she considered going over there. What would she tell her, though? What could she tell her? That now she too had unfounded suspicions about the man that Raymond had become? But with no proof to back up her misgivings, it was still all just conjecture on both of their parts. She hadn't been around during these past years, so there was still much she didn't know about what had happened to him. But that look in his eyes, it was one she had seen in her husband's eyes all those times before, and now it only brought back more memories of the trauma of the past.

She heard glass shattering as she stepped off the porch, causing her to turn back toward the door, thinking maybe she could say something to calm him down. But before she could take another step, she heard Raymond yelling and concluded it was best if she left him alone for the time being. She hoped he would come around and maybe even come find her once he had a chance to process the fact that she was back. But deep down, she knew whether or not she wanted to admit it, she had probably lost her son for good.

⚜

Walking down the front steps and across the street toward Delphine's, she rehearsed in her mind what she was going to tell her friend. Friend, could she even call her that now? After all the years and grief she brought on, their last meeting ending with declarations of never wanting to see each other again, it would come as no surprise if Delphine never wanted to speak to her again. But she had to try one last time. She owed it to everyone to attempt to explain and set things right if she could.

Approaching, she saw David and Evelyn's car parked in front of the house and thought 'Good, I can talk to all of them at once. They all deserve to know the full story.'

Delphine opened the door before she knocked.

"Genevieve, why am I not surprised to see you here?" Delphine said, not taking care to hide the disdain in her voice.

"Delphine, I'm sorry for coming by so late, but I feel I owe you an explanation. And an apology."

"Yes, it is late. But as you can see, none of us are asleep yet, so come in, I guess." She said, stepping aside to let Genevieve into the living room.

Evelyn, ever the one to notice what others may miss, noted the look of worry in Genevieve's eyes. Rising from the couch, she walked toward where Genevieve stopped.

"Dear, what is it? Something is troubling you, I can tell."

Genevieve shrugged and hung her head. "I'm not sure

where to begin. As I said to Delphine, I feel I owe you all an apology for leaving all those years ago, for showing up again unexpectedly, for seeming ungrateful for all the help you've given me."

Taking her by the arm, Evelyn steered her towards an empty chair, then returned to her seat on the couch next to David. "Nonsense, you don't owe any of us a thing. We were glad to help you get out of that terrible situation. But that's not really what's bothering you, now is it?"

"No, I..." she stammered. "I have to admit, maybe I was wrong. I'm worried about Raymond. There's something not right about him. I brought him home from the Gibson and tried talking to him, hoping I could make him understand. But he wouldn't give me the chance to even explain why I left, or what happened to his father. I saw something dark inside that boy, something I hoped I'd never see in him. I've seen it before, and Delphine, maybe you were right when you tried to tell me too. His father got that same look in his eyes on more than one occasion and I usually bore the brunt of the results of that mood on my body after he was done."

"I'm sorry, dear, but I'm not sure I'm following here. I understand that both you and Raymond suffered at the hand of your husband, but Raymond has been out from under his influence for many years now. What would give you the idea that he's following in that man's footsteps? Delphine, have you ever seen him with anyone around here? Or any indication of this behavior?"

Delphine, returning to her seat across from Genevieve, sat straight-backed, taking a deep breath before answering. "No. I've not seen him with anyone around the house, only the occasional girl at the Gibson. But I am relieved to hear that Genevieve finally thinks there is something not right about him. He's not the same boy I took care of all those years ago. From what little he has shared with me, I'm guessing he suffered some hardship while at the farm and perhaps also while he was on his own. He was a bit reserved when he was over for dinner, only giving me bits and pieces of what he went through, but what can you expect after so many years? I'm sure being back here is just a reminder of what he's lost." Turning to face Genevieve directly, she asked pointedly, "So what's changed your mind now?"

"I don't know how I can explain it, other than mother's instinct," Genevieve said. "As I was leaving, I could hear him in the house. I heard glass shatter, then he was yelling, almost howling, then pounding as though he was hitting the wall. What concerned me the most was the one phrase I clearly heard, and that was 'she will be mine'. I don't know who the 'she' is that he's referring to, but something about the tone of his voice was alarmingly different from anything I've heard come out of him before. Even when he was telling me to leave, I could hear the anger in his voice, but this was something more disturbing. And I fear for her, whoever she may be."

"Well, I don't know the man, other than when I met him as a boy. But if you two are worried, then perhaps it's best we keep alert. I can't say that there is much else we can do besides that, though," Evelyn declared.

"I suppose you may be right. I just wish I could just get through to him and help him see that I'm back and only want what's best for him. But Delphine, are you sure you don't have any idea who 'she' might be?"

Delphine stood up then sat down again, no longer able to hide the exhaustion she was experiencing. She picked up her glass, taking a long sip of lemonade, using the time to consider her words before answering.

"I can only guess. I say this cautiously and don't any of you dare repeat this. But there have been times I've seen him watching Simone. Not just a casual glance, but more intently. I brushed it off as just another guy admiring her at the bar, but now knowing that she was the one who teased him so mercilessly in school all those years ago, I wonder if he's been harboring thoughts of revenge all this time."

David, who had been sitting quietly and listening the entire time, spoke up. "If that's the case, then we need to do something. Either get the police involved, or at least somehow protect Simone."

"I'm not sure that's a good idea. I can't prove anything, it's only my speculation at this point. Besides, what would the police do? It's not like they did anything in the past." Genevieve replied.

Delphine's head snapped back from David to Genevieve, as she demanded, "Well then, what do you suggest we do? We can't just stop going out. That would raise even more questions. We can't sit idly by just waiting for something to happen, either. Just what do you propose we do?"

31

ow could it be? After all these years, just when he was coming to terms with Genevieve being gone for good, here she was, back again on his doorstep.

Raging with emotion as he paced back and forth, Raymond thought back on how Momma had instilled the love of music in him from such an early age. And now, all these years later, he found he was blaming her for losing that love as well. Granted, it had been daddy's fault. The physical abuse that caused him to lose hearing in one ear. But it all started with Momma.

'She taught me the love of all things to do with music. The rich sounds of each instrument, the emotions each one evoked. The stories that the singers shared through their words. It had been her obsession that she passed on to me. And now, because of her, because of that deep-seated love, when I can't hear the music, I have to find a way to capture it again. So, there it is. It's all her fault that I have to take the lives and the songs of all of those girls. Her and Simone. Yes. They both need to pay now.'

Sitting down at the small desk, Raymond began sketching out his ideas for revenge. He knew where Simone worked, and he figured it would be easy enough to determine where she lived as well. Many of the staff he knew lived at the house. If that was the case for her, then that could prove to be a bit more challenging, but nothing he couldn't overcome.

Momma, on the other hand. That retribution he wanted to take his time with. Perhaps maybe he should welcome her home first. Let her settle back into life here and allow her to think that all is forgiven. Yes, that could make the revenge that much sweeter. It wouldn't be hard to lull her into a sense of security. She would be so overjoyed to be home with her son again, he thought. She'd never see coming what he was planning for her.

He decided, starting right then and there, that over the next week he would spend all his free time repairing, painting, and cleaning the entire house in preparation to bring her home.

He started by disposing of what remained of his father's belongings, throwing away his few clothes, and burning the last of his papers. He didn't want any trace of the man or his presence in the house. He knew it had to be a clean slate for both him and Momma. There were too many unanswered questions, and he knew if there were any reminders of that awful man around, she may not be forthcoming with the answers he needed to hear.

Determined to rid the house of the musty smell that permeated the walls and furniture, he left all the windows open, day and night, regardless of the weather outside. He didn't want to have anything that might be off-putting for Momma upon her arrival. Everything had to be perfect.

He washed and dried what remained of her clothes and hung them back up in her closet, ready and waiting for her return. He made sure all the records were in the order that she had left them. He wanted her to listen to the music again. That was the key to making her feel at home again as quickly as possible.

Not once during this time did he touch a drop of alcohol or even go out for an evening of music. He was resolute on a mission to make sure that everything was in order for her return. Nothing was going to stand in the way of his eventual goal.

Once he felt the house was returned to a state that met his standards of satisfaction, he decided it was time to set out on his hunt to find Momma. He knew she had been staying not far away, just off of South Rampart Street. At least that's what she told him the night she came back. It was one of the few pieces of conversation he remembered. Most of the rest of the night had become a blur in his memory.

This wasn't the best part of town, that much was certain. The buildings themselves were soot covered, and the smell of human waste that hung in the air only added to the degrading atmosphere. The streets were populated with gambling houses, speakeasies, and women walking and working the streets, day and night. Looking around, he wondered why she chose to move there, surely she could have done better for herself. 'It doesn't matter now. She'll be home soon enough,' he thought.

Approaching the address where she was supposed to be staying, he stopped just short of the steps. His heart was pounding so fast and loud, he felt as though it would burst out of his chest. Surely those around could hear it, too. What was he going to say to her? Would she even come home with him? All the questions and no simple answers were running through his head. Taking a deep breath, he reminded himself of why he was here as he took the next step towards her front door.

"She ain't there," he heard a voice say.

Turning to see who had spoken to him, he questioned, "I'm sorry?"

"She ain't there. She left 'bout an hour ago," the woman on the next porch over told him. "An' just who are you, anyway?"

Stuttering, unsure of who this woman was in relation to Momma, he replied. "I, uh, I'm her son. Do you happen to know where she went?"

"Work I'm guessin', just like she does every day. Son, huh? She never mentioned you to me."

"Yes, well, I could say the same about you," Raymond tersely replied as he regained his composure. "Do you know where she works or when she'll return? It's rather important that I find her."

"She be back 'round supper time. Where she work, I don' know. Somewhere in the district, my guess," the old woman said, still watching Raymond with a wary eye.

"Well, thank you for your help. I guess I'll just come back later." He said, turning to leave. When he glanced back over his shoulder at the woman watching him, he thought, 'there's something about her, the way she's watching. Does she know me too from childhood? Or does she know something more?' Whatever it was, it was making him uncomfortable and nervous, as he quickly made his way back down the street.

Once he was out of the neighborhood, he began to breathe normally again. He hadn't realized how deeply the atmosphere of that area had affected him. After having maintained a certain level of mental quietness over the past weeks, he could hear the discordant music growing louder in his head again. 'No, I can't. I won't. Not now, when I'm so close to achieving my goal.'

He knew he had to get Momma settled in before he set the next phase of his plan into motion. There needed to be the necessary time to talk to Momma, to tell her all that had been going on in his life, about the time spent on the farm, living in Galveston, then finding himself back in New Orleans again. He wanted to tell her just how he envisioned the future for them, giving her that sense of security he knew she so desperately needed. He considered apologizing to her, but for what exactly, he wasn't sure. She was the one who had left him, after all. And in the end, everything that came after that, everything he did, was all her fault, he decided.

32

In keeping with the plan he had worked out so far, the next day, Raymond decided it was time to pay Simone a visit and drop off another package. Well, she wouldn't actually see him, but he would see her and put the next steps of what he had in store for her into play.

Arriving in the Garden District, he got off the streetcar at the stop just before the Batiste's house. He didn't want to risk being spotted by anyone, most of all Delphine. Keeping his head down, his hat just low enough to hide his eyes, to not draw any unwanted attention. He unhurriedly walked up and down the streets, only glancing up as if to check an address or street name.

Walking down Prytania Street, he found himself along the backside of the Batiste's property. He could see the stables from this vantage point, as well as the path that led to the back door. He wondered what was Simone doing right now? Is she even home or is she out somewhere, running her errands? Just then, he saw the door swing open and one of the stable hands walk out. He could hear laughter coming from the kitchen, Simone's distinctive voice ringing out over the rest. Ducking back behind a tree, he watched as the backdoor slammed shut, silencing the life that had just erupted from within. He found himself pinned against the tree, unable to move. That laugh bringing back memories of childhood torment, Simone and the others on the playground, teasing him, singing songs behind his back. The longer he lingered, the more deafening the silly childhood songs became.

In an effort to regain control, Raymond straightened up, pushing his shoulders back while muttering something unintelligible under his breath. Taking a deep breath, he stepped out from behind the tree, left the package at the door, and made his way down the side of the house. He knew if he kept on this path, it would take him back by the parlor doors, the same doors he had snuck in once before.

Approaching, he heard Delphine's voice, followed by a response from Simone. He could tell they were both in the same room now, but how close did he dare get? He couldn't run the risk of Delphine seeing him, if she did, his plans would be ruined, it would be all over before it even began. No, he had to make sure to stay hidden when he found a break in the bush and ducked in-between. Trying to blend in as best he could, he crouched down and listened.

"Here Simone. I brought you back that red cloth." He overheard Delphine saying.

"Did it not work out for you?" Simone asked.

"No, I'm afraid it was the wrong shade of red. But no matter. I'll just leave it here on top of your sewing basket."

"Thank you Delphine. I guess I'll just keep it for now. I still have no idea how it wound up here in the parlor. No one around here seems to know where it came from."

Hearing this, Raymond reached into his pockets, remembering having had a red napkin with him on one of his visits there. Now that he thought about it, he realized he hadn't seen it since. Had he dropped it there? Was this the same fabric she was talking about? Was it possible that Delphine had recognized it as one of his? He had to see this fabric for himself, to be sure.

Once satisfied that Delphine left the room, he peered out from his hiding spot to see that Simone stayed behind, and from what he could tell, she was working on her mending. Stepping out from his hiding spot, he took two tentative steps toward the side stairs, careful to not make any noise to give himself away. Fortunately for him, her back was to the window, and he could look in without revealing himself to anyone. There he saw the red napkin laying off to the side, now he was certain it was his.

Taking a step back, he bumped into a rocking chair, causing it to bang against the side of the house. Seeing Simone jump up at the sudden sound, he quickly made his way back off the porch and back to his hiding spot, out of sight, before anyone noticed him there. He wanted to wait and see her reaction to receiving the latest package. He didn't have to wait long. He heard someone call her back to the kitchen as he made his way back around the house.

"It would seem you have another mystery package," he heard an unknown voice say.

"Well, I hope this time there's a note at least," Simone replied.

Listening, he could hear her opening the box and letting out a gasp as the contents clattered to the floor.

"Oh my, who would send something like this? What are

they playing at? This note, I can't even bear to read it out loud. Please, just take this away." Simone cried.

Having had the pleasure of hearing her distress and not wanting to be caught, he made his way back to the street and strode on, head held high now, a more determined purpose driving each step. He knew now he couldn't wait any longer, it was time to make the last arrangements and set his plans in motion. He would return to Momma's run-down house tonight and bring her home where she belonged. Then, in due time, Simone would finally reap what she had sown all those years ago.

Returning home, Raymond took the time to slowly walk through each room once more, paying attention to the fine details. He wanted to make sure everything was in place for Momma's arrival. He straightened the quilt on her bed and fluffed the pillows one last time, then returned to the living room and moved a vase of flowers from the side table to the coffee table. He checked to make sure her favorite record was set up on the phonograph, ready for her to play when they returned. No detail was too small to be overlooked, everything had to be perfect.

Content with the state of the house, he set back out on his mission. Passing Delphine coming home from work, he greeted her warmly and bid her a good evening. Not wanting to raise suspicions, but not wanting to delay his mission any longer, he didn't give her a chance to respond, only acknowledging that he was on his way to catch the approaching streetcar.

⚜

Finding a seat at this time of day was a bit of a challenge. The car was filled with workers returning to their homes for the night. After a few more stops, most had exited and Raymond took a seat next to a window, allowing the breeze to cool him off and dry the sweat that had been dripping down his neck and brow.

Minutes later, as he approached his stop, the dingy atmosphere of the neighborhood that he observed the previous afternoon now had significantly changed. He couldn't say if it was the glow of the setting sun obscuring the grime on the rundown houses, the sounds of music and laughter pouring out of the open doors and windows, or perhaps it was the sense of determination on his mind, giving him this new outlook. But whatever it was, he was feeling as though he had transported to another place and time, as if he were back in the New Orleans he knew before everything had changed.

Shaking his head to clear it of the encroaching memories, he strutted toward the stairs of the house where Momma lived. The old woman he had seen earlier was nowhere to be found now. 'Good,' he thought, 'there was something not right about her.' Knocking on the door, he took one step back and waited. No response. Knocking louder this time, he heard footsteps approaching.

"Alright already. No need to break down the door," he heard the familiar female voice shout from inside.

As the door opened, Raymond was met by Momma, her hair tied up with a rag, dingy clothes torn and tattered. Taken aback, he wondered, what had happened to the woman who was always so put together?

"Momma?" He questioned.

"Raymond! Oh, my. I wasn't expecting anyone. Much less you. Son, what are you doing here?"

"I'm here to take you home, Momma."

Genevieve took a step back inside, grabbing at the apron hanging loosely around her waist, and started wiping her hands in an attempt to smooth out the wrinkles and dirt. She hoped to avoid letting him see how ashamed she was of how she must look to him now.

"Home? I don't understand."

Sensing her unease, he stepped toward her and smiled weakly. "Yes, Momma. Home. I've decided we've been apart too long now. It's time for you to come home and live where you were meant to all these years."

The tears that had been forming in the corners of her eyes started running freely down Genevieve's cheeks. A smile that first tugged at her mouth took over her entire countenance. Forgetting how dirty she was, she threw her arms around Raymond's neck and wept. At a loss for words, and unsure of how to respond, Raymond just stood, arms at his sides, wondering what to do next. He finally reciprocated with a brief pat on her back before disengaging himself from his mother's arms, then stepped back and said, "Come, let's get your things."

Wiping her eyes with her sleeve, Genevieve just nodded, leading the way to her room. As they walked, Raymond looked around, noting the peeling wallpaper, the layer of filth covering every imaginable surface. He was pleased with himself when he thought of all he had done to prepare the house for her. He knew she would be so much more comfortable sleeping in her own room, cooking in a well-stocked kitchen, and most of all having her music back again, too. He could feel the giddiness rising in his chest as he pictured the scene in his mind.

"I'll only be a minute," Genevieve said, snapping Raymond out of his daydream.

"Of course. Anything I can help with?"

"No dear. I don't have much," she replied as she busied herself throwing her belongings into a tattered satchel.

While she finished, she sent Raymond back out to the porch to wait. Questions running through her mind distracted her for a moment as she changed into better clothes, but she fought to push them away for now. She didn't want to second-guess what had changed his mind. There would be time enough for them to talk once they were home.

She stopped by the proprietor's room to let her know she was vacating. Once that last task was done, she was by his side, ready to return home and to her life once again.

33

Sitting out on her front porch, Delphine was enjoying the late evening air when she saw Raymond and Genevieve, carrying a small suitcase, approach the house. Overwhelmed by their surprise appearance, she hastily turned her head to the side in order to not betray her curiosity at what she could only describe as a dizzying turn of events.

"What's going on? Did Genevieve actually agree to come back here?" she mused. How did Raymond convince her to come back? Or did he force her?

Once she knew they had passed and entered the house, Delphine turned her head back, and continued watching the activity across the street, observing lights turning on in each room as they were entered or occupied. Delphine was full of questions, with no simple answers in sight. Glued to her seat, her rocking chair squeaked louder on the old wooden porch as she fidgeted, trying to figure out a way to go over and glean more information regarding this sudden change.

'Is it possible he threatened her?' Delphine's thoughts took a dark turn. She was afraid for her friend now. Maybe she hadn't come back on her own accord. If that was the case, what did Raymond have planned for her? Not able to sit still any longer and not caring how late it was getting to be, she picked herself up and walked across the street.

Halfway over, she saw the living room light go out. She knew Genevieve's old room was the one in front, while Raymond's was in the back corner of the house. She could see a light still illuminating what she knew to be Genevieve's room, and a shadow passing back and forth behind the curtain. Uncertain of what was taking place and how she would explain her sudden arrival at this hour, she turned back toward her home. She paused at her door for a moment, looking back over her shoulder once more, before going inside.

Figuring she'd be unable to sleep, Delphine paced the floor, keeping a watchful eye on Raymond's house. She chided herself, knowing there would be nothing she could do if Raymond was truly the monster she believed him to be.

Having worn what would amount to a new rut in her floor, she finally felt as though sleep would overtake her. Despite the promise of a few hours of uninterrupted slumber, her dreams did more to frighten her, causing her to wake on more than one occasion. As dawn broke, she concluded it was probably best to get up and begin her day, knowing that the nightmares would only continue the longer she lay in bed.

⚜

Hearing someone whistling outside, Delphine glanced out her front window, spotting Raymond walking down the street. He appeared to be in a buoyant mood, one she had not seen in him for a long time. Unsure of how long he would be gone, she hastily dressed and ran across the street, frantically knocking on the door.

After what felt like an eternity, Genevieve answered, making it plain to Delphine that she had awoken her.

"Delphine. Good grief! What time is it? What day is it?" Genevieve asked, rubbing the sleep from her eyes.

"Genevieve. Oh, thank goodness. I was worried something happened to you last night. It's just past six, Saturday morning. I'm sorry. I didn't mean to wake you. But I saw Raymond leave, and I just had to make sure you were okay."

"I'm sorry. But what are you going on about?" Genevieve asked, finally getting her wits about her, but was still having trouble making sense of what Delphine was trying to say.

"How long will Raymond be gone, do you think?" Delphine inquired, shifting her weight from one foot to the other.

"I don't know. I didn't even know he was gone. I was asleep, after all. Look, everything is fine. I'm guessing he must have just gone to pick up some food. Why don't you come back later when he's home? Better yet, why don't you come over for dinner tonight? The three of us can have a nice meal together, just like we used to do before I left."

Delphine looked at her friend, unsure whether to blurt out her concerns or continue to keep them to herself.

"I'm not sure I can. Work is going to be busy these next few days."

"Fine. Fine," Genevieve huffed. "I should be done with work early today. I'll come by the Batistes' and give you all a hand. I'm guessing you could use the help, yes?"

"Yes. That would be wonderful. Are you sure you're okay?"

"I'm fine, Delphine. Just tired from being woken up from one of the better sleeps I've had in a long time. Now, if you don't mind, can we finish this later?"

Before Delphine could answer, Genevieve closed the door, ending any more chance of discussion. Shaking her head, she said "okay," to the closed door and turned to walk back home. She was thankful to see Genevieve unharmed, but still had many questions that hopefully would get answered later that afternoon.

Looking back over her shoulder at the closed door, Delphine bumped into Raymond as he was coming back down the street.

"Delphine, good morning. How are you on this fine day?" Raymond asked cheerfully, shifting a bag from one hand to the other.

"Raymond, oh, I'm sorry. I didn't see you coming. I'm fine, thank you," she stammered.

"I'm surprised to see you out this early. Are you on your way to work already?"

Delphine paused, trying to decide what exactly she should say. She couldn't let on that she knew Genevieve was back. Not until she had a chance to actually speak with her and find out if she was really okay staying back at the house.

Deciding it was best to keep her thoughts to herself, she replied, "Yes, but I realized I had forgotten my bag. I was in such a hurry to get out the door today that I would have left my head behind if it weren't attached. It's a busy day at work and I really must be on my way."

"Of course. I understand. Please, don't let me keep you any longer. I also need to get home. I have a lot to prepare for." Raymond replied, tipping his hat to Delphine and turning up the walkway to his house. Glancing back over his shoulder, he saw her still standing in the same place on the sidewalk, just watching him. Unsure if the look on her face was one of curiosity or just disorientation from her scattered brained morning, he nodded again as she smiled back at him and made her way back across the street.

Reentering her house, she quickly made her way to the closest chair, dropping into it while letting out the breath that she had been holding all the way back. Her head was spinning from the encounters, first with Genevieve, and then with Raymond. There was something about the way he said that he had things to prepare. What could he mean by that? Surely now that Genevieve was back, he wasn't planning on harming her. He had missed her so terribly when he was a child, he should be overjoyed to have her home.

Maybe the suspicions she had been harboring about Raymond had been wrong this entire time. But there were still unknown questions rattling about in her head, not to mention the way she had seen him looking at Simone at the Gibson. Something about that made the hairs on the back of her neck stand on end.

'No,' she thought. 'There is still something off about this and I am going to get to the bottom of it, if it's the last thing I do.'

❦

Genevieve was trying to go back to sleep after Delphine left, but just as she was dozing off she heard Raymond come in the house. In her sleep addled haze, she wondered where had he gone? Why had he left so early in the morning, or had he gone out the night before and was just now returning home? Following a rabbit trail of thoughts, she then began asking herself, were the suspicions Delphine alluded to worth considering? No, surely Raymond had just been out that morning running an errand and there wasn't anything more devious going on. After all, he was her son, a good boy, and now that they were back together again, all would be right with the world.

Deciding that staying in bed was no longer an option, she got up and began getting ready for her day. She knew she had to go to work and now that she promised Delphine she would come by the Batiste's house and help there, it was now going to be a longer day than she first hoped for.

She had wanted to make a special breakfast for Raymond that morning, it was the least she could do on their first day back together. Remembering that she had seen a fairly well-stocked pantry when she had been there before, she quickly got dressed before making her way out to the kitchen.

Entering, she was surprised to find the table already set and Raymond at the stove, cooking breakfast for the two of them. Where she once had seen the little boy standing before her, now, here was a grown man, capable of taking care of himself, and apparently her as well.

"Raymond, my goodness. You didn't have to go to all this trouble. I was going to make breakfast for you this morning," Genevieve declared.

"Momma, please. Sit down," he urged. "I don't want you

to have to worry about taking care of me and yourself and you having to go to work, too. I have the entire day off ahead of me with only a few chores to take care of around here. Please. Coffee is ready, and the rest will be on the table in just a couple of minutes."

Shaking her head, she did as she was told, sitting in what had been her normal seat all those years ago.

"Raymond, I can't tell you how happy I am to be back here. For us to be together again. I feel just terrible for leaving you all those years ago. We have so much to catch up on. What have you been doing all this time? Where have you been living?"

Not wanting to let him know how much she knew, she continued. "Did you stay with Delphine? I knew she would take care of you. She was always such a wonderful neighbor to us."

"No, well, yes. It's a lot to explain. But let's just have our breakfast first. We can talk about our plans for today and the next few days as well. Then, this evening, we'll have plenty more time to catch up on all the past details. For now, I just don't want you to worry about anything."

Genevieve looked over at Raymond as he turned back to the stove, considering his stance and demeanor. He had grown up into a fine-looking man, she thought. But there was a tone in his voice, she couldn't quite figure out. As though he wasn't being completely honest with her about his motives for finding her or bringing her home. What could he have gone through in those years that she was gone? Delphine had told her of his going to that bastard of an uncle, but what took place after he was able to get away from there and come back here? Was he working? So many questions. Her head was spinning again.

Raymond set down a plate in front of her, the smell of freshly cooked bacon, eggs and biscuits, breaking her wandering train of thought. She looked up at him and smiled as her way of saying thank you. She didn't think she could find the words or her voice at that moment. Raymond smiled in return, but she could see the happiness wasn't reflected in his eyes. It was as though he had pasted a smile on his face, but wasn't feeling it with his entire being. Genevieve shook her head to clear the darkening thoughts and began to eat the food he had prepared for her.

"Will you be going to work today?" Raymond inquired in-between bites.

"Yes. I have a busy day today. The family I work for will be leaving town next week. So we have to get everything in order today and tomorrow for their departure. Since they will be gone for ten days, I will be home more after that."

"Hmm. That's good," he murmured, not looking at her, his focus somewhere off in the distance.

"I'm sorry?"

Turning his attention back to Momma, he said, "Oh. No. I was just thinking that will be good for us. Since you won't be working much next week, it will give us time to spend together. I tell you what, don't worry about dinner this evening. I have already taken care of it as well and I'll handle the cleaning up this morning too. You just worry about what you have to get done at work these next couple of days. I don't want you to feel as though you need to take care of me as well."

"Raymond, I can't let you do that..."

"Nonsense. It's my turn to take care you Momma. I know it's been a long time, and you must be feeling, well, some guilt, I'm guessing. But I don't want you to. I want you to know that everything is going to be okay now."

He paused, taking in a deep breath, and continued, "We'll talk some this evening, I promise. But for now, you just go about your normal routine and let me take care of everything else. Okay?"

Genevieve looked at him with lingering thoughts somewhere between curiosity and disquiet, hoping it wasn't showing on her face. "Very well. But if there is anything you need me to do, please, let me. I can't let you take all of this on yourself."

Raymond nodded and returned to finishing his breakfast. He had noticed a look in her eyes, but wasn't quite sure what to make of it. Was she lying to him about something? Or was it just the apprehension of being back here after all these years? This house surely held many memories, both good and bad. That will all change soon, he thought. New memories will be made and will replace all the bad ones from the past.

Finishing her meal, Genevieve excused herself from the table and returned to her room. Hurriedly she got ready for work, then gathered up her hat and bag before returning to the living room.

"Goodbye dear. I'm off. I'll see you this evening." She called out.

"Goodbye Momma," he replied from the kitchen.

Walking out on to the porch, she felt as though a weight was lifting off of her shoulders. Could it be that they were returning to a normal family once again? She longed for that to be true. But she also knew she would have to deal with Delphine and her crazy suspicions first. She would put those to rest once and for all this afternoon.

34

During a break just after lunch, Delphine took Simone aside for a chat.

"Simone, I have to apologize for my behavior lately. I don't want you to worry about me or anything else that may be going on."

Simone looked inquisitively at Delphine before responding. "I don't understand Delphine. I mean, you've been out of sorts lately, and there was our conversation that we had the other night. I haven't been able to get that out of my mind. Even though you told me not to worry. But you have to know, if there is something going on, regardless of what's going on in my life, you can talk to me. You are my dearest friend, after all, and I will always be there for you."

Delphine hung her head, ashamed of the secrets she had been keeping all this time. But she knew it wouldn't do any good to burden her with that information now.

Looking back up and smiling weakly, she responded, "You also are my sweetest and dearest friend Simone. I don't know what I would do without you. But regarding anything that I have said before, please, I implore you, put it out of your mind. In just a few days from now, you will be marrying that wonderful fellow of yours and beginning a new chapter in your life. That is all you should be concentrating on now."

"Yes, I suppose you're right. There is still so much to be done."

Delphine stood and smoothed the front of her dress. "Now, I have to go run an errand. Should Cook or Evelyn ask after me, please let them know I'll be back shortly."

"Of course. Is it anything I can help you with? I have a little more free time this afternoon. Much to my surprise, everything I needed to do is just about done, ahead of schedule."

"No, no. I'll be fine. It's just something I need to take care of on my own. Why don't you go sit outside and enjoy the afternoon for a bit? It's a lovely day, after all." She took Simone's arm and started guiding her toward the side porch of the house, as though she were trying to steer her away from something or someone she didn't want Simone to see.

"Thank you, Delphine. I think that's the best idea I've heard yet," Simone said as she settled down into one of the rocking chairs.

⚜

Once satisfied that Simone was staying put, Delphine quickly made her way back in to the house, through the parlor and into the kitchen. She threw a quick wave to Cook, who was too busy with her duties to notice the urgent pace that Delphine was moving. Just as she came down the outside stairs, she about ran headlong into Genevieve, who was coming to meet her for their agreed upon appointment.

"Delphine, my goodness. You nearly bowled me over. What's the hurry?"

"Genevieve, thank you. I mean, I'm sorry. I was trying to get out before Simone came back. I knew you were coming to the house, but really, we can't talk here. There are too many people about and this is a conversation we have to have, just the two of us. Please, quickly. Let's walk down the street a ways," Delphine implored.

Once she felt they were far enough away to talk comfortably without being overheard, Delphine slowed her pace and found a shady oak they could stop under.

"Okay, Delphine. What is this all about? You are not acting like the woman I used to know," Genevieve impatiently demanded.

"Why are you back at the house, Genevieve? Did Raymond threaten you? Are you sure you're okay? The last time you were there, you were beyond drunk. Now I see you coming home with him last night and, well, I am left with a lot of questions." Delphine asked in a rush, only stopping because she was running out of breath.

Shaking her head, Genevieve sighed. "Yes. I'm fine. And yes, the last time you saw me there, I was not in a good place. But things have changed since then. Raymond came to find me over where I was staying and asked me to come home. What was I going to say? No?"

Pausing, she looked imploringly at Delphine, then continued. "He's my son Delphine. I've been waiting so long for this reunion to happen, that once I got past the initial shock, I, of course, went right away. To be back in my home, with all of my things, and my music. Can you believe he still had what remained of my records after all this time? Yes, it's been a little awkward, of course, we really haven't had a chance to process it all. But in time, we'll be back to the mother and son relationship we used to have. I really don't understand why you are so concerned about me and him."

Delphine paused to consider what Genevieve just said before she replied, knowing she had to be sure of her tone and posture regarding what she was about to say and the potential ramifications of the accusations she was about to lodge.

Shifting her weight, she looked hard at Genevieve, exasperated at having to have this conversation again.

"Where do I begin? You've missed so much. And a lot of it is not good. I only know bits and pieces myself, but what I do know makes me wary. He's been back here longer than he's let on and during that time I've seen him, on more than one occasion, at the Gibson. I'm sure you know, or have at least heard, about the dead girls that they've been finding, too. Of course, the police don't care anything about them. That comes as no surprise to anyone. But, Genevieve, I've started to notice that when some of these girls have come up dead, it's been close to there and often when we've been there, too. And when Raymond has been there."

Hearing these unfounded accusations that Delphine was leveling at her son infuriated Genevieve. Taking a step closer to Delphine with her fists clenched, Genevieve gritted her teeth and growled. "How could you even think that? You have no cause to say it's been Raymond. You think you can just throw out an allegation like that and no one is going to call you out?"

Standing up straight, not ready to back down, Delphine replied. "I know, I know, I have no proof. It's just that awful feeling in my gut. There have been a couple of times I caught him watching Simone. He had the oddest look on his face, as though, well, I can't describe it. It was just terribly unsettling and when I found out that it was him, back after all these years, and knowing the history of your husband and his temper, I just..." Delphine trailed off, finding herself now unable to complete her thought as she saw the hurt in Genevieve's eyes.

"I refuse to believe that Raymond could ever hurt someone in that way. Yes, his father was a terrible man. But he was only around for what I would call a brief period of Raymond's life. He was gone more than he was there, so I don't really think he had that much of an impact on him."

"Okay, now Genevieve, how can you say that? He was there when Raymond was young and growing. Consider the times he was home. The beatings Raymond would witness or be on the receiving end of the fights you and Walter had. That's a lot for a young boy to experience and not let affect him somehow. And what about the time on the farm with those awful relatives? And where has he been all those other years in between? I know he was back at the house a few times, but he was gone more than he was here. Who's to say what happened to him in those years?"

Genevieve raised a hand to cut Delphine off. "I admit, the time he spent on the farm was probably one of the worst things that could have happened to him. Had I known that was going to happen, I might not have gone away, or at the least I would have tried to get back sooner. But I didn't think through many of my decisions over those few days and, as you know, circumstances beyond my control came into play as well."

Pausing, she stepped back and took a deep breath. "I guess life was hard for him those years. Especially if he was on his own and at such a young age. But until I get the story from him, I just can't bring myself to give any credibility to your suspicions of my son. It's not like you did much to help him, either."

Delphine stared at Genevieve with a look as though she had just been punched. Unable to contain herself any longer, she poked Genevieve in the chest. "How dare you say I didn't do anything to help him? I took him in when you disappeared. I kept an eye on your house while you were both gone, who knows where. When he did show up again, I tried to do what I could without overstepping. I also kept your secret all these years, too. Looking back, maybe I should have done more. But don't you dare tell me I didn't do anything!"

Seeing the pain she reflecting in Genevieve's eyes, she lowered her voice before she continued. "Alright. I've said my piece and I see that you are at least physically okay. But I just can't ignore this feeling in my gut and with everything else going on at the moment, I don't have time or energy to spare. I hope for you sake that I'm wrong and that you and Raymond will get back to the relationship you once had."

Genevieve considered the woman she once thought of as a friend for a moment, wondering what was to become of them now that these accusations had been made. Taking a deep breath before responding, she looked at Delphine with sadness and loss. "Raymond and I do have plans for dinner this evening and we're supposed to take some time to talk over what's happened all these years. I can't say that

I'm going to bring up what you've just told me, because I still refuse to believe that he could be responsible for any of it. But I will hear him out and hopefully he will hear me out too. As to my invitation to you about coming over anytime soon, I think it best that we don't do that for a while. Not until cooler heads can prevail."

Delphine just nodded as she started to leave. Taking a step, she paused and turned back. "I hope you find what you are looking for, really I do."

Genevieve biting her tongue as she watched as Delphine walk back to the house, just stood there, knowing that no matter what else she said, nothing would change Delphine's mind.

35

As he set the flowers on the table and straightened the place settings once more, Raymond ran through the menu in his mind, making sure he had all of Momma's favorites prepared for that evening. He wanted everything to be perfect. No detail was too small to be overlooked.

Stepping back, he glanced around the house and was overcome with the memories of childhood that these walls contained. Most were good, he had managed to push down as much of the bad as he possibly could. Having gotten rid of the remaining items that had belonged to his father was the last cathartic step in dealing with his past. From here on out, it would be all-new. New memories to be made with Momma and revenge against Simone that would brighten the dark places in his soul and quiet the dissonance that was ever present in the background of his mind.

He found that having the two of them to focus his thoughts on helped to keep his other urges under control. It had been almost a month now since he had last been out and collected any more songs from the Doves. While he could still hear those songs he had already collected in his mind, they had become fainter, as though the music was playing from some distance away and not right in front of him.

As he tenderly picked up one of Momma's favorite records and placed it on the old phonograph, he was reminded of the time when Daddy had thrown a lot of Momma's cherished records across the room. The sound of them shattering as they hit the wall and crashed to the floor reverberated through his head. He must have been 4, maybe 5. But even at that young age, he knew how important the music was to Momma. She didn't have an extensive collection. What she had, she had scrimped and saved for months to buy, and every one was to be treasured and enjoyed. With each record that Daddy flung, Raymond saw the pain reflected in her eyes as though her heart were shattering on the floor alongside the broken pieces.

Oh, how he hated that man for all the misery he caused them. Raymond knew that whatever fate had befallen his daddy had been a punishing one. He certainly deserved it. But now was not a time to reflect on the past. Now was the time to look toward the future.

Returning to the kitchen, he finished dinner preparations, seasoning the greens one last time, pulling the freshly baked cobbler from the oven. The smells of home permeated the room and brought a sense of peace over him again.

Right on time, Genevieve came home from work as though it had been any other day. Walking into the house, she was greeted by the aroma of dinner waiting to be served, the sight of fresh flowers on the table and her beloved music playing in the background. Tears immediately rose in her eyes and rolled down her cheeks. How she had missed this, her son and her home. She stood there for a moment, taking it all in, thinking to herself, there is no way that the man that did all this could be responsible for any of the things Delphine had tried to convince her of.

"Raymond, I'm home," she called, still not having moved from her spot just inside the front door.

Calling out in a cheerful tone, Raymond replied, "I'm in the kitchen, Momma. Please, go ahead and sit down. Dinner will be out in just a minute."

Taking off her coat and setting her purse on the sideboard, she made her way to the dining table, smiling to herself. "This is how life is supposed to be," she murmured as she sat down.

Raymond came out of the kitchen carrying two plates loaded with roasted chicken, mashed sweet potatoes, and collard greens. Setting them down, he returned once more to the kitchen and came back with a pitcher of lemonade. Once satisfied that everything was present and accounted for, he sat down in the chair across the table from Momma. Smiling at her, he said, "I tried to prepare all of your favorites. I hope you like it."

Genevieve looked at her son and beamed. Here was a fine young man sitting across from her, no evidence of any emotional scars or lasting negative results of his upbringing. She knew she had little part in the man he had become, but she was proud and would tell that to anyone that asked.

"Raymond, you have outdone yourself. I am overwhelmed by what you have prepared here. Everything looks and smells wonderful. I can't wait to eat."

"Well, don't delay any longer on my part. Let's enjoy," Raymond replied, pouring lemonade for the both of them.

As they ate, Genevieve started asking Raymond general questions. She didn't want to jump right in with Delphine's suspicions, she still couldn't believe this man sitting in front of her was capable of those atrocities. Instead, she asked how long had he stayed with Delphine after she disappeared. What did he do after that? Was he working now?

In between bites, Raymond shared his story with Genevieve, requesting that she not ask questions while he told the tale, there would be plenty of time for those later.

He explained to her that Delphine had done the best she could to take care of him, but that once summer had come, she didn't think it fair to him to be cooped up alone in her house every day. She had reached out to the only aunt and uncle he could remember and asked if they could take him in, at least for the summer.

"We both thought or hoped that maybe you would return sooner, rather than later, and I could come home again and go back to school in the fall. But that wasn't to be the case."

He had said it took him a while for him to forgive Delphine for sending him to the farm, even though there was no way she could have known what that journey held in store for him. Glossing over some of the more despicable details, he told Momma about the backbreaking work he was made to do, picking vegetables in a field one day, the next one spent hoeing and tilling, and yet another day being sent out to an outer field to plant and eventually harvest cotton. It was never the same job twice in a row and it didn't give him a chance to learn one skill sufficiently.

He shared how this, of course, infuriated his uncle, who

would beat him in an attempt to teach him a lesson. "It was during one of those beatings that I wound up with this," he said, gently touching the scar on his temple. "He was usually careful not to hit me around the head, but this one time, he had a board that had a nail sticking out and it scraped my skin deep enough to draw blood. Of course, Aunt Flo didn't do anything to help. It was then I vowed to get away from them, whatever it took. This is the only reminder I carry with me of that time."

Genevieve tried to apologize, but Raymond cut her off. "No, it's long past now. Nothing you can say will change anything."

He continued on, telling her of his return to New Orleans for a time, then moving on to live in Galveston, and his eventual return home once again.

"Even during all the time I was gone, Delphine must have been keeping an eye on the house, because when I came back, everything was still as it had been. I don't think I ever properly thanked her, Momma. Maybe we should invite her over for dinner some night soon?"

Genevieve tried not to show her dismay at the idea. After her conversation with Delphine earlier that day, she didn't think that would even be possible now. Stifling a sigh, she smiled to hide her true feelings and said, "I think that would be a lovely idea, Raymond. It's been such a long time since I've seen her. I don't know that I could ever repay the kindness she did by taking you in."

Raymond paused, looking at Genevieve, knowing the smile on her face and what she had just said was not all together true as he remembers that she been with Delphine and the others that night at the Gibson. Not wanting to betray his thoughts either, he nodded in acknowledgment and waited to see if she would continue. When she didn't, he picked up his tale again, keeping this reaction of hers in the back of his mind.

"I've been back for a while now. I started out working mostly odd jobs, then went on to pick up day labor construction jobs. With so much growth in the city, it's easy enough to find work when I want or need to. It also allowed me to take time off and try to find you, too. I've never stopped looking, Momma. I always thought you were still out there."

Bowing her head, Genevieve tried to hold back the tears she could feel welling in her eyes. The guilt she was feeling for having left him alone for so long was starting to over-whelm her.

Looking back up, she wiped her face with her napkin and asked, "What about someone special? Surely you must have a girlfriend you haven't yet told me about. A fine looking man such as yourself."

"Momma, I," Raymond stuttered. "No, not really. Well, sort of."

Genevieve looked at Raymond, the inquisitiveness apparent on her face, but she hoped not betraying her true motive behind the question. Finally, he continued.

"Well, there is someone. And I want you to meet her, Momma. I really think she's the one."

Smiling broadly, thinking this was a sign Delphine was wrong, she giddily declared, "Oh Raymond, that makes me so happy to hear. When do I get to meet this mystery girl of yours, then?"

Pausing to take a deep breath, Raymond replied, "Soon. Very soon. And I know you'll love her just as much as I do. Oh, we'll be such a happy family."

36

Later that afternoon, Simone went to seek out Delphine, wanting to talk about the remaining last minute plans. She noticed Delphine hadn't been around much of the day, and when she was, she had been acting rather peculiarly. Finding her in the study, with her back to the door, Simone quietly asked, "Delphine, do you have a minute?"

Delphine, jumping at the sound of Simone's voice, dropped her feather duster. "Oh! You startled me."

"Sorry, I thought you heard me come in. What's got you so jumpy?"

"Nothing. I..."

"No, I know you, and I know something is wrong. You haven't been acting like yourself lately. What is going on?"

Delphine looked around, attempting to find something else that she could occupy herself with, to avoid these probing questions.

She looked apologetically at Simone and smiled. "I'm sorry. I've just been busy. Between here and my house, it seems that my chores have been never ending lately. Really, there's nothing more than that going on."

Not accepting this answer, Simone looked directly at her friend. "No, Delphine. I've known you long enough now to tell when you are keeping something from me. The look on your face when Genevieve showed up at the Gibson, well let's just say your face gives away more than you know. Now today you rushed out, and it seems like you've been avoiding me. Spill it. What is going on?"

Taking a deep breath, Delphine steeled herself. "You're right. There is something troubling me. But this isn't the place to discuss it. What do you say to dinner at my house tonight? Just the two of us."

"Are you sure you're not too busy?" Simone replied bluntly.

Taken aback by Simone's tone, Delphine nodded. "No. You're right. We need to talk. This conversation is long overdue. And we really should have it before your wedding, too."

Her concern growing, Simone took a step closer. "Okay, now you're starting to worry me. What is going on?"

"Just come over for dinner tonight. I'll fill you in on everything then. But please, keep this between us for now, okay?"

Simone, growing more impatient, protested. "I don't know how much more of this secrecy I can take. Between the mystery packages, and that note, and now you being so evasive. Why can't you just tell me now?"

"Listen, we have work that needs to be done, and now is not the place to have this conversation. I'm sorry, but you are just going to have to wait until tonight." Delphine's tone showed she was losing patience and wouldn't tolerate any more questions.

Unsure why Delphine was being so secretive, Simone reluctantly agreed. Delphine was, after all, had become her dearest friend in such a short time. If she was asking her this one favor, surely she could oblige.

When everyone was coming into the kitchen for the staff dinner, Simone made her exit, hastily throwing out an explanation that she needed to take care of some wedding preparations. Frederick stepped in front of her, saying he was unaware of anything else that needed to be done.

"It's nothing that you need to be there for. I just have a couple of last-minute details to see to before we go home this weekend. Really. It's fine. I'll see you tomorrow," she replied, as she gave him a quick peck on the cheek.

Walking toward the streetcar, Simone had an uncanny sense that someone was watching her, a chill running down her spine. Looking back over her shoulder, she didn't see anyone obvious, just a few neighbors taking their usual evening stroll and some of the other household staff heading home for the night. Still, she couldn't shake this feeling until she arrived at Delphine's house and found herself safely inside.

Delphine was quick to answer the door and let Simone in. She glanced around outside as she did, as if she were expecting someone else to be there, then hastily shut the door.

"Simone, I'm glad you made it. No one else knows you're here, right?"

"No. I told Frederick I had to take care of a few wedding plans, nothing that he had to be involved in. He questioned it at first, but seemed to accept that answer. But why are we being so secretive about this? I mean, we've had dinner together before."

"Yes. I just, well, this is a sensitive topic, and not everyone else agrees with me that I should even tell you, and I just wanted you to hear from me first. I know you'll have plenty of questions, more than I can answer right now." Delphine stopped abruptly, noticing the concern rising in Simone's posture.

"Okay. Now I'm really confused. You've been acting strangely lately, but now you are starting to scare me, too."

Softening her tone to put her friend at ease, Delphine said, "Please, let's sit down to dinner and I'll explain."

Making their way to the table, Simone was trying her best to maintain an appetite. Once seated, Delphine served them both, and then began sharing her concerns.

She started out explaining just who Genevieve was in relation to herself and their shared past. She had taken care of a young boy who was Genevieve's son for a period of time. She had lost track of both of them some years ago when Genevieve disappeared and Raymond had been sent to live with other family members.

She pointed out that Simone had, in fact, knew Raymond as a child, whether she remembered it or not. When Delphine first met Simone, she didn't recognize her and didn't have any cause to associate her with what took place at the school all those years ago. And as for Raymond, Delphine hadn't recognized him and didn't have any cause to associate him with any of the current events that had been taking place, either.

Now that Genevieve was back in town, after having been away for all those years, she was attempting to rebuild her life. Delphine made sure to leave out the more grue-

some details of Genevieve and Raymond's experiences. Simone, sitting straight-backed in her chair, was pushing the food around on her plate, not actually eating. She had a look of skepticism on her face, that Delphine noted.

"So, what has this got to do with me?" Simone asked. "I don't understand why this has got you sound wound up."

"Since he's been back, I've encountered Raymond on more than one occasion. He's not the same young man that I once knew. There's something dark inside of him. And it's given me pause. Genevieve, of course, is trying to repair her relationship with him. When I raised my doubts about him to her, she naturally reacted as any mother would, and declared there was no way he could be the man that his father once was."

Simone pushed her plate away, signaling that she wasn't going to be able to eat anything more. Shifting in her seat, her agitation with her friend increasing, "Again, I ask, what does this have to do with me, though?"

Delphine sighed and pushed back her chair. "I'm getting to that. And this is where I can't prove my suspicions, but here they are. I've seen Raymond watching you when we've been at the Gibson. He tries not to be obvious about it, and I think the one time that you two did encounter each other on the dance floor, that seemed to set him off balance a bit. I can't say for sure. Again, it may just be my mind playing tricks on me. But the way I've seen him looking at you, it gives me an ill feeling. And now these mystery gifts you've been getting. That book, you said it was something you remember from grade school, right?"

"Well, yes. But a lot of kids read that."

"Okay, sure. But that last package, the note. It made a reference to playground games. If I remember correctly, the

incident between you and Raymond as kids took place on the playground."

Holding up her hand, Simone interrupted, her voice rising. "Wait a minute. So if I have the story right, you think he's been watching me this entire time? But why would he do that? And why now? I mean, the playground stuff was so long ago. And it was just me trying to get his attention, well, because I thought he was cute."

"I don't know. Like I said, the interactions I've had with him haven't led to much information about what he's been doing or anything about his life. But, and here's where I hesitate to say this," Delphine paused, trying to gather her thoughts before making her next statement. Looking around as though she expected someone to be in the next room listening in, she lowered her voice and continued. "The girls that they've been finding, the timing of those, and when we've been out, and I've seen him, well..."

"You can't seriously think he, what's his name again, Raymond, has anything to do with those?" Simone exclaimed.

Shaking her head, Delphine said, "I don't know. I mean, I hope not. But I'm just not sure anymore. I know just enough about his father, and the man that he was, that it wouldn't be a far stretch."

Simone jumped up from her chair and started pacing the length of the table, stopping in front of Delphine. Her voice shaking, she asked, "So I'm in danger? Does Frederick know? Who else knows?"

Delphine got up and moved her chair around to the side of the table. Reaching over, she took both of Simone's trembling hands into her own. "I don't think Frederick knows about Raymond or my suspicions about him. As to my

concerns, well, they are just that, mine. I shouldn't have burdened you with them. Evelyn and David know a little too, but I just need to talk to Genevieve and keep everyone else out of it."

"But I feel like I need to say something to Frederick now. Or maybe you do, since you know this guy and his mother. I just don't feel right about him not knowing or keeping secrets from him..."

"Simone, listen to me. I don't think you need to have a conversation with Frederick. Just let me handle this first."

"Yes, but Delphine, you're worrying me now. If this guy is as dangerous as you say he is, then aren't you in trouble too? And shouldn't we tell Frederick about him, so he can keep an eye out too?"

"No. I don't want to worry him needlessly. I can't prove anything. And I don't know how he'll react to my suspicions, and I sure don't want him doing something stupid. I need to have another conversation with Genevieve, and possibly with Raymond too. See if I can't get them both in the same room and talking."

"But don't you think that could lead to even further trouble?" Simone's tone was one of genuine concern for her friend now, since there was still the unanswered question of how this could all end.

"For now, you need to put this out of your mind, you need to focus on Frederick and your preparations. This is my bailiwick, and all this going round and round won't do either of us any good. Now, let's try to eat. We both are going to need our strength for these next few days."

37

The celebratory evening before the wedding had finally arrived. All the chores completed, all the errands run. The only item left on the list of preparations was the wedding itself.

David had insisted on driving his new-to-him Model T, picking everyone up at their homes instead of making them all come to the house first. He hadn't had the car long and wanted to show off the shiny black machine to everyone. Just as they were leaving Delphine's, the car sputtered and stalled.

"Of course, tonight of all nights, this piece of junk would decide to act temperamental on me," David declared, throwing his hands up in the air. "Why did I ever let you talk me into this worthless piece of machinery?"

"Me? I seem to recall you were the one who said this would revolutionize society, dear," Evelyn replied, trying to stifle a giggle.

"I say we just all go back to the horse and carriage, such

a more genteel way of traveling," David said, lifting the hood and trying to figure out what had gone wrong.

Frederick stepped up and looked over the engine for a moment. Reaching in, he wiggled a loose wire. "There. That should fix it."

Incredulous, David tried cranking the engine and, to his surprise and the delight of the others, it roared back to life. "Quick, everyone in before it decides to conk out on us for good."

After a bit of good-natured ribbing and debate over the pros and cons of the various means of transportation, they arrived at the Gibson. The music was pouring out from the open door, announcing the band was already in full swing. By the time they got in, it was standing room only.

Handing off their coats to the check stand attendant, David apologized to the group once more. "If it hadn't been for that breakdown, we would have been here in plenty of time to get a table."

Frederick patted him on the shoulder as Simone told him not to worry about it. "The important thing is that we're here together. Now, let's go have some fun!"

Making their way to the dance floor, Evelyn spotted a small, empty table, barely big enough for two. Though it didn't have enough chairs for all of them to sit, at least they could put their drinks down, and one could take a turn sitting while the others danced.

Delphine offered to stay at the table and order the first round of drinks, while the two couples joined the rest of the dancers. "I'll be fine. You go ahead. Have fun."

Simone glanced at her friend, an eyebrow raised, as though to say, 'are you sure?' Delphine smiled and shooed her away. Once she was sure they were deep on the dance floor surrounded by others, she took her time looking around the room. She hadn't spotted Raymond when they first came in, but in this crowd, it would be hard to find anyone that easily.

She speculated things had must be back to normal over at his house now that Genevieve was back. She had seen lights on when they left that evening and heard music coming from an open window. Whether they were both home, or it was just one of them, she didn't know. But she didn't spot either of them here, so maybe she was just worried about nothing. 'Soon now, it won't matter, anyway. Simone and Frederick will be married, setting off on their honeymoon and out of harm's way. Perhaps I should take this as a sign that things are finally going the right way,' she thought.

No sooner had that thought exited her mind, she saw Raymond stride in through the front door. Dressed to the nines, he had an air about him that exuded a new confidence, yet the look she saw in his eyes was still unsettling at the same time.

She watched him looking around, his eyes surreptitiously scanning the room. Quickly turning her head to the side, she hoped he hadn't noticed her. Not seeing Genevieve with him, another pang of fear stirred the bile in her stomach.

Using a fan to hide her face, she watched while Raymond made his way to the bar. Delphine glanced quickly back at the dance floor to make sure of where her friends were, before turning her attention solely back to Raymond. She couldn't shake the feeling that something was wrong, but with nothing to back up her hunch, she resolved to just stay alert and protect those that she cared about most.

Lost in concentration, she didn't hear Evelyn and David return to the table.

"May I have this next dance?" David inquired.

Delphine jumped. "I'm sorry. What?"

"Delphine, dear, we didn't mean to startle you. What's wrong?" Evelyn asked.

"I'm sorry. I just thought I saw Raymond..." she said, looking over in his general direction.

Evelyn turned to see where she was looking and spotted Raymond across the room. "Oh. Oh, I see."

"So about that dance?" David interjected.

"I'm sorry David. I think I'm just going to stay at the table this evening. I'm not sure I'm feeling up to all that. But I didn't want to disappoint the lovebirds."

"Dear, why don't you go refresh our drinks? I'll stay here with Delphine and keep her company until you return. Maybe I can convince her to take the next dance with you," Evelyn said, shooing David away. "Okay. Now that he's gone, what's going on Delphine? And don't tell me it's nothing. I've known you too long."

Delphine leaned over the table, trying to keep her voice low. Despite the music being loud, she didn't want to risk anyone else hearing what she had to say.

"You know Genevieve is home with Raymond now. And while it all looks normal from the outside, there is this feeling I have about him, I just can't seem to shake. And tonight, when he walked in, well, there was just something different about him. Honestly, Evelyn, I don't know anymore if I'm over-reacting or what. But I just want to see Simone and Frederick happy."

Evelyn patted Delphine's hand to console her. "I know

that Genevieve is back at the house with him, but I've heard she's also still showing up to work and from what I can tell, seems to be in fine shape. I haven't had a chance to talk with her again, but I'm also starting to think your suspicions may be unfounded."

"I really hope that is the case, Evelyn, but I just don't know. I confronted Genevieve the other day, and she said she was having dinner with Raymond that night. They were supposed to talk, but she was pretty upset when we parted. I doubt very much that she..."

Before she could finish, David was back at the table. In addition to the drinks he had in hand, he also returned with another person. "Evelyn, dear, and Delphine, please let me introduce you to Raymond. Raymond, my wife, Evelyn, and our friend, Delphine."

"A pleasure to meet you both," replied Raymond with a little bow, not giving away the fact he already knew Delphine. "You seemed to have lucked out getting this table, I don't think I've ever seen this place quite so full."

"Yes, it was a stroke of luck," Delphine replied icily, while wondering why he didn't point out they were already acquainted.

Clearing his throat to break the obvious tension, David said, "Well, Delphine, if you aren't going to take me up on the dance invitation, I suppose I shall take my wife back out to the floor."

"Yes, that's a good idea," Delphine replied. "Not to worry. I'll be here when you return."

"Delphine--" Evelyn started.

"I'm fine. Go. Dance with your husband and have a good time."

As David and Evelyn returned to the dance floor, Delphine turned her attention to Raymond, who was still standing awkwardly behind the chair Evelyn had just vacated. Unsure whether to ask him to sit down or leave, she chose the former. Raymond was taken aback by the invitation, but sat down anyway.

"Delphine, I--"

Interrupting him, Delphine started. "Before you start trying to explain anything more, Raymond, let me stop you right there. I don't know what you are up to. I don't know your intentions. All I can say is I hope that what I'm sensing about you is wrong. That you and your momma have reconciled and are on a good path now is good news, I guess, though I still worry about both of you. I also know you've been back in town longer than you've let on when we had dinner. And I've kept my questions to myself out of respect for you and your privacy. I figured if you wanted to stay in touch with me, you would have. Aside from what little you've told me, I don't know what's happened to you in the years you were gone. And it's none of my business either."

Stopping to catch her breath and take a sip from the drink David had brought her, she looked at Raymond over the top of the glass, trying to judge his reaction.

"Delphine, I feel as though I owe you an explanation and perhaps an apology. Yes, you are right, I've been back longer than I first told anyone. And I appreciate you keeping your distance. I have no good reason for why I didn't come over sooner other than I was still angry about, well, everything. But things are going to be different now.

Momma is home with me where she belongs and we are becoming a family again. You'll see. Soon, life will be perfect for all of us."

"I'm not sure what you mean by everything, but there is something different about you. Maybe it's just because you're a man now, all grown up, and I still think of you as the boy I took care of." Delphine was being careful in choosing her words, she didn't want to disclose any of her suspicions just yet.

"There was a lot that happened to me over the years I've been gone and even during the time I've been back, some of which you already know. I also never gave up hope that I would find Momma again, and now that I have, well, I'm just trying to put things right again."

"But Raymond, I've also seen you here many times, and I'm sure you've seen me too, because I've also noticed the way you've looked at Simone."

Trying to feign indifference, Raymond considered Delphine before answering. "Simone? Oh, is she your friend? Yes, she's a very attractive girl. How could I not help but notice her?"

"Yes, she is. But let me tell you this and hear me clearly. She is my dearest friend and is getting married this weekend, and I won't stand for anything that could possibly ruin her day."

Raymond was taken aback by her sudden shift in tone. Fidgeting in his chair, he paused, considering his words and the pronouncement of Simone's impending marriage, before answering her accusations.

"Delphine, I don't know what I may have done to give you pause. But I have no intention of causing any sort of turmoil for you or any of your friends.

Before she could reply, Raymond stood. "I apologize for intruding on your evening. I didn't mean to cause you any agitation. I bumped into David at the bar and I mentioned you looked like someone I once knew. He invited me over and to decline, well that would have been rude. Now that we have had our chat, I will take my leave. Please extend my thanks to him. And perhaps one of these evenings soon, Momma and I will have you over for dinner."

Raising his glass in a small toast, he nodded his head and turned to walk back toward the bar, leaving Delphine with her drink and thoughts.

38

As the band wound down to take their next break, the two couples returned to the table to find Delphine alone.

"I thought that nice young man Raymond was still here with you?" David asked. "He said he thought he knew you. Was that the case?"

"Yes. It's been years since I had seen him, though. He was still a young boy the last time we met. As it turns out, Genevieve is his mother."

"Well, now it's all starting to make more sense. No wonder he recognized you then. You took care of the boy when she went away."

"Yes. For a time. But I lost track of him and it would seem he's been on his own much longer than anyone realized. But now that Genevieve is back home again, they are making a go of being a family once more." Delphine mused. "But enough about that. Tonight is supposed to be about Simone and Frederick and celebrating them."

Simone smiled, hoping to hide the unease she suddenly felt, and looked adoringly at Frederick, causing him to stutter. "I still don't know what I did to deserve a woman such as her. But as far as I'm concerned, I'm not going to question fate and I'll let nothing stand in the way of our wedding tomorrow."

"Here, here," echoed David. "I don't know what you did to deserve her, either. But a toast to the both of you. May your lives together be long, happy, and full."

Raising their glasses, Evelyn, Delphine, Simone, and Frederick cheered David's sentiment.

Setting her glass back down, Simone turned to her friends and said, "On that note, I don't mean to be a party pooper, but I think I should be getting back to the house. The last thing I want to do is not get my beauty sleep the night before this biggest day of my life."

"At least let me see you home," Frederick said as he moved to help her from the chair.

"Or I can drive you home if you like," offered David.

"No, thank you. I'll be fine taking the streetcar. Besides, after the ride over, I'm not sure you'd make it back again to pick up the others." Turning toward Frederick, she smiled and said, "And you, don't you know the groom isn't supposed to see the bride before the wedding? I will stay for one more dance, and then I will be on my way. The rest of you stay and enjoy what remains of the night out. You deserve it all after the work you've put in helping us get ready."

"Fair enough. You have a point. But you shouldn't go alone." David agreed.

"David's right. You shouldn't be going alone," Delphine said. "I'll accompany you back to the house."

"No, Delphine, really, I'll be fine. It's been so long since you've had a night out. Just enjoy yourself, please."

Delphine protested again, not wanting to let Simone out of her sight, but Simone wouldn't listen to any of her objections, instead she made her way toward an empty spot at the bar to get her friends one last celebratory drink.

⚜

After a few futile attempts to get the bartender's attention, she turned back toward the bandstand. The break was over and the musicians were readying for the next round of music and mayhem. Turning back to the bar once more, she accidentally bumped into the gentleman to her left.

"I'm sorry. Excuse me."

"No, excuse me. I didn't mean to encroach," he replied, turning to meet her.

Coming face to face with the dapper man standing before her, Simone explained. "Sorry again, I'm just trying to get a few drinks for my friends before I have to leave."

"Leave? So soon? Why would you want to leave when the party is just getting underway?"

"I have a big day tomorrow that I must get home and finish preparing for. Otherwise, I would stay," she demurred.

"A big day? Well, let me at least buy you a drink as my way of saying congratulations," he said, signaling the bartender.

"Thank you, that's very kind. But I really shouldn't. I told my friends I'd get drinks for them before I left. Though I don't see them at the table any longer. I guess they've gone back out to the dance floor."

"Allow me then. You order your drinks for your friends and the waitress can deliver them. In the meantime, one small celebratory drink with me, and then you can be on your way. Where's the harm in that?"

Whoever this gentleman was, he certainly was persistent and wouldn't take no for an answer, Simone thought as she studied his face. "Very well. One small drink. I'm Simone, by the way. And you are?"

"Simone, what a lovely name," he offered his hand, while avoiding answering her question at the same time.

After the drinks were ordered and sent on their way for delivery, Simone turned her gaze back toward the dance floor. Not seeing any of her friends in the crowd, she shrugged her shoulders and turned her attention back to the mystery man.

In an effort to act surprised, he asked, "So you were saying tomorrow is a big day? May I ask what makes it so?

Smiling at the thought, Simone said, "Yes, I'm getting married."

"How wonderful for you. A toast then, to the lovely bride who I'm sure will be more beautiful than the loveliest of doves. And to her future life. Cheers." He replied, a feigned smile crossing his lips and the scar on his temple changing color.

Considering his words, a shiver to ran down Simone's back as she noticed his reaction. Just as quickly as the look had appeared, it was gone. Lifting the glass to her lips, she said, "cheers," and downed her sweet champagne cocktail quicker than she probably should have. Setting the glass down, she checked with the bartender to make sure the drinks for the others were taken care of, and then turned back to this mystery man. "Thank you again for the drink and your kind words. But I really must be going now."

"Of course. It was my pleasure," she heard him say as she made her way toward the coat check and door. She could feel his gaze following her across the room, only adding to her growing discomfort. Wondering if perhaps she should take David up on his offer of a ride, she looked around, trying to spot him in the crowd. Unable to find him, she decided she was being foolish and would just take the streetcar home, as she had planned.

Once outside, Simone noticed the gas lamps appeared to be dimmer than when they first arrived. What had been bright and illuminating earlier now appeared shrouded and obscured. She felt unsteady on her feet, but attributed that to her swallowing her last drink too quickly. She told herself she was being silly and that all she had to do was get home. Nothing was going to interfere with her wedding day tomorrow.

Walking toward the streetcar stop, she stumbled and instinctively reached out, hoping to find something to stop her fall. As her dress swung, a piece of it snagged on the building while her right hand came in contact with the arm of someone who had come up behind her at that precise moment.

"Thank you," she slurred. "I..." she tried to continue, now finding her tongue thick in her mouth.

"No worries, Dove. I'm here now."

Turning her head to see who her mysterious benefactor was, she came face to face with the stranger from the bar. That insincere smile that he wore when she left was now replaced with a look of mania and enthrallment. It was the last thing she saw before everything went dark.

39

Raymond spent most of the night sitting up, watching Simone sleep off the effects of the bromide. Giddy with excitement, he replayed in his mind over and over how easy it had been to get her back here. Just as he exited the Gibson, he saw her stumble, and quickly made his way to her in order to catch her, should she have fallen. This excitement, mixed with the desire for revenge, kept him awake throughout the night.

Though he was exhausted and desperate for just a couple of hours of sleep, he knew the next 24 hours would be the most crucial to his plans. As long as he could keep her quiet and undetected during the day, he would sleep deeply that next night.

When she began to stir, he stood up from his chair and stretched. Seeing a strand of hair hanging across her face, he reached over to brush it away. Thinking this might alarm her more, he withdrew his hand and just watched her a moment longer before turning his attention to their breakfast. Not having the means to prepare a proper hot meal, he laid out a few slices of bread with jam, two cups of water, and a jar of peaches. Patting his pocket once more to reassure himself the vial was still there, he returned his attention back to Simone. He didn't want to have to resort to drugging her again, but kept the option close at hand, just in case the need should arise.

He saw her eyes were open now, frantically looking around the room and squirming against the ropes that he used to bind her wrists and ankles.

"Good morning Simone. I do hope you slept well. My apologies for the gag and binding, but it wouldn't do either of us any good to have you shouting or attempting to leave." He whispered.

Trying to yell or at a minimum speak, she found the handkerchief in her mouth muffled even the most guttural of noises.

Approaching her, he pushed back the hair that had fallen in her face. "There, there. Just calm yourself. There's no need to struggle. I don't mean you any harm. Surely you should know that by now."

Shaking her head violently trying to dislodge his hand, she attempted to push herself up into a sitting position against the headboard, as far away from him as she could get.

Undeterred, he continued, "As you can see, I have everything you need here. There are fresh clothes in the closet, a basin you can wash up in, and though it's meager, breakfast is ready for you as well. I do promise to come back later with a hot meal. After all, you must be famished. But, I must insist, when I take the gag out of your mouth, you won't make a fuss. Can you do that for me?"

Simone looked at Raymond, then around the room, then back at Raymond again, nodding her head in agreement.

Smiling as he reached over, he murmured, "Good girl. Lean forward just a bit and we'll get this out so you can eat. I must, however, leave your hands bound. But don't worry, I will take care of you and all of your needs until you are ready."

As Raymond removed the rag, Simone stifled a yelp caught in her throat. Now able to breathe freely, she greedily gulped in the air. Upon finding her voice, she croaked, "What have you done to me? Where am I?"

"Nothing that will cause any long-term harm. You're safe here, Dove. Specifically where you are, well, that's not important right now," Raymond said as he sliced a piece of the peach and held it out for her to eat.

"Drink?"

Noticing how dry her throat was, she nodded, gulping the water he offered, when she began to choke. Raymond pulled back the glass, allowing her to catch her breath, wiping her chin when she finished. Once satisfied she had enough to drink, he offered another bite of peach, then bread, alternating until she had consumed everything.

"I seem to be having trouble remembering some things. Have we met before?" Simone asked as shifting back into the corner of the bed, all the while keeping her eyes on him.

Raymond leaned back in his chair, choosing his next words carefully before replying. "Yes, but I'm not surprised you don't remember. One of the side effects of the bromide you took last night."

"Bromide? Why? What? I don't understand. Why am I here?" She sputtered.

"All in good time Dove, all in good time," Raymond replied as he smoothed down the bedspread by her feet.

Shuddering at the tone of his last statement, Simone pulled her feet back closer to herself. She had heard the stories of the other girls who had been killed outside of various clubs around town. Though the deaths weren't widely reported or even investigated, the few stories that she heard circulated had nicknamed the killer "The Jazz Killer" based on the time of death and location of the bodies. Wondering if he had anything to do with those, she tried hiding her fear, she attempted to change the subject.

"Can I... um, would it be possible for me to use a bathroom?"

"Of course. But promise me you won't try anything foolish now."

She nodded, showing her compliance while holding her hands and feet out in front of her, waiting for him to untie the ropes.

Leading her to what barely could pass as a bathroom, it was more of a closet, barely big enough for one person, with a chamber pot and washbasin, he stuck his foot between the door and the wall keeping the door from closing all the way. Laughing, he said, "Don't try to lock the door. I won't look, but I'll be waiting right here."

Continuing to talk from behind the door, she hoped to appease him, maybe even prompt him to let his guard down. Trying to use as sweet a voice as she could, she started by asking, "So, what are we going to do today?"

Surprised by her sudden change in attitude, Raymond shifted his foot slightly, allowing the door to close. He hadn't expected her to be compliant so quickly.

"I, well, I..."

"You mentioned something about a hot meal. That sounds like it would be delightful," she continued melodiously.

Still unsure of how he should respond, he let out an unintelligible, mumbled response. As Simone opened the door, she noticed he was pacing rapidly back and forth. Clearly, she had upset him. Unsure if she should continue her with her compliance or try a different tactic, she decided to try to play on his sympathies.

"As for today, the only reason I ask is, well...."

Before she could finish, Raymond stopped in his tracks, turned and glared at Simone.

"Don't you worry about what we're doing today. We are well hidden here. No one will find us. Now, let's get you back to your bed," he insisted, grabbing her by the wrist.

Hissing, Raymond gave her a shove back onto the bed. "Listen to me. You are going to stay here and you are going to be quiet. I have to go out for a little while. When I get back, we will have a pleasant meal and then decide what's next. You understand me? Not a sound."

He was striding around the small room like a caged animal, covering the length and width in just a few steps. Glancing out the only window, making sure it was still locked, he then returned, standing in front of her.

"Do you understand?" he demanded.

"Yes." She acquiesced.

"Good. I don't want to have to gag you again. I'm trusting that you will think about your behavior while I'm gone. In the meantime, you can forget the plans for your wedding today. Oh, yes, I know you were supposed to be getting married today. It's not going to happen." He wickedly declared as he stomped out of the room, slamming the door behind him.

40

Delphine arrived at work early the next morning in order to help Simone get ready for her big day. Most preparations were already done, and the wedding was going to be a small affair. Just family and friends. The Batistes had been gracious enough to offer the use of the back courtyard and kitchen for the wedding and reception.

Cook was busy preparing the food, while Evelyn and David were setting up the chairs and tables outside.

Climbing the back stairs, Delphine was humming to herself, a song she had heard last night. She wondered if Simone had heard it, as the band had just started playing it when she left. It was something new, nothing any of them had heard before, but was sure to be a hit based on the reaction from everyone there.

Knocking on Simone's door, she called out, "Good morning miss bride. Are you ready for today?"

Not getting any response, she tried knocking again. "I'm

coming in Simone. I certainly hope you don't have Frederick in there."

Pushing the door open she found Simone's bed neatly made, her wedding dress handing from the wardrobe, and the flowers standing ready in the vase, but no sign of Simone.

"Huh, that's odd. Where could she be?" Delphine mused.

Making her way back down to the kitchen, she asked Cook if she had seen Simone that morning.

"No. Evelyn took the flowers up earlier and said her bed was already made and she wasn't there. I thought maybe she went out for a walk. Maybe the butterflies are getting to her? You don't suppose the girl got cold feet, do you?"

"No. She was so excited last night. I don't think anything, not even a hurricane, could stop her and Frederick from getting hitched today. No... something is just not right." Delphine was worrying. The nagging thoughts about Raymond's behavior, the girls that had been found dead around the quarter, too many unanswered questions were causing her to have concerns.

"I'm going to go check with Evelyn and David. Maybe David drove her over to Frederick's this morning. Even though she knows the groom isn't supposed to see the bride before the wedding"

Finding David in the yard, Delphine asked if he knew where Simone went.

"No. Evelyn asked me the same thing. No one has seen her this morning. And no one heard her come home last night either. Which is odd, because she left way before we did and someone should have still been up when she got back." Taking a deep breath, David continued, "Delphine, you don't suppose that - ". He stopped before he could finish his thought, but Delphine knew what he was thinking.

"I don't know. I don't want to think that. But I have this feeling in the pit of my stomach. Something is not right, and I fear that Raymond might be involved. I don't know what to do. Do we tell Frederick, go to Genevieve's, or just sit here and hope that maybe she's just out for a walk and will return soon?"

Coming in at the end of the conversation, Evelyn, ever the practical one, said, "How about you and David go to Genevieve's and see what's going on there. I'll wait here until Frederick and his family arrive. In the meantime, maybe Simone will just show up and all this worry will be for nothing."

Delphine tentatively agreed, still having the unsettling feeling that no, this worry wasn't for nothing.

⚜

The drive back to the house was tense and quiet. Too quiet for Delphine. As soon as Genevieve opened the door, Delphine began peppering her with questions.

"Where is Raymond? What has he done with Simone?"

"Wait, what? I don't know what you're talking about. He went out last night, but if I had to guess, he's sleeping it off in his room right now. But what does this have to do with Simone? Isn't she getting married today? And why do you think Raymond has anything to do with anything?" Genevieve barked.

"Ladies, this speculation and accusation is getting us nowhere. Genevieve, would you be so kind as to go see if he is indeed sleeping? Though I imagine with all this fuss, he's bound to be awake by now," David implored.

Genevieve went to Raymond's room and knocked. Receiving no answer, she gently pushed the door open and was met with an empty room. The bed undisturbed, Raymond's work clothes hung over the back of a chair.

Returning to the living room, she looked at both Delphine and David before telling them what she hadn't found. "He's not there. I don't know where he is. But what you are suggesting is ridiculous. As to where Simone is, well, I have no idea. Maybe she and Frederick ran off and eloped. But I will not stand here and listen to you disparage my son any longer. Now, if you both will please leave."

Delphine started to protest, but David just gently took her by the shoulder and turned her towards the door. "Thank you for your time. We'll show ourselves out."

Ever the diplomat, David escorted Delphine to the car before he said anything else.

"Delphine, I know your concerns. I share them. But until we have any sort of proof that Simone is actually missing, we have to just return to the house and wait."

"I know he has her, David. I don't know why. But something in my gut is telling me he's got her." Delphine sighed.

Pulling up to the house, they found Frederick pacing the driveway, kicking at the stones. Running to the car, grabbing at the door, he called out, "Simone?"

"No dear, I'm sorry," Delphine replied, stepping out of the now open door.

"Where is she?" Frederick shouted, preparing to sprint down the sidewalk.

"Calm down son, that's not going to do anyone any

good," David said, taking Frederick by the arm. "Let's all go inside and work this out. We'll find her."

Yanking his arm from David's grasp, Frederick started back down toward the street. "No, I have to go look for her. She could be in trouble, or worse yet. Well, I don't want to say."

"Frederick, please. Let's go inside and discuss this. Surely there has to be some logical explanation as to where she is." David said as he steered Frederick back toward the house.

"No, Frederick is right, David. And you are too. We need to go in the house and tell him about Raymond." Delphine whispered from behind the two men.

Frederick, now frantic, turned to face Delphine. "Wait! What? Who the hell is Raymond and what does he have to do with any of this?"

"Frederick, we owe you an explanation." Delphine started as they walked into the kitchen, to find Cook and Evelyn waiting at the table, the look of worry clear on their faces.

Trying to take control of the group, David insisted everyone sit down. Frederick refused, continuing his erratic walking around the table, then heading towards the door again.

"Frederick stop. We have kept this information from you and Simone both. And in hindsight, that was a mistake."

"Start talking, David, or I'm out that door and will find her myself."

"Okay. First off, Raymond is Genevieve's son. Delphine has had some suspicions about him. I don't know all the details other than she knows his family history, the abuse he suffered at the hands of his father and others, but she, well, we think maybe he has Simone."

"But why would this Raymond guy have taken her, and where? You're not making any sense," Frederick demanded.

Delphine interrupted, "He's been at the Gibson recently and I've seen the way he's been looking at her. It was enough to make the hairs on the back of my neck stand up. And well, they knew each other as children. She was rather mean to him in school and I don't know, but I have to think he has decided to get his revenge against her and maybe, somehow, got her to go with him last night."

"Delphine, please. This speculation is getting us nowhere," David interrupted. "Now, we can only go based on what we know. Simone left the Gibson last night, just after midnight. We'll start there, ask anyone who might have seen her, and then trace the route she would have taken home."

"I never should have let her go by herself," Frederick admitted, dropping into a chair.

"If it's anyone's fault, it's mine," Delphine confessed. "I tried telling you all before, but I wasn't adamant about it. I should have made you all listen. I knew Raymond was there, and I sensed he was up to no good. But I let my judgment slip, trying to give him the benefit of the doubt. I now see I was wrong to do that, and I have to live with that decision."

"Delphine, don't go beating yourself up. We should have listened to you when you first brought this up," Evelyn said, trying her best to comfort her friend.

Frederick started for the door, but David stood in his way.

"Stop, man, before you go flying out of here. We have to

let clearer heads prevail here. First, let's go back to the Gibson like we discussed and we'll see where that leads us."

Grumbling, Frederick agreed. "Fine. But if Raymond or whoever is involved even puts a hair out of place, or does anything to Simone, I will kill them myself, with my bare hands."

⚜

Unsure if they would find anyone at the Gibson so early in the day, they were relieved to find the coat check girl and bartender there when they arrived. They found out that Simone had been seen talking to a man fitting Raymond's description at the bar, but had left alone. According to the bartender, the gentleman had left shortly after she did, but in what direction he went, he couldn't say with any certainty.

Underwhelmed by the response they received, they walked back outside. Delphine stopped by the lamppost. "So, she would have walked this way towards the streetcar stop. Would the operator remember her?"

"If it's the usual guy, then probably so. But the only way to know for sure is to head over to the depot and see who had that route last night. How about Evelyn and I head over that way? Delphine, you and Frederick, why don't you two walk around here a little more? Maybe we're missing something," David offered.

Frederick, getting more agitated by each moment that passed, agreed that walking might help him focus better. As he and Delphine set off down the sidewalk, he spotted a small piece of fabric caught on the side of the building.

"Delphine, does this look like it could be from Simone's dress last night?"

Taking the piece in her hand, she turned it over, choosing her words carefully. "I suppose. But remember dear, there were a lot of people here last night and any one of the other ladies could have had been wearing something similar."

"Yes, but it could be Simone's too!" he shouted as he took off running down the alley leading back to a courtyard behind the building next door to the Gibson.

Trying to decide whether to follow or keep looking in the area for clues, Delphine opted for the latter, thinking there might be something more to show where Simone went next. If her suspicions were true, Raymond wouldn't have taken her far. 'But how would he have gotten her to go along with him?' Was the question she kept asking herself. Surely Simone wouldn't go along willingly. After all, today was supposed to be a big day for her. No, he must have slipped her something. And if that was how he convinced her, then that should narrow down their search area, too.

Looking down the street, she didn't see where Frederick had gone. Calling out, "Frederick! Come back. I think I have an idea."

41

Running back into the house, Frederick found Evelyn and David telling Cook what they had found.

"Tell me you found something. Tell me you found Simone!" He demanded.

"No son, I'm sorry. I was just telling Cook here that the regular driver was indeed on the route last night, but he didn't pick up Simone or any other passengers at that stop. He did notice a couple walking down the street in the opposite direction that he was traveling, but didn't get a good look at them. The gentleman was on the street side and obstructed the view of whoever was on his arm." David explained, trying to steer Frederick to a chair while Cook brought him a glass of water.

"That had to be her! But who is this guy? Is it this Raymond that everyone is talking about? What does he want with her? Where would they have gone? I have to go back out and look for her again," he exclaimed, pushing the chair back and turning toward the door.

"Frederick, sit down," Delphine bellowed, coming into the room.

This tone of voice was enough to command everyone to stop everyone in their tracks. Never before had anyone heard her this loud. "This rushing around is not going to do any of us any good. I am just as worried as the rest of you, if not more so. I feel completely responsible for letting her go alone, knowing that Raymond was there. If anything happens to her, I will never be able to forgive myself. Now, please. Let's all sit down and decide what to do next."

Frederick slouched down into a chair, not happy to be sitting still, but deferring to Delphine's take-charge order for the moment.

She showed David, Evelyn, and Cook the fabric piece that Frederick had found by the Gibson. "It's not much to go on, but it's a start. I can only surmise she stumbled and caught her dress on the siding of the building. If that's the case, and since the streetcar operator saw a couple walking, then they must not have gone far. My guess is he overpowered her somehow. She certainly wouldn't go willingly."

"Based on that, then, we should be able to narrow down the search area. But there are so many boardinghouses and rooms for rent down there. Where do we start?" Evelyn asked.

"We have to go back to Genevieve. Even though she doesn't want to believe her son could do something like this, we need to get her involved. Where was she staying before she came home? Could she have any idea where he might take her? Is it possible that he went back to where it all began? Where his daddy met his untimely end?" David asked.

A look of bewilderment crossed Evelyn's face. "You don't suppose that he knows where that was?"

Delphine nodded. "Actually, I do know that he knows. At least where Walter had been living before someone killed him. The police came by once when he was staying with me. They had found his daddy's belongings at an old boarding house and Raymond had to go pick up what he left behind. I don't know if the same old man is still running the place, but it would be a place to start."

"Alright. David will take you and Frederick there and drop me off at Genevieve's in the meantime. Maybe Raymond has come back by now, and god willing, Simone is there as well. Safe and sound." Evelyn offered.

Eager to get back out and find Simone, Frederick was the first one to the door, just about knocking Cook over in his haste to go.

"Sorry, Cook. Are you alright?"

"Yes dear. I'm fine. You go on and find her now. I'll hold down the fort here."

The others quickly rising from their seats, looked at one another, hoping for the best but fearing the worst. Cook took Delphine's arm just as she was walking out the door.

"She's going to be okay. I just know. Down in my bones. The child will be fine."

"I certainly hope you are right, Cook. I really do. In the meantime, please let Simone's family know what's going on. Her parents are already worried enough and I don't want to worry them any further, but they need to know what we've found out. And I know they are going to offer to help, but please do your best to keep them where they are."

Reaching Genevieve's house, Delphine was surprised to

not find anyone home. She returned to the car and directed David to the old boarding house. It was easy enough to find, but upon arriving, they found it in a more dilapidated state than Delphine had seen before.

"Something is not right here. Those boards weren't there a few weeks ago. And where is the old man that runs this place? He should be around somewhere too." Delphine observed as she tried the front door and found it locked.

Frederick, having gotten out of the car, was pacing frantically up and down the sidewalk, yelling Simone's name. Turning to Delphine and David, he asked, "Now what do we do?"

Delphine was quiet, standing on the porch, debating what to do next. Turning to Frederick, she told him to hush. Looking at the house, she turned to David. "David, would you be so kind as to walk around back with me, please?"

"Of course. But may I ask why?"

"Look around at all the other houses. Tell me, what do you see?"

Both David and Frederick looked up and down the street, noting that all the other houses were occupied, or at least had signs of life. Flowers were growing in yards, windows open and curtains rustling in the breeze. Looking back at the boardinghouse, David now saw what Delphine was pointing out. "It seems as though these boards on the windows are new. They aren't showing any weathering. Even the yard still looks well tended. I'm thinking that someone is trying to hide something."

Frederick, starting up the stairs, was ready to pound on the door when Delphine admonished him again. "Frederick, stop!"

"But if Simone is in there, what if she needs our help?"

Frantic, his head swiveling back and forth between Delphine and the house.

"That's why I want David to walk around back with me, so we can take a look and see what's going on. You, on the other hand, need to calm down before you do something rash. We're all anxious here, but please, for Simone's sake, let me do this first."

Frederick, grumbling under his breath, nodded, coming back down to the sidewalk.

"Okay, now David, let's take a look around back," Delphine said, pointing at a walkway between the house and the next one over.

Careful of their steps, not wanting to alert anyone who may be around the backside, they crept down the walkway until Delphine could peek around. Seeing no indication of anyone back there, she tried the back door and found it unlocked. Pointing this out to David, she looked at him questioningly. He indicated they should return to the front of the house where they could then decide what to do next.

"What did you find?" Frederick demanded when they returned.

"Someone must be here. The back door opened easily. But that still doesn't tell us who might be living here now. I would feel better if we could get in touch with the proprietor before we just go busting in there. There's no telling what or who is inside, or if it's even safe to go in there," Delphine explained.

"I'm going in," Frederick asserted, starting toward the steps.

Blocking his way, Delphine insisted, "No Frederick, stop. Think this through."

"I'm done thinking this through. It's time to act. The

longer we wait, the more danger Simone is in. We're supposed to be getting married today! I'm not going to allow something to happen to her on what should be the happiest day of our lives."

"Frederick, Delphine is right. We can't just go barging in there." David interjected.

"Then what do you suggest we do?" he snarled.

"I think we go back home, get everyone together, find Genevieve, and figure out what's next. Not necessarily in that order. But running off at the first sign of an open door without any other information is liable to get one of us hurt, or worse," David acknowledged.

Frederick, stomping back and forth like a caged lion, felt as though he were being held back on a leash. "But if Simone is in there, we need to go get her. Now!"

"We have to trust that she is still safe. From everything we know so far, there is no indication that if it is Raymond, that he would want to hurt her." David, taking Frederick's arm, steered him back toward the car. "Come on, let's get back to the house. Then we can get some of the others to come with us, too. There's greater strength in numbers."

Not satisfied, but seeing the wisdom in David's words, Frederick stormed toward the car without another word. Delphine looked at David and just shook her head, as if to say, 'I hope you're right.'

42

As promised, Raymond returned that afternoon, bringing with him a hot meal consisting of fried chicken, greens, potatoes and even a strawberry cake for dessert. 'Wherever he got the food from must be close,' thought Simone, 'because it's still too warm for him to have traveled far. Or maybe there is a kitchen downstairs that I don't know about. But surely I would have heard him down there cooking if that were the case.'

Sitting with her back up against the wall in the farthest away corner of the bed, she kept these thoughts to herself. She didn't want to make any sudden movements or do anything else that might upset him again. During the time he had been gone, she didn't know how long that was, she decided her best course of action would be to play docile and agreeable. Maybe that would win him over enough to at least untie her again.

"Good afternoon Simone. I trust you had a quiet day?" Raymond inquired while setting the food on the table.

"Yes. I suppose it was. Um, I'm sorry, I still don't know your name. What should I call you?"

Deflecting her questions, he commanded, "Please, stick out your feet and I'll take the ropes off now. Then you can come and join me at the table. We don't want the food to get cold now, do we?"

'Yet again. Why is he avoiding telling me his name,' she wondered? Complying, she pointed her feet straight out in front of her, then offered her hands as well. Pausing for a moment, he considered her outstretched arms, then nodded in agreement.

"Alright, we'll see how it goes. I suppose it will make the meal more enjoyable for the both of us," he noted, removing the ropes from her wrists, too. "But one wrong move, and that is the end of dinner." He admonished in a blood-chilling tone.

"I understand. Thank you." Simone stood cautiously. Having been in pretty much the same position all day, she was unsure how steady she would be upon standing.

Raymond, feigning being the gentleman, pulled out her chair for her to sit down and placed a napkin on her lap. "I'm sorry. I don't have anything more than water to drink. I had hoped to bring some tea or lemonade as well."

"This is fine, thank you. It all smells and looks delicious. I don't think I realized just how hungry I was until I smelled the food."

"I hope you will enjoy then. I do know these are your favorites after all."

Simone studied him carefully. How did he know so much about her? Trying to keep the conversation light-hearted, she remarked, "Oh, yes, the strawberry cake especially."

"Yes, I knew you would like that most of all. But as Momma always told me, you must eat your greens before you can have any dessert."

Complying, she took a large bite of the greens and attempted what she hoped came across as a genuine smile, even though that wasn't what she was feeling inside.

She saw Raymond watching her before he resumed eating. She hoped that her countenance and behavior came across as genuine and not just an act. If she could keep putting him off long enough, maybe she could find a way out.

Putting his fork down, Raymond turned his attention back to Simone. "I thought perhaps we would listen to the radio after dinner. After all, it's music that makes everything right in the world, isn't it?"

Waiting a beat before answering, she replied, "I suppose it is. At least for me anyway, I can't imagine life without it."

"Yes, just another thing we have in common," Raymond drawled.

Maybe the meal and warmth of the small room were making him tired, Simone hoped. Could this be her opportunity to get away?

The rest of the meal was spent in silence, both Raymond and Simone engrossed in their own thoughts. Simone pushing her food around on the plate, trying to find her appetite, knew that she would need her strength for whatever was to come. The meal reminded her of Cook and all the wonderful dishes she was always preparing. Trying to hold back tears, she thought of her friends and, most of all, Frederick, imagining what he must be going through right now.

When she found she could no longer eat anything else,

and it appeared as though Raymond had finished, Simone stood and began clearing their dishes, stacking them back in the basket he had used to bring in the food.

Standing, he tuned in the radio, finding a song he knew they both had heard before. Now more steady on her feet since she had eaten, Simone hummed along and began dancing around the room, keeping an eye on Raymond the entire time. She saw his lids growing heavy, then shaking his head as if to wake himself again.

Not wanting to get her hopes up at a chance for escape, she quietly suggested, "Perhaps you'd like to lie down for a little rest? I'm sure that you must be tired after your day."

As if he were contemplating the ramifications of taking a nap, Raymond nodded. He wanted to believe everything would be okay. "Promise me you won't try to leave?"

Taking in her surroundings, noting the position of the chairs and other furniture, the one window near the bed, and the only door leading in and out, she replied, "Of course not. I will stay right here in this chair the entire time."

Glancing from her to the chair, then the door, Raymond paused another beat. "As much as I'd like to believe you, I'm afraid I will have to secure you to the chair before I can sleep at all."

"But, I promise, I won't leave." She implored.

"I'm sorry, Simone, but this is the way it has to be. Only for a little while longer now. Soon we'll go home. You'll see. Everything will be as it should be."

'Home?' she thought. 'What could he possibly mean by that? Is he just trying to keep me off balance? Surely he's not letting me out of here alive.' Knowing that she shouldn't push her luck any further, Simone sat heavily in the chair, allowing Raymond to tie the ropes once again. She winced as the rope came in contact with the welts on her arms and ankles, tenderer to the touch now that she had been without the bindings for a time.

"Just a little nap. Then you may have the bed again for the night."

After he drifted off, Simone shifted herself around in the chair. If she could just reach the hem of her dress, maybe, somehow, she could wiggle her way out of the ropes that were tied close to it. She still had no idea where she was, or how she would get away, but she had to do something more than just sit here.

Now that her head was clear of whatever he had dosed her with, she saw his demeanor as even more unsettling. One minute he was gentle and sweet, tenderly feeding her this morning, bringing her favorite foods for dinner. Yet in the blink of an eye, she could see madness shadowing his face, his voice taking on a disturbing timbre. The way he talked about going home. Where was home? And what was he planning to do next?

Finding a small hole in her dress, she wondered if it could have been ripped last night? Yes, now bits and pieces were coming back. She had been at the Gibson but left before the rest of her friends. She remembered being outside, stumbling, and someone coming to her aid. Her dress had caught on the wood of the building, too. Picking at the hole some more, she could slip her finger through. Ripping ever so slowly as to not make any noise that might wake him, she managed to tear off a strip and balled it in her hand. She had no idea what exactly she would do with it, but there it was.

Raymond stirred, mumbling something unintelligible.

Should she try to get him to talk in his sleep? No, it probably was best not to push her luck. So far, he hadn't harmed her. Aside from brushing the hair from her face and removing then retying the ropes, he had barely even touched her. No, she would remain here in the chair until he woke, then allow events to unfold from there.

Waking in the bed the following morning, she wondered, had he drugged her again? She found herself still wearing her same dress, only her stockings had been removed. The smell of coffee permeating the room. Becoming more clear-headed, she detected other scents of breakfast as well. Opening her eyes, she saw Raymond at the table set with food, watching her.

"Good morning Simone, I trust you slept well."

"I'm sorry. I must have dozed off. But I don't remember moving to the bed."

"It was late, and you were sound asleep when I awoke. I simply moved you so you would be more comfortable."

"Thank you. You didn't have to do that."

"Of course I did. I told you, I don't want you to worry about anything at all. Today I will bring in some hot water and you can bathe yourself. There are clean clothes for you to change into as well. I noticed a rip in your dress."

'Oh no. The piece of fabric she had worked loose last night. Where did it go?' She felt around under the quilt, hoping maybe she had lost it in the bed somewhere. What must he have thought if he had found it in her hand? There was nothing in his tone or demeanor that would lead her to believe he had.

Just then, her fingers brushed over something, hanging off the edge of the bed. Shifting to her side in an effort to conceal her true movements, she fingered the scrap and tucked the fabric down toward her feet, where she hoped she could retrieve it later. She still had no idea what she could do with it, but for now, it had become her touchstone to the life she was supposed to live and to the loved ones she knew must be looking for her.

After finishing breakfast, Raymond returned to the room with the promised hot water. Allowing Simone privacy, she was able to clean herself and change into the clothes he had provided. A simple shift dress and shoes, appearing to be new and her exact size. That he knew this and that he had removed her stockings during the night more than disturbed Simone again. How long had he been watching her? How did he know these most personal details?

She knocked on the door to let him know she had finished. Entering, he took a moment to admire her and the outfit she had chosen.

"Do you like it?" He asked eagerly.

"Yes, thank you. It's lovely," she replied, hoping her demeanor would continue to win him over.

"I'm so glad. And the fit is perfect too. So, now that we've had our breakfast, and you have had the chance to clean up and change, what shall we do today?"

A look of surprise crossed Simone's face. This was not a question or anything she had anticipated. Was he actually offering to take her out somewhere? Could this be the opportunity for her to signal for help, or even possibly get away?

As though reading her thoughts, Raymond chuckled and continued, "A game, perhaps. Or maybe you would like to read a book? I am sorry to say we can't leave here just yet."

Trying to hide her disappointment, Simone nodded once. "Of course. May we turn the radio on again?"

Crossing the room to the radio, Raymond fiddled with the dial until he could tune in a station playing only music. With his back still turned, he said, "I need to go out again, just for a little while. I find I will have to leave you bound again, but I will leave out the gag, provided you will not do anything foolish. If all goes well, then perhaps tomorrow we will go home."

'Home,' thought Simone. 'Wherever could that be?' Trying to compose herself and not let the fear and trembling in her voice slip through, she could only reply, "Thank you."

43

It was decided that Frederick would go back once more to Genevieve's and see if she was home. Maybe his being alone would convince her to talk to him, take pity his bride was missing, and perhaps divulge something to him she wouldn't share with the others. It was a long shot, but one he was willing to take.

He was mentally beating himself up as he got off the streetcar, walking towards Genevieve's house. "I shouldn't have let Simone leave alone. I should have at least walked her to the stop and made sure she got safely on the streetcar. At least then she would have made it home." He kept muttering to himself. Banishing any thoughts of what might be happening to her at that moment, he steeled himself as he knocked on the door. He had to remain calm and composed, if he was going to get anything more out of that tight-lipped woman.

As she answered the door, Genevieve was wiping her hands on her apron. Surprised to see him there, she looked around. "Frederick, what are you doing here? Have you found Simone?"

"No. Not yet. And quite frankly, I'm out of ideas where to look for her. That's why I'm here. I'm hoping that you might have some idea, based on your experience, that is."

Looking back at him, trying to determine his motive, before inviting him inside, she opened the door further. "The porch is nowhere for this conversation. Come in, let me get you something to drink."

Stepping inside, Frederick looked around at the house. It was neat and orderly, no sign of anyone else that he could tell. Trying to be casual in his conversation, he admired the living room, noting the record collection. "Any favorites?"

"I'm sorry," Genevieve called from the kitchen.

"The records. Any favorites you have there?"

"Oh, I don't think I could pick just one," she replied, coming back out and handing him a glass of lemonade. "I don't have many, but that is one thing I can't live without. My music."

Frederick walked over and picked one up at random. Not really looking at it or registering who the artist was, he turned it over and over in his hands. He was considering smashing it. That certainly would get her attention, he thought. Instead, he put it back where it belonged, walked back, and sat down in the chair across from her.

Trying his best to contain his anger, he cleared his throat before starting. "Genevieve, I need your help. I know you've been away for a while. I don't know all the details of your life and I don't need to. But I thought maybe you might have some idea of where Simone might be. Or who could have taken her? If that is indeed what happened."

Genevieve was unsure of how much Delphine or the

others had told Frederick. Playing it safe, she simply said, "Frederick, I'm so sorry. I really don't have any idea. You don't think she could have just gotten cold feet, do you?"

Glaring at her, unable to hide the contempt he was feeling, he sputtered. "No. Well, the thought crossed my mind, but no." Seeing her shift in her chair, he softened his tone. "We were both excited about starting our life together. She was planning how she was going to decorate my, no, our house. She had the most beautiful quilt that she had sewn years ago that she was eager to display. So no, I don't think it was cold feet."

Genevieve sat looking at Frederick, waiting for him to continue.

His agitation growing at her non-committal response, his voice rose. "And of course, there's been all those girls they've been finding. As you know, the police don't really seem to care about investigating. I've walked around to all the places those poor girls have been found and didn't see anything to indicate..."

Putting up a hand, Genevieve stopped him. "Don't go there Frederick. I'm sure she's fine."

Looking back at her with a haggard look, he reached over and picked up the glass of lemonade that was sitting on the table. His hand shaking so hard that he thought he'd spill it, he set it back down again without drinking.

"No, I, well, while Delphine and I were searching, I did find a scrap of what I think is her dress on the side of the Gibson. But that's the only clue we've had so far. Genevieve, I'm sorry to ask this. I know Delphine has already asked you before. But I have to know. Is there any possibility that your son could have something to do with this?"

"Why on earth do you all think that Raymond has

something to do with this? What has he ever done to anyone that would give you all the thought that he would hurt Simone? I am getting really tired of all these accusations you all are throwing out there," Genevieve exclaimed.

Frederick, taken aback by her sudden outburst, sat back in his chair. Just as he was considering his next words, he heard a noise on the front porch and turned his head toward the door. Seeing Raymond walk in, he just about leapt out of his chair.

"Why you son of a--"

Genevieve was on her feet in an instant and in-between the two of them before he could take a step further. "Frederick, I suggest you either sit down or leave. I will not have you speaking to my son that way." Turning her attention towards Raymond while still keeping an eye on Frederick, she went on. "Raymond, you're back. You had me worried, son."

Raymond looking from his momma to Frederick and back to Momma spoke his next words carefully. "Yes. Um, sorry momma. I was out on a job. But it looks like I came home just in time. This fella giving you trouble?"

"No dear. He's an acquaintance whose fiancé is missing. He's friends with Delphine, and since he's not originally from around here, he thought maybe I might have some ideas of where she could be."

"I see. And do you? Have any ideas that is?"

"No, as I was just explaining to Frederick here, I don't have a clue. Have you heard anything?"

Raymond turned and closed the front door, trying to keep his composure. The last thing he had expected was to find Frederick in his living room with his momma.

"No, I haven't heard anything. Of course, I've been out of town, so I doubt I could be of much help."

Brushing past Frederick, he walked over to his mother, gave her a quick hug, then continued on toward the kitchen, leaving Frederick and Genevieve facing each other, staring one another down.

Frederick, unsure of what to do or say next, walked back to the table where he had left his lemonade. Picking it up, he drank it down in two gulps, then forcefully set the glass back down. Turning his attention back to Genevieve, he said in a low voice, "If I find out that you have any knowledge as to what's happened to her, so help me."

Before she responded or Raymond could return from the kitchen, Frederick made his way to the door. He stopped for a moment, considering saying something more to Raymond, instead, walked out, slamming the door closed behind him.

Raymond, returning to his momma's side, asked, "What was that all about?"

Genevieve just shook her head. "Raymond, we need to talk."

His pulse quickening, he took her hand. "Momma, what's wrong?"

"Son, I know you've been hanging around the Gibson. So I know you've also probably seen Simone. She is a lovely young woman, who is supposed to be on her honeymoon now with that man that just left. However, it seems she's gone missing. I don't want to believe what others have been saying, but I have to ask Raymond--"

Dropping her hand and taking a step back, Raymond interrupted, "Ask what? You surely don't think that I had something to do with it? What lies has that fella been trying to feed you?" He started towards the door as though he were going to run after Frederick.

"Raymond, calm down. Frederick isn't the one putting ideas in my head. He's just looking for his fiancé. No son, Delphine seems to think that you may have had something to do with Simone's disappearance, and god forbid, those other young women they've been finding, too. I told her, time and time again, that she's wrong. I can't begin to believe that you would have anything to do with any of that. But that fool has got this idea in her head and just won't let it go," Genevieve said, sinking down into her chair, exhausted by the turn of events of the evening.

Drawing a measured breath, Raymond walked over to the chair vacated by Frederick. Taking hold of the back as to steady himself, he looked around the room, unable to meet his Momma's inquiring eyes. How could he possibly tell her about Simone now? Now, in that moment, he found himself in a position he had not considered before.

44

Running over to Delphine's house, Frederick was unsure of what his next move was going to be. He had not expected to come face to face with Raymond. Nor had he held out much hope that Genevieve would have any information, but he had to do something. Furious at letting Simone leave by herself, he continued the mental dressing down he had been giving himself. 'What was I thinking? I should have gone with her. If I had, none of this would have ever happened.'

Pounding on Delphine's door, he pushed his way in as soon as she opened the door. "That no good, son of a--" stopping himself before he cussed.

"Frederick, what is going on? What did Genevieve tell you?" Delphine asked, leading him to a chair.

Slamming his body down, pounding the armrest, he burst. "Nothing. She told me absolutely nothing. She seems to think we're all ganging up on her son. That he couldn't possibly have anything to do with Simone's disappearance.

And then he showed up! Right there, in the living room. It took everything in me to not beat him to a pulp."

A look of alarm crossed her face. "What? Raymond is back? Are you sure?"

His voice rising to a shout, "Yes, I'm sure! He said something about needing to pick up clothes or some such excuse and was also just checking in on his momma. But Delphine, I tell you, there is more going on there. I don't know what it is, but I'm thinking your suspicions are right. He's involved somehow." Leaping from the chair, he exclaimed, "And I'm going to find out once and for all!"

"Frederick, sit back down. Flying back over there, half cocked, is not going to get you anywhere. Now tell me exactly what happened and let's figure out a plan from there."

Recounting his brief visit with Genevieve, the interruption of Raymond's unexpected return, and smug manner, he lamented. "Why Simone?" Rubbing his hands over the stubble, adding to the fatigue showing on his face.

"Alright, listen to me. This is what we are going to do. I want you to sit back down. You've been pushing yourself non-stop, and I'm guessing you haven't eaten much either." Frederick protested. "No, don't argue with me now. I'm going to fix you supper and you can keep an eye on the house over there. If there is any movement or indication of anything going on, we'll follow him."

❧

From the kitchen, Delphine watched the house across the street as well. Lights were still on in Raymond's house, and she could see shadows moving back and forth, but was unable to determine who exactly they belonged to. Though she didn't let on to Frederick, her first instinct was to march over and demand an explanation. But she knew with no proof to back up her accusations, anything she said or did would only be met with denial.

Thinking about the old boardinghouse, there was still a nagging thought she couldn't shake. Places like that were too profitable for the owner to just leave it all behind. Then again, didn't David say something about the boards appearing to be new? If that were the case, then perhaps it wasn't truly abandoned. Maybe someone just wanted it to look that way.

Taking the food back out to the living room, she and Frederick started planning what to do next. She suggested possibly returning to the boarding house, taking a better look around, seeing if they could get inside again. Frederick jumped up, ready to leave right then, when she reminded him that Raymond was still across the street. They hadn't seen him leave and wouldn't it be better to see what he did first?

Finishing their meal, they continued to sit and watch as, one by one, lights went out throughout the neighborhood. When the last light was extinguished at Raymond's house, they realized no one had come or left since they began their vigil.

Delphine, feeling the tiredness taking over, knew she couldn't allow herself to close her eyes, even for a minute. The cover of darkness would be the perfect time for Raymond to make a move, she thought. And if he does, I'll be watching.

Startled by a loud bang that sounded like a door slamming, Delphine discovered she had dozed off. Chastising herself, she looked at the clock and found it was just after three. How long had she been asleep? Calling out to Frederick, she found he wasn't there. Where could he have gone? Did he see something and go after Raymond himself? Looking around, she didn't find any sign of a note or where he might be. "Oh Frederick, please don't do something stupid," she said to the empty room.

⚜

Frederick had been sitting in the chair, watching the house across the street. Dozing off and waking himself up with a start, he chastised himself again. Now was not the time to be taking a nap. He saw Delphine was asleep in the chair across from him. The entire street was dark, no signs of anyone out. Even the birds were still quiet at this hour.

Unable to sit still any longer, he went to the bathroom sink and splashed water on his face, then looked at himself in the mirror. "Simone, I will find you today, my love. I will do whatever it takes to bring you home and put an end to this once and for all."

Quietly, he crept out to the kitchen, picking up a peach from the counter, then walking back to the front door. His plan was to go sit outside, hidden by the gardenia bush, and keep an eye out for Raymond to leave the house. Just as he was settling in, he heard a rustling and saw a shadow moving across the street. Pushing aside a branch, he saw Raymond leaving, walking in the direction of Back o'Town.

Dropping the half eaten peach, he followed, putting just enough distance between them so not to be seen, yet continuing to keep an eye on his subject. He knew he should have gone back in to tell Delphine what was going on, but he couldn't take the chance that Raymond would get too far ahead and he would lose him.

Following Raymond, he wondered exactly where they were going. The circuitous route made it seem like he didn't have a specific destination in mind. It wasn't until Raymond took a turn down Perdido Street that Frederick knew he was on the right path, this was the street where the boarding house was located.

Looking ahead, Frederick was trying to figure out a way to get there in advance of Raymond when he accidentally kicked a pebble into a step. This noise was enough to make Raymond quickly turn his head. Frederick hoped he was far back enough to hide in the darkness, but now he couldn't take any more chances.

Keeping perfectly still, he waited until Raymond started on his way again. From what he could see of Raymond's reaction, the interruption didn't seem to slow down his journey. It appeared he was satisfied no one else was around as he resumed walking towards his destination.

Taking a deep breath, Frederick continued on, taking slower, more deliberate steps, shifting his view back and forth between the sidewalk and his subject, careful to not make any other noise that would give away his presence.

When he was half a block away, he watched Raymond go around the backside of the boarding house. Realizing he had no weapon other than his own hands, he quickly glanced around to see if there was something he could use in the case of having to defend himself. They were pretty evenly matched as far as size and weight from what he could tell, but anything to give himself the advantage was all the better.

Approaching the house, he noticed the board leaning against the railing. 'This will do,' he thought, as he picked it up and made his way around to the back. Would Raymond have left the door unlocked as he had the last time? There was only one way to find out.

45

Raymond had a sense that someone might be following him, but every time he turned around, he was only met with the darkness of the night. "Must be my mind playing tricks on me," he mused. He knew he shouldn't have stayed home as long as he did, but he had to make sure that Momma was sound asleep before he left again.

After that Frederick guy had left, and Momma had shared her concerns, he assuaged her by telling her yes, he was familiar with who Simone was, but had no idea who could possibly want to cause her, or any of those other poor young girls, harm.

Hoping to distract her from the unfolding events, he shared with her a little more information about his time living in Galveston, and what he had been doing since she had left. How life there had been hard when he first arrived, not knowing anyone or anything about the city, and how at night he would sit outside a club close to where he lived, in order to listen to the music the bands would play. No matter what else happened, music was still important to him. It was something the two of them still shared.

After a while, he knew it was time to return to New Orleans and home. He had been hoping to find her there, waiting for him when he returned, and how disappointed he had been when she wasn't. He made sure he left out the part about knowing his father was dead, and the old boarding house. He couldn't give her any ideas about where he was when he wasn't home. She seemed to accept his story, and by the time they went to bed, she expressed her joy at their being a family once again.

Tossing and turning, he was sleeping fitfully, when he decided enough time had passed that he could leave again. He left a note telling Momma that he had to go again, but not to worry, he'd be home soon.

He took his time circling the boardinghouse once before going in through the back door. 'Now that I know people are out looking for Simone, I'll have to be more careful of my comings and goings,' he thought. Picking up a candle in the kitchen, he lit it with a match as he crept quietly up the stairs. Though no one else other than Simone was there at the time, he thought it best to keep any noise to a minimum.

Stopping on the landing to look out between the cracks of boards that covered the window, he still couldn't shake the feeling of being watched, and thought he saw a shadow pass below, causing him to do a double take. He didn't want to risk opening the window or removing a board in hopes of a better view, instead, extinguished the light and continued up the remaining stairs. If there was someone out there, he would have a better vantage point from one window on the second floor that wasn't covered. He was starting to question whether boarding up so many windows had been such a good idea.

Looking into the room where he had sequestered Simone, he found her sound asleep on the bed. From this vantage point, she appeared to be still tied up and in the same position as when he had left her. Satisfied, he turned and made his way to the room next door. There, he had an unobstructed window with a view of the street out front. Gently raising the window an inch, he was hoping it would allow him to hear if anyone was creeping around, while he looked back and forth as far as the view would let him.

Not seeing anything out of place, Raymond tiptoed back to the door. Standing with his hand on the knob, he contemplated his next move.

Approaching the side of the house, Frederick saw a flicker of light, then darkness again. He could only assume that Raymond had lit something to illuminate his path, until satisfied with his steps, put it out again. That was one advantage Raymond had over him, he was familiar with the layout of the house. Frederick would be going in blind and would have to give his eyes time to adjust to the darkness inside before he could make any moves. He was hoping the element of surprise would work in his favor, but he would have to prepare himself for whatever the outcome would be. Saying a silent prayer under his breath, he murmured, "I'm coming for you, Simone. Hold on."

Starting up the first step, he heard a scurrying noise coming from the front of the house. Should he go look or continue on? Waiting, he strained to hear any other noises.

Satisfied that all was quiet, he resumed his cautious steps. Trying to handle of the backdoor, he found it unlocked. Hesitating, he took a deep breath, slowly pulling the door open. As he did, a cat ran out, yowling in surprise, loud enough to silence any noise he might have made opening the door.

Trembling, he stretched his hands out in front of himself, making sure he wasn't about to walk into anything, or more importantly, anyone. His eyes quickly adjusted to the darkness inside, different from what he had expected. The lack of illumination from any outside sources only helped to intensify his other senses. Listening, he could hear footsteps above him. One set only. Too heavy to be Simone, that must be Raymond walking around up there.

Frederick made his way through the kitchen and into a hall, keeping as close to the wall as he could. He could now make out the front door, and what he perceived to be a room off to his left and one to the right. There were stairs in the middle, leading up to the rest of the house. Was there another staircase? He wondered. This main one was too exposed for his liking.

Listening again, he heard a door open, then close, and footsteps moving again. Which way were they going? Towards the stairs or perhaps into another room? Were there more people here than just Raymond? Frederick was starting to think coming by himself had not been the best idea. There's no turning back now, he silently admonished himself. Gripping the board tighter in his hand, he made his way towards the stairs, listening in between each step.

⚜

Raymond paused, the hair on his arms standing at attention, all of his senses were on high alert. Of course, that cat yelling had done nothing to calm his nerves, either. Now he was sure he heard someone downstairs. His sensitivity to sound had been his best and worst asset all his life. Having lost hearing in one ear, he found his right ear compensating more, and his other senses heightened as well. He could listen to a piece of music just once, and then could replay it in his mind, over and over again, hearing each note of each individual instrument. At the same time, if something was out of tune, he would hear that too, and it would upset the precious balance he tried so hard to maintain.

Slowing his breathing, listening, waiting. Hearing the slightest creak of a floorboard validated his suspicion that someone else was in the house now. Knowing that someone would hear his footsteps downstairs, he slipped out of his shoes, pushing them up against the baseboard before opening the door. Sliding on the hardwood floor in his stocking feet, he maneuvered down the hall toward the top of the stairs. From there he would have a line of sight able to see the intruder first, hopefully being able to move fast enough to knock them back down to the first floor.

Hearing the footfalls approaching, halting at every other stair, he could tell whoever it was must not be able to see very well, or was being extremely cautious. Did they suspect someone else was in here, or were they just breaking in and looking to take whatever they could get their hands on? Or worse yet, was it Frederick or Delphine, come looking for Simone? Surely they didn't know where he was. Then again, he had that sense that someone was following him. Could it have been one of them this entire time? Feeling around in his pockets, he came up empty, finding he had nothing he could use to defend himself.

Another step. How many had that been now? He guessed whoever it was had maybe five more to go before they were at the top of the stairs. Sliding yet another foot down the wall, Raymond was now able to see an approaching shadow. Based on the size, he determined it was not Delphine, and it was only one person. Preparing himself, he decided it must be Frederick. How would he deal with him without waking Simone? Any noise they made surely would rouse her. Even though he had tied her to the bed prior to his leaving, he knew if she heard noises, that would be her cue to try making some other sound to attract attention?

Raymond heard three more steps taken in quick succession. Was the intruder growing careless now? Or were they more confident in their direction? Either way, he was prepared. It would all be over soon.

46

Realizing that Frederick was gone too, Delphine could only surmise that he had seen Raymond again and took matters into his own hands. She threw on her housecoat and ran across the street to Genevieve and Raymond's house. Not waiting to be let in, she barged into Genevieve's room, shouting, "Genevieve! Where's Raymond?"

Startled from a deep sleep, Genevieve muttered, "Since he came home last night, I assume he's asleep in his bed."

Running out, Delphine pounded on Raymond's bedroom door, calling, "Raymond, wake up. Are you in there?"

Receiving no response, she shoved open the door, only to find a neatly made bed.

"Genevieve, he's not here," she exclaimed. "We have to go. Now!"

Rubbing the sleep from her eyes, she looked at the state Delphine was in, still tying to make sense of the situation. "But where? How do you know where he is, Delphine?"

"The boardinghouse where your no-good husband holed up all those years ago. Come on, I'll explain on the way." She said, grabbing Genevieve by the hand, dragging her toward the door.

Running the entire way, for what felt like miles, but was only in fact six blocks, they arrived, spent and out of breath. Cautiously, they circled around the house, trying to breathe normally. It was then Delphine spotted something hanging from a shrub on the side of the house. Picking it up, she recognized it as a piece of Simone's dress.

"Now do you believe me?" she implored, waving it in front of Genevieve's face.

"That still doesn't prove anything," Genevieve insisted, walking back to the sidewalk. "There could be many girls with that same dress."

Delphine just looked at her incredulously, shook her head, and pushed Genevieve back toward the front of the house.

Pointing at the house, Delphine forcefully whispered. "Who else would know about this place? You do realize it was your son who came here all those years ago to collect Walter's belongings. Genevieve, you have to believe me. I didn't want to believe that the young boy I knew and cared for all those years ago could do something like this. But we're here now. And one way or another, we have to find out what's going on and, more importantly, Simone."

Looking at the house, then back at Delphine, Genevieve was trying to come to terms with what she still didn't want to believe. "I - I didn't know."

"Of course you didn't. You weren't here." Delphine spat. "Come on, we're going in."

Reaching the top of the stairs, Frederick's eyes adapted to the darkness. He could now see a hallway stretching out on either side of where he was standing. A sliver of light shining in the window to his left illuminated the shorter section and one doorway directly across from him. Turning toward the right, he saw a longer hall, with three, maybe four more doors. Unsure what room Simone may be in or if any of them were occupied by anyone else, he stood still, waiting. Just then, a glimpse of what appeared to be a shadow along the wall caused him to take a step back.

In the split second he took to breathe, the shadow came around to meet him face to face.

Without considering who it might be, Frederick swung the board, coming in contact with the side of the shadow's head. It was enough to knock whoever it was off balance, allowing Frederick to ascend the last step and gain access to the hallway. Now he could see exactly who he was up against. Raymond.

"Simone! Where are you? Where is she?" Frederick growled, charging at him.

Raymond, lunging back at him, snarled. "Wouldn't you like to know?"

Frederick lifting the board to block his outstretched hands, used the force to push Raymond back against the wall, pinning him in place, the board across his chest.

Leaning into Raymond's face, his voice low, he snapped. "If you have hurt one hair on her head, I will destroy you, piece by piece. You will know pain as you have never known before."

Raymond, using the wall to brace his foot, pushed back,

causing Frederick to stumble and crash into the door behind him. It was then he heard Simone cry out, "Frederick, I'm here! Help me!"

Frederick, turning his head toward Simone's voice, gave Raymond the advantage of distraction. Charging at Frederick with all speed, he shattered a wall sconce with Frederick's head. Frederick could feel a piece of the glass slice through his skin and blood running down the back of his head. He, in turn, swung the board, attempting to come in contact with any part of Raymond's body that he could.

Simone continued calling out, "Oh my god, Frederick! What's going on out there?"

Ducking to avoid the board, Raymond replied, "Simone, dear, everything is fine. Don't you worry now."

"Please, don't hurt him!" she cried.

"Simone, I'm here. I'm coming for you!" Frederick shouted.

Back and forth, the two men continued to brawl, falling on a chair and shattering it, giving Raymond the opportunity to pick up a piece of the broken leg. With the jagged edge outstretched, he charged toward Frederick, puncturing his shirt and pushing the wood into his stomach.

Just as Frederick fell to the floor, the downstairs door flung open with a bang, Genevieve and Delphine rushing in. Groping around in the dark, Delphine found a switch turning lights on the stairs going up in front of them, prompting Genevieve to call out, "Raymond, son, are you here?"

A crash, and the sound of glass breaking, was the only response she heard. "Raymond," she cried, rushing toward the stairs. Delphine grabbed her, pulling her back to keep her safe.

"Momma?" Raymond gasped, followed by a yowl, then silence.

Genevieve, pulling free of Delphine's grasp, raced up the stairs, stopping when she saw both Raymond and Frederick sprawled out on the floor. Frederick was holding the remains of the chair leg protruding from his gut, while Raymond was curled in a fetal position, blood pouring from his head, the board broken in two next to him.

"Raymond, son, my son..." Genevieve cried, prompting Delphine to rush up the stairs to see what was happening.

"My god, Frederick! Raymond! What?" Delphine asked, bending down to check on Frederick. Finding him bleeding profusely, she was relieved that he was conscious and talking. Just as he started to speak, she heard Simone calling out.

"Hello? Frederick? Someone? Anyone! Please, help me!"

"Simone? Keep talking," Delphine replied, making her way down the hall.

"Delphine? Is that you? What's going on? Where's Frederick? Is he okay?"

Stepping around Genevieve and Raymond, Delphine reached the door where she heard Simone's voice coming from. Finding it locked, she turned back to Raymond. "Where is the key?"

Leaning against Genevieve, his breathing labored, Raymond looked at Delphine, shaking his head in defiance.

"Damn it, Raymond!" Delphine demanded. "Where is the key?"

"Son, give her the key. Then this can all be over. You can come home, and everything will be fine," Genevieve cooed while cradling Raymond in her lap.

Raymond looked at Delphine, then at Momma, and

back to Delphine. Gasping, he said, "If you hadn't butted in, none of this would have happened. But you just had to stick your nose in and ruin everything."

Delphine turned, starting back toward Raymond, exclaiming, "Why, you no good... And you, Genevieve? Have you been covering for him all this time?"

Genevieve, shutting her down with a look, turned her attention back to Raymond, quietly saying, "Raymond, son, none of this is your fault. I should have never left you all those years ago. But right now, you need to end this and give Delphine the key."

Struggling to reach into his jacket pocket, he produced the room key. Delphine approached, trying to take it from his hand, finding him clutching it. "Momma, the music. It was all about the music. And Daddy... he tried so hard to destroy all that. I'm so so sorry momma. If she hadn't teased me all those years ago. It's her fault. And the other girls. It's their fault too."

Yanking it from his hand, he yelped when she drew blood. Glaring back, she lowered her voice. "Raymond, I don't know what you are talking about. But if you have hurt her in any way, you will pay for it the rest of your life. Do you understand me?"

Seeing that she had the key in her hand, Frederick attempted to stand, only to fall back down again.

"You stay put. I'm getting her out, then we'll get help." Delphine admonished, unlocking the door, finding Simone tied to the corner of the bed.

"Simone! My god, are you all right?"

"Delphine, oh! I'm so happy to see you," Simone wept. "I've never been so frightened in all my life!"

Running to her friend, she quickly untied the ropes. "Did he hurt you?"

"No." was all she managed before bursting into tears.

Delphine pulled her into a hug. "My dear girl, you're safe now. I'm here, so is Frederick, but we need to get help. "

"Frederick? Where is he? What's wrong? Tell me!"

"He's out here in the hall. Just come with me now."

Making their way out of the room, Simone found her strength, rushing past Genevieve and Raymond, throwing her arms around Frederick's neck. "I thought I'd never see you again," she wept, when she noticed the chair leg sticking out of his stomach. "Oh my, Frederick! You need help now! Delphine!"

Frantically running downstairs, Delphine found a phone and called the police. Once satisfied that they were on the way, she placed a second call to David and Evelyn, briefly explaining what had happened, before running back up to tell the others.

Frederick groaned as he tried to push himself up again, trying to soothe Simone's fears. "I'm here Simone. I'm so, so sorry. I should have never let you go home by yourself."

"It's not your fault. You had no idea. None of us did. All that matters is we get you to the hospital now."

Looking down the hall toward Genevieve, Frederick asked, "What of Raymond there?"

Simone, turning back to face him, implored. "Raymond, so that's your name. I don't understand any of this. Why me?"

Raymond, struggling, looked back at her with deep longing before answering. "Because, Dove, it was your fault. All those years ago on the playground. And then when we danced together at the Gibson, I knew. I've spent years searching for the one who gave life to those voices in my head. All those other girls, none of them could do for me what you were going to do. I collected their songs, hoping that the clamor would stop. But it never did."

Turning his face toward Genevieve, Raymond cried. "I don't hear anything. I don't hear the music anymore, Momma."

47

Evelyn and David arrived just as the police were pulling up. Frantically, they rushed from the car, finding Delphine standing on the front porch, shaking and waiting. Throwing her arms around Delphine's neck, Evelyn gasped, "Is everyone alright?"

Looking at Evelyn and David, then over at the police, Delphine said, "Frederick is hurt pretty bad. He's upstairs. Simone has some rope burns and welts, but she'll eventually be fine."

"Raymond?" David asking with trepidation clear in his voice.

"He's alive. Genevieve is up there with him. She's still in denial. But the police will take care of him."

As two of the officers went upstairs, Delphine remained on the porch, explaining to the third what happened. As she was talking, she watched Simone coming down the stair, accompanying Frederick on a stretcher, leaving for the hospital with David and Evelyn following in their car.

Knowing she still had to remain behind, she excused herself for a moment, setting off to find Genevieve.

Walking in the front door, she came fact to face with a patched up Raymond, being escorted down the stairs, his hands cuffed behind him. Mumbling and singing incoherently, the only decipherable words being 'music' and 'it was her'. They had deemed his wounds superficial enough to not warrant a trip to the hospital, the police leading him to the waiting cop car while Genevieve followed along, wailing and imploring them to not hurt her baby.

Looking at Genevieve with sadness and disbelief, Delphine stepped in front of her. Taking a deep breath, she opened her mouth as if to say something, instead biting her tongue, holding back her words.

Moving aside, she watched as an officer led Genevieve away. She was left wondering, after everything she'd just seen, how could she possibly still believe that Raymond wasn't the monster they all thought him to be?

Returning to the officer, Delphine continued giving her statement, outlining all the times she had seen him at the Gibson, how those times coincided with the killings of some of the other girls they had found, and how she found everyone at the boardinghouse.

Once satisfied she had told them everything, they allowed her to leave and join her friends at the hospital. David was in the waiting room when she walked in, meeting her with the news she was hoping to hear.

In one long breath, he told her, "Frederick will be fine. He's lost some blood, but the doctors seem to think he'll make a full recovery. Simone is with him now. They've already bandaged up her wrists and ankles. Evelyn is on the phone with her parents."

Finding her shaking, David led her to the nearest chair. "It's all my fault, David," she said, dissolving into tears.

Placing his arm around her shoulders, he offered her his handkerchief. "No, it's not. We should have listened to you sooner. But all that matters now is everyone is safe, the police have Raymond, and he can't hurt anyone else."

"I certainly hope you are right. Genevieve was still defending him, even as they were leading him away. I can't understand how..." she trailed off, noticing Simone walking out of a room.

Rushing to her friend, she hugged her hard until Simone was gasping for air. "I'm fine, Delphine. Or I will be." She said as she held up her wrists. "Frederick will be here for a few days, but after that, we will be married. Nothing is going to stop that."

48

The entire way to the police station, Raymond kept humming to himself, a mash up of songs, indecipherable to anyone else but him. He remembered the Doves he had killed and could hear their songs playing out in his head. The officer driving kept telling him to quiet down, but he wouldn't comply. It wasn't until they had locked him in a cell that he began shouting. "It's her! Only her. Only Simone and I can share the music."

Pounding the wall until he scraped his fists raw, he moaned and crumpled to the floor, resuming the humming, "She's Crying For Me," the song he always associated with Simone, over and over again.

Genevieve, in the other room, was still trying to explain to the officer that it had been the abuse at the hands of his father and the influence of others over the years that made him this way—anything she could think of to excuse his behavior. But try as she might, in the end she knew that nothing she could say would convince them he hadn't done what he stood accused of.

Dejected and disheartened, she took one last look at him in the cell, finding him curled up in the corner, still humming to himself. Crying silently, she left him once more, returning to the house they once shared, now a hollow reminder of the life that could have been.

Placing a record on the turntable, she walked to the couch, as the tears fell and "West End Blues" began to fill the cracks left in her soul. Music, as it always had been, would be her solace once again.

Acknowledgments

Where to begin? There are so many people to acknowledge, some may not even realize their contribution and may be surprised to find themselves mentioned here.

First, of course, is my family. Their unwavering support and belief in me has kept me going, especially when I felt like giving up. That inner voice, or inner critic I should say, can be a pretty powerful deterrent at times. But I prevailed and have shut her up, at least for a little while.

To my wonderful beta readers, Brandy, Garret, Beth, and Judy. Your feedback, enthusiasm, and honesty helped me figure out some of the things that I had definitely missed in all of drafts of this novel.

To Amber who has been a source of encouragement, inspiration, sounding board, and most of all friend. I can't wait to see the results of your creative mind unleashed on the world.

To the writing communities I've been a part of. Everyone at The Write Practice. There are so many members there that if I tried to list everyone who helped me I know I would miss someone. You were my earliest readers of the story and your critiques and support taught and encouraged me so much. I am thankful. All the people I met with: agents, editors, and writers, at the Pacific Northwest Writers Association conferences. Every year I attended was a wonderful experience and I can't recommend it enough.

To the teachers and librarians who showed me the worlds contained in stories, both fiction and non-fiction. You encouraged and challenged me in your teachings and book recommendations, and instilled a love a reading that will never die. You truly are unsung heroes.

Most of all, thank you to you, my readers. For investing the time it took to read this book, that for so long only lived inside my head. I do hope you've enjoyed it. And if you would be so kind, drop a review wherever you purchased it, so others can find it too.

About the Author

M.E. Cooper has been making up stories since childhood.

Her stories transport readers through time and across continents. Drawing inspiration from her extensive travels, she brings vivid settings and rich cultural textures to each novel. Her work spans decades, seamlessly blending historical authenticity with deeply personal character journeys. Whether set in mid-century Las Vegas or the jazz-infused streets of 1920s New Orleans, Cooper's novels delve into the inner lives of her characters, exploring identity, memory, redemption, and the human spirit. When she's not writing, she can be found wandering through hidden alleyways in unfamiliar cities, always chasing the next story.

You can find all of her books at your favorite retailer. And if they aren't available there, ask them to carry her books. Or drop a line with any recommendations of where you think she should sell her books.

Drop by and visit her author site at http://me-cooper.net

There you can buy books direct, sign up for her e-mail newsletter, read short stories and get all the news on upcoming books and more.